D1110375

More praise for
Glad News of the Natural World

"You'll laugh yourself silly, as you always do in a Pearson novel—but you'll also find yourself touched by the author's great affection for his characters. *Glad News of the Natural World* is glad news indeed for Pearson aficionados—wickedly funny, deeply compassionate and wise beyond words."

—Polly Paddock,
The Charlotte Observer

"Louis Benfield is back and grown up (more or less) in this hilarious . . . tale of a modern-day Southern slacker. . . ."

—*Publishers Weekly*

"Pearson delivers a quirky view of the world in extraordinary ways: he deploys reinventions of meandering Proustian narration, serpentine Faulknerian sentences and sharp Swiftian satire. Readers who expect a simple tale . . . will instead be surprised by Pearson's unique narrative style, chaotic plot structure and colorful characterizations. Readers . . . ought to enjoy Louis Benfield's kaleidoscopic adventures."

—Tim Davis, *BookPage*

"Just as truth is often better than fiction, or in the hands of an adept memoirist more entertaining, the 'reality' of all these people, and the backgrounds that Pearson invents (or remembers) for them, are engaging and promising. . . ."

—Donald Harington,
The Atlanta Journal-Constitution

"Pearson's writing is satirical, humorous, irreverent and endearing; his characters are over-the-top caricatures of good and the bad, sane and insane, saints and sinners. Readers will be led to unexpected places. Highly recommended."

—Joanna Burkhardt, *Library Journal*

"Riding the wave of [Pearson's] highly spiced prose is still a pleasure...."

—*Kirkus Reviews*

GLAD NEWS
OF THE
NATURAL WORLD

T. R. PEARSON

SIMON & SCHUSTER PAPERBACKS
New York   London   Toronto   Sydney

SIMON & SCHUSTER PAPERBACKS
Rockefeller Center
1230 Avenue of the Americas
New York, NY 10020

First Simon & Schuster paperback edition 2006

SIMON & SCHUSTER PAPERBACKS and colophon are registered trademarks of Simon & Schuster, Inc.

For information regarding special discounts for bulk purchases, please contact Simon & Schuster Special Sales at 1-800-456-6798 or business@simonandschuster.com.

DESIGNED BY LAUREN SIMONETTI

Manufactured in the United States of America

1   3   5   7   9   10   8   6   4   2

Library of Congress Cataloging-in-Publication Data
Pearson, T. R.
Glad news of the natural world / T. R. Pearson.
p.   cm.
Sequel to : A short history of a small place.
1. Eccentrics and eccentricities—Fiction. 2. City and town life—Fiction.
3. North Carolina—Fiction. I. Title.
PS3566.E235G58   2005
813'.54—dc22   2004059042

ISBN-13: 978-0-7432-6463-1
ISBN-10:   0-7432-6463-0
ISBN-13: 978-0-7432-6464-8 (Pbk)
ISBN-10:   0-7432-6464-9 (Pbk)

*For the good people of Neely,
North Carolina—wherever they may be*

GRAVEYARD
OF THE
ATLANTIC

1

I AM DISTINGUISHED BY my penmanship. By the hang and hue of my suit coat. The sophistication of my haircut. The silken luster of my tie. Instead of cumin or clove, bright-leaf tobacco, essence of jasmine car freshener, I smell judiciously of Kiehl's cucumber talc, Italian shoe leather, pilfered motel soap.

My colleagues slouch against the railing that corrals us while I stand apart with my Lucite sign held level at sternum height. They grouse and carp in Pushtu and Slovak, Arabic, Mandarin, Hebrew, Yoruba. They've made their signs with pen and pencil on whatever has come to hand. With a grease marker, I've written "Shapiro" in, effectively, Baskerville.

She's due from Paris in the company of a Pomeranian, Mrs. Gloria Shapiro of York at Eighty-ninth. And though I've tried to imagine the woman as some manner of savory heiress, a handsome creature in her middle years with a haberdashery fortune and an appetite for slim discriminating gentlemen like me, there is a practical limit to my baseless optimism. Mrs. Gloria Shapiro is flying, after all, into Newark with her dog instead of into Kennedy with retainers. I spot her coming out of customs long before she has noticed me.

She is bone thin, knobby, a haute couture refugee who'd rather be dead than lack the upper-arm tone to go sleeveless. She has conscripted a hapless skycap into Pomeranian duty, a lanky black kid in an oversize hat with his trouser cuffs dragging the floor, who dangles the dog before him at arm's length.

3

The creature is rheumy-eyed and grizzled, with nails like talons and amber teeth. He looks conspicuously unhappy and nearly old enough to vote.

Mrs. Gloria Shapiro spies her name on my square of milky Lucite. She snaps her fingers at me and says by way of greeting, "You."

As I take her dog, the skycap favors me with information. "He bites," he says and shows me a punctured finger. "Leaks some too."

I hold the dog beneath his forelegs, and every time he squirms and growls, he looses a freshet of urine onto the grimy terminal floor, onto the sidewalk, generously onto each of the three arrival lanes, onto the cement rental-bus island, onto the short-term parking lot, onto the leather upholstery of my Crown Victoria passenger seat. I've been told his name is Ashton and he'll reliably spew kibble if not permitted to be an irrigating menace in the front.

Even on the short trip back to the terminal to collect Mrs. Gloria Shapiro's luggage, Ashton snarls and snaps and urinates with such animosity as to prompt me to wonder what life might be like with arms that end at the elbows.

Mrs. Gloria Shapiro has been led, she informs me, to expect a limousine. I don't have a limousine. I don't even have a Town Car. I have the Crown Victoria I'm driving, and it's not even black but more the shade of grayish brown you might find in a septic system. I apologize to Mrs. Gloria Shapiro and tell her the limo is in the shop.

"Where are you from?" she asks me. It comes out in the form of an accusation.

"North Carolina," I say which, for Mrs. Gloria Shapiro's purposes, might as well be Alpha Centauri. I stand revealed as the cracker import she's condemned to depend upon to haul her clear from greater New Jersey to York at Eighty-ninth which, for all she knows, I might attempt by way of Philadelphia. And, worse still, not in a limousine but in a sludge-brown Ford.

She presses her lips together and grimaces. Mrs. Gloria Shapiro snorts with articulate force enough to insinuate the bitter anguish of disembarking from Premier Class into the care of the likes of me. I take occasion to picture Ashton winging westward in the cockpit, showing his grim teeth to the flight crew while moistening the controls.

We are hardly out of the airport proper before Mrs. Gloria Shapiro is abusing me over her cell phone to some Upper East Side friend. Her name is Enid, and she and Mrs. Gloria Shapiro forgo the splendors of Paris to indulge instead in galloping mutual abject mortification once I've elected to take the turnpike instead of 1&9.

In a stage whisper, Mrs. Gloria Shapiro floats the theory that it's my habit to pad my charges with unwarranted turnpike tolls. She's glaring at me from the backseat when I find her in the mirror. The toll plaza's vapor lights lend iridescence to her hair and cause her surgically tautened facial skin to look slick and extruded.

I hear her tell Enid, "I don't know. Georgia or somewhere."

I lay a careless hand on the console as we cross the Passaic River, and Ashton nips my wrist. He breaks the skin.

Mrs. Gloria Shapiro insists I take the tunnel until I take it and we find traffic backed up all the way to Kennedy Boulevard, occasion for Mrs. Gloria Shapiro to wonder pointedly of Enid if a capable driver wouldn't have known to take the bridge instead.

All down the ramp, Mrs. Gloria Shapiro points out gaps in

adjacent lanes and has me shift and weave to gain a half a car length here and there. She comments uncharitably to Enid on the quality of my driving, and the two of them have a rollicking laugh together at my expense. I hear the sound of Enid cackling over the staticky phone connection with all the ladylike grace of a cowhand.

In the city Mrs. Gloria Shapiro has her sanctified routes and detours which, apparently, she expects me to divine. As I work north along the avenues and east on clotted cross streets, Mrs. Gloria Shapiro reveals to Enid the way she would have gone. She and Enid enjoy some galvanizing sisterly outrage over the roadwork I get mired in at Sixth and Fifty-seventh, the carting truck I fall behind on Seventy-eighth.

They conclude they should have expected as much from the pride of Alabama.

Not a block and a half from his building, Ashton sees fit to throw up which Mrs. Gloria Shapiro lays to my hectic brand of driving and claims to be a little turbulent herself. I see that Ashton has doused the front-seat beading with residual bile, has deposited the bulk of his discharge onto the carpet. He missed the floor mat altogether and hit instead the drive-shaft hump. I make out nova and milk chocolate, the odd macadamia nut. The stink of the stuff gives remarkable instantaneous offense.

Mrs. Gloria Shapiro's doorman wears siege-of-Stalingrad livery with epaulettes and showy stamped brass buttons on his skirted greatcoat, a modified busby on his head with both a chin strap and a plume. He is massive and Teutonic, has Eastern European bridgework and the good sense to hoist Ashton out of my Crown Vic by his scruff. Mrs. Gloria Shapiro calls him Lenny and says that Enid tells him "Hey" as he unloads the luggage from the trunk and motions for help from the lobby.

The concierge comes out with a bellman's cart and an air of imposition. He's a pudgy Cuban interrupted halfway through his *Daily News* who Mrs. Gloria Shapiro hardly greets and fails to call by name. He joins Lenny with his cart at the lip of the trunk and has Lenny to understand that, in his estimation, baggage hauling is beyond the scope of his duties. He takes the unenterprising layabout's view of conciergerie which I hear him elaborate on as Mrs. Gloria Shapiro signs her ticket and, by way of a tip, visits upon me advice.

"Ammonia," she says, and then leaves off to entertain input from Enid. "Nonsudsy," she tells me along with instructions for blotting Pomeranian effluvia. I have just ginger ale and a cast-off *Wall Street Journal* under my seat.

I've got the doors and windows open and am grinding vomit into the rug with a page of market indicators and selected small-cap stocks when Lenny leans against my fender well and offers me a cigarette. Mentholated, I notice. Generic. Lenny sets his hat with grave custodial care upon my hood before confessing he once attempted to drown Ashton in the gutter. A fire crew had come along to open the hydrant up the block while Lenny had charge of the creature out front on an airing. Drowning him, Lenny informs me, had seemed the merciful thing to do.

Lenny pauses and puffs. He shakes his head, flicks ash off of his greatcoat. Sounding for all the world like Henry Kissinger, Lenny says, "He floats."

I light up off Lenny's butt and come empirically by knowledge that mentholated generic cigarettes taste decisively both at once.

Lenny proves to hail from Schrankogel in the heart of the Tyrol, and he tells me he made a sort of a living for some years as a boxer. Not a champion or a contender or a respectable stooge opponent but instead a sparring partner for journeyman tomato cans. Gym suet, a sluggish ambulatory punching bag for hire. Lenny boasts that he's been sutured in most capitals of Europe and had his fractured jaw wired in Atlantic City. He balls his massive hands into fists and strikes his boxerly pose, carries his left so low I'm sure that even I could catch him flush.

In my turn I allow I'm driving as a favor for a friend and reveal to Lenny that, in fact, I am a working actor. "Stage," I tell him with a sniff, and describe for Lenny without prompting the role that promises to occupy me for the coming weeks which I choose to inflate and lard with fabrication. I will, in truth, be holding a pewter tankard, wearing a vest and pantaloons and trying to look for nearly a half an hour stupendously jolly about as far downstage as an employed opera chorister can get and still qualify for union wages.

I give myself out to Lenny as a man on the cusp of dramatic triumph and declaim for him a scrap of monologue I used in a showcase once.

Lenny instinctively knows better than to bother to believe me, has kept company with a vast wealth of pretenders in his day. Instead he opens his mouth and laughs, reveals his dental metalcraft in its gaudy range of alloys, ores and hues. Lenny says that in the coming weeks he hopes to wed a Hapsburg and live in regal splendor in Vienna. He flicks his smoldering filter out into the street, shoves his hat onto his head and punches me fondly on the shoulder to almost chiropractic effect.

Lenny returns to his post and mans the door of Mrs. Gloria Shapiro's building while I sit in creeping glacial traffic on the FDR from Fifty-ninth Street to the Brooklyn Bridge.

2

I CAN'T HELP BUT believe I was intended for better use than I've gotten. Not celebrated achievement or selfless Christian industry but some manner, at least, of steady worthwhile employment. As it is, I'm largely wasted, only spottily engaged and, for a robust thirty-four-year-old, almost criminally unambitious.

I didn't move, like people tend to, to the city with a dream. I wasn't propelled by a nagging itch for fame, an appetite for self-expression, an overstimulated ardor for all things cosmopolitan. I can't remember ever hoping to abuse the rubes back home with galling displays of the polished urban sophisticate I'd become since, but for my father, I very probably would have stayed a rube myself. He made me come to the city, arranged for a job and dispatched me to fill it.

He was hardly the sort with call to address his own regrets through me. He'd seen a fair bit of the world, both as an airman in Korea and as the husband of a woman prone to fits of wanderlust who'd bound herself in holy wedlock (as my father told it) to her porter. My mother was regularly exposed in the beauty shop to travel magazines and attended missionary slide shows in the Methodist fellowship hall which had the effect of aggravating her sense of personal stagnation until her longing to be at some remove from where she'd ended up could only get stifled and tamped down by an actual vacation.

They toured Sicily, my parents did. They camped in the Transvaal. They cruised the Yangtze River and took a flat in Bu-

9

dapest. They spent a week by the Scapa Flow up on the Orkney Islands when two days would have very likely served them, celebrated an anniversary in Lisbon, another in Vancouver, saw a total eclipse from Tenerife, a fer-de-lance in Costa Rica, ran across a woman they'd gone to high school with at Walton-on-the-Naze who confounded them by not being dead the way they'd heard she was, proved alive enough anyway to borrow train fare from my father.

Until she was too infirm to manage it, my great-aunt would come and keep me which was a little like being tended by a perfumed chifforobe. Aunt Sister was gouty and diabetic, almost morbidly short of breath and plump, she liked to call it, though she had passed plump some years back and had realized in her dotage junior sumo girth and heft. She'd collapse onto the sofa in the TV room midmorning and stay there usually until I'd helped her up to go to bed at night.

Aunt Sister took exercise in the form of adjusting the hassock to suit her, rolling her stockings up and down depending on the humidity and shifting between her *Guidepost* and her *Greensboro Daily News* wherein she'd read the obituaries and make a hash of the crossword puzzle. She didn't cook and seemed content to exist on a diet of Ritz crackers, never quite figured out how our front door locked and couldn't see to dial the phone. I could have done virtually anything with Aunt Sister's blessing and permission since regardless of what I'd propose to her, I'd get the same reply.

I'm going down to the store, out to the park, over to the neighbors. I'll be in the driveway disassembling my mother's Pontiac. I'm having a divorcée in for a spot of unseemly debauchery in the tool shed. I'll be in the basement making a portable thermonuclear device. I'm heading out for a pint of scotch. I'm going to have my tonsils removed. I'll be on Guam if you need me and don't intend to come back until Tuesday next.

Invariably Aunt Sister would do me the courtesy of stopping what she was about. She'd leave off, that is, with her daytime drama, interrupt her reading, allow her stockings to go unadjusted barometrically and indulge in what looked, for all the world, like genuine cogitation before telling me, "Well," and telling me, "All right."

I shopped. I cooked. I locked up nights. I vacuumed, and I dusted. I seethed over the deplorable hands my parents had left me in, and it was some years later before I came to see how shrewd they'd been. There they were off in the wide world eating their haggis and watching their eclipses while I was back home as harried and undone as a trauma nurse. They must have known I'd have no ready opportunity for mischief, would be checked and stymied by Aunt Sister's wholesale fecklessness.

They never even brought me back anything much. Nothing, that is, worth having. I'd get a slurry of leftover pocket change, shoehorns from hotels, the odd appalling gift-shop trifle (the Euro equivalent of coconut heads) and only once a handsome bottle of fine Swedish aquavit. My father stored it in the freezer for safekeeping against the day when I'd be old enough to drink it, and he sought my permission for every dram it took him to empty the thing.

My parents, then, were hardly the sort to be suspicious of worldliness which—along with doubts about the value of postgraduate education, indifference to symphonic music, contempt for federal institutions, baseless allegiance to margarine and high-test gasoline—was a long-standing and respectable local custom. The conventional thinking went that the world at large teemed with the stripe of people who could have stood more soap in their bathwater, less flavor in their food, and would all have moved here anyway if we'd known the stomach to let them.

I'm sure my parents inspired no end of whispered criticism for going, like they did, all over the place. Most particularly my father, who had scant use for civic diplomacy and so would return from a trip and tell to about anyone who'd listen how the virtues of where he'd just been far outstripped the ones at home. My mother, for her part, was perfectly capable of a cozy bromide, could fix her mouth and insist that an evening at a Palermo café table with a view of sunset on the Tyrrhenian Sea was nice enough in its way but could hardly compete with the pleasures of life back in Neely among her neighbors and her many cherished friends.

This was not the brand of sentiment she would air in front of my father because she knew he'd say, "Christ, woman!" no matter where they were.

He had a cynical streak, my father did, an acidic sense of humor, a talent for lively improvisational deflating commentary, a decided preference for native decency over organized religion, a profound aversion to nostalgia, little use for politics, an abiding and largely unindulged enthusiasm for cribbage and a deep affection for flue-cured burley tobacco in the form of Tareytons.

My father disapproved of sneakers on any human over forty who was not in the verifiable care of a licensed chiropodist. He followed the Cardinals but only through box scores and only in September, owned on vinyl the complete recordings of the Harmonicats and observed a lasting moratorium on transactional palaver once the cashier at the Big Lots, when he'd asked her how she was, had passed a quarter hour in breathless clinical description of the fallout from her hysterectomy.

My mother was always, I think, a little surprised she'd fallen for my father. She was guilty of an indefensibly sunny disposition, had been raised to an uninhibited fervor for her Holy Savior and had grown, I suspect, to anticipate she'd take up with a man who shared her faith and embraced her optimism. Instead my father had come along with his faintly pagan roguishness and, the way my mother told it, an impossibly dapper pair of pleated trousers.

We had for years in an end table drawer a snapshot of my father wearing those cavernous pants while posed before an oleander bush. He always looked to me a little like a camel driver, hardly formidable competition for the righteous Son of God, and I do believe that my mother endured lifelong disappointment over the fact that most everything she'd been brought up to believe had been thwarted by a droopy pair of powder blue serge pants. She regretted, I think, a certain want of spine in her convictions, wished sin were less delicious and Christian virtue not so dull.

I doubt they ever mustered between them concrete misgivings about their marriage. They suffered through the usual upsets and abrasive interludes, but my mother and father were each ideally suited for the other in that she instinctively curbed him just when he had need of curbing and he checked her when she'd earned cause to be checked.

My father enjoyed dismantling people the way a man might demolish a barn. He'd start with the trim and the hardware, take issue with stray fond beliefs, but gingerly and in a cordial manner, before setting about to remove the siding a clapboard at a time. He'd ask after the car a fellow drove, the religion he subscribed to, the shows he watched, the work he did, the hobbies he pursued. And once my father had made his way entirely down to the raw framing, he'd locate the posts or stays or trusses holding the structure up and proceed to explain to the candidate at hand why his core convictions were benighted rubbish.

My father considered this sort of thing philosophical inquiry, and he chose to believe that most people would be gratified to learn where their joists were racked, their sills bug-eaten, their rafters out of true, where they'd departed from sound judgment and right thinking. My mother, for her part, considered "gratified" an extravagant reach. She allowed my father his interviews, the odd genial belittling jab, but once he'd laid the groundwork for wholesale demolition, my mother would ordinarily intervene.

From across a room, a patio, a lodge hall, a restaurant table, my mother would tell my father, "Louis," with enough emphasis and bend to snare his undivided notice and arrest his line of talk. Then she would train upon him the special puckered face she pulled as a reminder he'd "gratified" a man into his grave already.

Yes, my father had once subjected a Hazlip to philosophical inquisition on an occasion when there had been a dearth of sounder people about. My father always insisted he was only trifling with the fellow, had been driven into that Hazlip's company out along the street once the town band had struck up (with its usual overabundance of brio) a brassy Benny Goodman medley.

After the icehouse burned, the two-acre lot it had occupied in town had been turned into a park with a burbling fountain and a band shell which had proved to be a thoroughgoing acoustical fiasco due to the reverb from the bank facade directly across the street. So the band would be revisited by the phrases it had played mere moments after it had finished playing them, most usually while it continued to lacerate a melody. The music, then, the band was playing and music it had but recently butchered (wholly unimproved by its visit to the bank across the street) would meet together the way sedans will sometimes meet out on the highway, which is to say catastrophically.

The way my father described it, enduring a concert at the icehouse park was the musical equivalent of eating Waldorf salad—all sorts of unsavory incompatible items together at once.

The only remedy was to sit as near as possible to the stage to allow the band the chance to drown itself out, but given the caliber of local talent ordinarily on display, about the only thing worse than hearing the Neely band play with an echo was hearing it play up close and unobscured. Year in and year out, that ensemble could claim a couple of good musicians, but, as is the way of the world, the flat unrhythmic mediocrities always played just loud enough to swamp them.

It was relatives mostly who sat up close, spouses and cousins and offspring along with civic boosters like my mother who insisted on believing that everything homegrown was better than it was. My father attended because the park was in a seedy part of town, so he couldn't in good conscience let my mother go alone. But she preferred him wandering loose rather than perched up front beside her where he'd wince over artless phrasing and actively bemoan arrangements. She decided she'd rather have him cadging cigarettes by the street.

My father had contracted some years back a nagging case of walking pneumonia which my mother had seen as an opportunity for him to give up smoking. She always insisted that her father had died from some manner of nicotine poisoning. He smoked Luckys and dipped Tube Rose and stayed phlegmy and congested but expired, in point of fact, from comprehensive arterial blockage and so was a victim more of bacon drippings and chicken-fried cube steak.

Now if my father had been a smoker in the conventional sense, he likely could have found some way to give his Tareytons over. He might have taken nicotine supplements or undergone hypnosis, sought peer support in the musty basement of the YMCA. In point of fact, though, he was more in the way of an avid tobacco enthusiast. He enjoyed the trappings and the rituals of the smoking life. Tamping the pack and peeling the band, tearing the foil along the stamp edge, bucking a cigarette free of its brethren and running the length of it under his nose. He appreciated the futile wishfulness of matchbook advertising, the rasp of match head against striker, the smell of paper and leaf once fired.

He never really drew on his cigarettes in the common local manner, as if he had need of burley-tobacco smoke to keep him alive. My father was more in the way of a cigarette aficionado. He was equipped to admire the delicate striping of the rolling paper, the bouquet of the blend, the column of ash, the tang of the smoke on his tongue. If my mother had not been seized by such a blind distaste for smoking, she might have noticed that my father, even once he'd lit one up, hardly by local standards smoked his Tareytons at all. He savored the scent and feel, the ceremony of the undertaking. He had cigarettes instead of NASCAR or the mysteries of high church.

Initially my mother attempted to curb him with disapproval alone before she graduated to overt acts of frustration. She'd snatch away my father's ashtray once he'd ground a butt out in it, would dump it and rinse it and leave it to drain in the basket in the sink. My father merely added retrieving the thing to his host of Tareyton trappings. In response my mother began to break my father's ashtrays. I do believe she accidentally fractured his scallop shell, the one with GRAVEYARD OF THE ATLANTIC painted on it in gaudy scarlet. It was brittle and thin and went to pieces at last against the sink edge, but a few of the subsequent ones were plastic and called for directed hammer blows.

My father never offered to rise from his chair in the den and intercede. He confessed to me once that he found my mother's pluck a little stirring and then winked in a fashion, I have to say, I wish he hadn't winked. He carried a box of ashtrays home one night from the grange hall, little accordion-folded items made of glorified aluminum foil. For every one my mother crumpled and dispatched, he had a dozen more.

That's when my mother took to hiding matches and throwing Tareytons out—half-finished packs for the most part, but an entire carton once. Then she met at a women's circle meeting with authentic ammunition, learned that the husband of a cousin of a woman she had met had been diagnosed with a malignancy. Or semiauthentic ammunition, that is, since it was a testicular tumor, a fact which my mother omitted from the version she favored my father with.

She took to fretting over my father's health, and when she fretted, she wasn't plucky, and when she wasn't plucky, my father found he was insufficiently stirred. So the gesture my father made for my mother, his pledge to give up smoking, was a little in the way of testicular itself.

Of course, he didn't actually quit but did become discreet and cagey. He secreted Tareytons and matches away all around town and would produce them as he circulated from mailboxes and tree cubbies, had packs hidden out of the weather deep in mausoleum niches and under memorial headstone overhangs. So a stroll with my father was often a lesson in vice-fueled legerdemain.

The trouble was, he earned in time a reputation for ghoulishness. People, most particularly widows, would drive out to the cemetery to pay what they called their respects to their late husbands and various kin which involved usually a spot of groundskeeping informed by abuse. In Neely sudden death routinely functioned as a prelude to resentment. Husbands (as a rule) would keel over with a rupture or a blockage, with their worldly affairs a little wide of tidy and resolved, leaving their wives alone to negotiate the local stages of grief which tended to open with numbing shock and culminate in indignation.

The women who visited the municipal cemetery with the greatest frequency were, by definition, the angriest of the lot. Their husbands had left them with second mortgages, car payments, Visa debt, the occasional long-standing girlfriend in Danville or Winston-Salem who'd shown up at the funeral to stake her romantic claim. They'd found by then the pornographic fetish magazines, dollar chips from Biloxi casinos, hidden fifths of Everclear, the odd paternity subpoena in a furnace-filter box.

Their husbands, in short, were not anymore the men who they had buried, and on trips to the cemetery, they would inform them of as much. Impolitely, as a rule, and with an overabundance of venom which my father was, a little too frequently, handy to hear them at. They'd see him and seethe and think poorly of him, if for no other reason than he was an actual living man convenient to be thought poorly of.

Talk, naturally, circulated about his preference for the graveyard, talk originating with and colored by women who knew scant use for men, and it was enough to cause my mother to take charge of his cigarettes. She kept them for a while in a drawer in their mahogany secretary, thereby prompting my father to leave off with the graveyard altogether and spend his leisure snooping around for the key to the filigreed lock.

Since my mother was stingier with his Tareytons than he cared for her to be, my father took to bumming smokes from citizens on the street. That's how my father fell in with that Hazlip at the icehouse park who gave him a Carlton and then set in to speaking at some length of assorted wretched choices he had made throughout his life. Automotive and matrimonial. Educational. Tonsorial. Moral. Civic. Legal. Dietary. That Hazlip owned up, apparently, to being severely blue and sought from my father advice on how to cope and what to do.

My mother took the view my father should have bucked that Hazlip up, should have visited on him a splash of even wholly fraudulent sunshine, but my father had been preoccupied with the effort a Carlton requires for a human of normal lung capacity to draw smoke through the filter, so he'd hardly heard that Hazlip and had no notion what to say. When that Hazlip drove his Fiesta into a pond on the way home and went unmissed and undiscovered for about two weeks together, my mother preferred to believe that my father had at least partially killed the man. As the keeper of his Tareytons, she blamed herself a little and decided to let my father at his cigarettes again.

She revealed where she kept the key to the filigreed lock of the secretary, in a small ceramic jug on the kitchen windowsill that contained otherwise a few paper clips, a little grit and lint.

My father humored my mother at first, and whenever he wanted a Tareyton, he'd waste a solid quarter hour shaking the key from the jug. One evening, however, he chose instead to extract it through the bottom. He brought to bear the very hammer my mother shattered ashtrays with.

3

SO WITHOUT ARTICULATE COMMENTARY, discussion really beyond a snort, they went back to their pre-testicular-tumor life together. My father indulged, whenever he wished, in the rituals of smoking while my mother actively disapproved and made his ashtrays scarce which frequently functioned for them as a manner of foreplay. They were, then, affectionate as a rule and pretty happily bound together with few regrets that they had settled and stuck just where they'd ended up, but even still they weren't so terribly anxious for me to imitate them. My father in particular expected me to range wide and explore, even decreed and organized it for me once I had resisted.

I was back at the time to seeing a girl I'd dated in high school. I'd gone to college halfway across the state, had come home with a degree but precious little professional ambition. I'd reoccupied my old bedroom, reclaimed my chair at the breakfast table and was working with a guy I knew installing kitchen counters. Or rather he was installing kitchen counters that I would help him carry when I'd not been sent instead to fetch a tool out of his truck.

I met up with Fay again once we'd been called in by her aunt to replace the butcher block on her pass-through with artificial stone that looked a bit like granite until you touched it. Back in high school, I'd been Fay's boyfriend for almost an entire month while she was in between linebackers. She'd spent the first two weeks complaining to me about the one she'd dropped and the last week and a half ensnaring the one she claimed for a replacement. I got to drive her around in my father's sedan and keep her in barbecued Fritos. She'd leave most nights the orange imprint of her lips upon my cheek.

She was sunning herself at her aunt's poolside in just bikini bottoms, was nut-brown and blond and tattooed on the blade of her right shoulder. Not a flower or a butterfly but some strain of jungle cat large and colorful enough to have graced a gunnery sergeant.

"Is that Fay?" I asked her aunt, and she and Buddy, the guy I worked with, glanced out the window as Fay flipped onto her back. Buddy groaned involuntarily at the sight of Fay's bare chest.

The aunt flung open her sliding door, and we heard her say, "Fay, honey," and watched her join her niece out by the far end of the pool. She pointed back toward the house as she described, we had to figure, the pair of us in her kitchen with our adenoids on display. Fay sat up, bare-chested still, and peered immodestly our way. She rose and dabbed sweat from her cleavage with the towel she'd been sprawled on, stood uncovered while she cast around for her bikini top.

Fay only got the thing tied once she'd reached the kitchen door, and she proved happier to see me than I'd any right to hope for. She screamed, "Louis!" and charged directly over to throw her arms around me, kissed my cheek and left a greasy fragrant smudge of Sea & Ski.

It turned out Fay was suffering through a rather extended linebacker drought. She'd had a marriage annulled already. Fay anyway chose to call it annulled, though I'm not entirely sure that Baptists recognize the concept. Her husband had blown a knee out in 49er training camp and, following surgery, had gone to listless blubber and been cut. When the remaining defensive backfield proved immune to Fay's various charms, she moved home with a signing-bonus ragtop and a notarized Nevada divorce along with quite sufficient detached indifference toward her former husband to permit Fay to believe that her vows hadn't counted because they hadn't stuck.

She set herself up as a bachelorette and reconstituted virgin and took to trolling for the variety of neckless lout that she preferred. In keeping with local tradition, though, we had few athletes to boast of—chiefly a girl with uncommon field-hockey skills at the private middle school. The men of Fay's vintage who'd known some degree of glory on the gridiron had taken jobs, for the most part, at car dealerships and had gone, without exception, to seed.

I, however, was essentially everything I'd been in high school. Meek and wiry, that is to say, polite agreeable company. So Fay proved keen to rekindle the relationship we'd enjoyed, but with Jose Cuervo this time around instead of Frito-Lay. I didn't have anything else going on, and she'd hugged me in her bikini which, for practical purposes, had the same effect as a collar and a leash.

It didn't hurt that Buddy resented me. While he loved his wife and son, he had the capacity still to work up bile for a friend and employee who was wholly unfettered and of clear interest to a situational virgin with a deep tan, a diamond navel stud and a Bengal-tiger tattoo. For almost two months solid after we'd finished work on Fay's aunt's pass-through, Buddy regularly sent me to fetch back tools from his truck he didn't need.

The trouble was that Fay had neglected to evolve appreciably more than I had, so she routinely searched for her next linebacker while in my company. The adult part of her allowed for both an intimate relationship with me (conducted acrobatically in the wayback of my Civic) and an appetite for sporting behemoths out on the horizon. I would catch Fay, however, gazing intently upon me from time to time as if considering me for a compromise choice and measuring me for fit. She was maturing, apparently, into the grim capacity to suspect that there were only so many strapping defensive specialists to go around.

My mother didn't care for Fay. She considered her loose and vulgar, had been reared in an age when felons and drunken seamen got tattoos, not decent young ladies from proper homes, even ones with Baptist annulments. Her constitutional optimism, though, permitted her to hope that Fay was pliable enough for alterations and redemption. I suspect that my mother prayed for Fay to accept Christ as her Savior or, at the very least, reject the tube top as proper public attire. She probably dispatched a petition or two to the Lord on high as well to tempt me to see the virtues of the Messick she preferred who was untattooed and unannulled, pierced only in her earlobes and would as soon have walked to Sacramento in her stocking feet as service a fellow by way of recreation in his Civic.

My father, naturally, was equipped to appreciate Fay's allure. He was a man, after all, and so maintained a sliver of his brain for the raw unsavory objectification of women. He proved qualified, then, to recognize Fay as both a poor matrimonial prospect and effectively impossible to quit. Those occasions my mother would sigh and wonder what I saw in the girl, my father would mute the television or peer out from behind his paper and fix my mother with one of his concentrated incredulous glares.

Only once she'd begun to shift and squirm would he tell her,

"George Maharis," by way of reminding her that she herself had previously craved a man for his anatomical superstructure and precious little else. My mother, then, was reduced to fretting and prayer and scattershot hopefulness which left my father to the actual enterprise of leading me from temptation. It turned out he'd known in his salad days a variety of Fay. A Carol, in fact, with ginger hair and trifling inhibitions who'd proven weak against my father's pair of impossibly dapper pants. Apparently Carol was both lovely and fond of vigorous use, liked her fun back in a day when women were hardly encouraged to. And once my father had enticed her (assisted by his baggy trousers), she'd responded with displays of her ungirlish appetites.

My father, I recall, convened a chat devoted entirely to Carol. He asked one evening if I wouldn't care to join him for a walk, but once we'd left the house and crossed the porch, we stopped on the front steps. He perched upon the third tread down, and I sat alongside him in what had become the traditional family spot for sensitive exchanges.

My mother kept ferns on the capstones either side of the stairs, and, like her mother before her, she fertilized the things with chicken manure. Not dry inoffensive composted manure in bags from the garden supply, but mucusy aromatic droppings more recently in a chicken. My mother's ferns were robust and bushy, a thriving sight from the street but a bit of an eye-watering trial to tolerate up close, and over time we Benfields had taken to using the thick ammonia stink as a form of conversational insulation.

Two gentlemen having a confab between my mother's ferns weren't likely to be plagued by interlopers.

My father, consequently, felt free on the steps to speak to me of Carol more frankly than he would have spoken of her in the house. He'd won her, as it turned out, from a boy with pants less dapper than his own and had enjoyed her devotion for almost a year until a fellow with a Malibu had come along to trump my father's trousers. They'd been happy in their time together, my father and this Carol, and he cataloged for me Carol's charms and Carol's skills and enticements with the pitch of detail a man with a wife in the house behind him had need of the intervention of a chicken-manure cloud to discuss.

"She was something, all right," my father told me, and, after a moment of pining nostalgia, he listed a string of men that Carol (following him) had been something with.

Then he told me how he'd run across her at a Christmas show in Charlotte, a seasonal retail monstrosity at the War Memorial Coliseum which my mother had dragged my father to when Mrs. Phillip J. King fell ill and pronounced herself too gastrically unsettled for the trip. As a rule my father was constitutionally incapable of Christmas cheer, most particularly in the first week of November. So he remained in the car in the lot for a while in a sullen display of pique until abject boredom drove him onto the coliseum floor proper, where he searched for my mother among the booths and the ghastly Christmas displays.

The way my father described it, he got waylaid by a Christmas product on offer. He strayed across a table freighted with assorted yuletide icons (elves and reindeer and fir trees and Santas) all made with felt and buttons and glitter and cotton and fuzzy lengths of yarn, the types of items he guessed he could find back home if he rifled a drawer or two. There at the Christmas show, though, he could buy that stuff for thirty dollars and change along with glue and blunted scissors in a pasteboard "kit," they called it, from a woman by the cash box at the table end.

She was leathery and peroxided and hardly looked like she once had, but my father recognized her nonetheless. "Carol?" he said, and endured a spot of squinting contemplation.

Theirs was not, by my father's account, an exceedingly fond reunion. At first Carol couldn't place my father, though she eventually remembered his pants, and only after she'd studied him mercilessly did she claim to recall him as well. There were numerous gentlemen otherwise she could conjure far more clearly, particularly the six she'd taken in wedlock, including the two she'd married twice. They'd inflicted upon her all manner of unhappiness which would be in addition, my father learned, to Carol's ingrate children.

"Larry, is it?" she asked my father.

He shook his head and told her, "No."

My mother found him wandering the coliseum floor with his arms full of Christmas "kits." He kissed her with a passion he usually reserved for occasions she'd broken an ashtray, and she could see in his boxes through the cellophane facing what looked even to her like crap.

My father didn't trouble himself to draw the parallels. Once we'd left the fragrant front-porch steps and struck out along the roadway, he failed to moralize, and he neglected to instruct. He didn't predict what he suspected would become of me and Fay, didn't ask me to trust his wisdom and his judgment in such matters, refused to let on he was favoring me with guidance of any sort. Instead he wondered about the purpose of groundhogs in the Savior's divine plan, puzzled over the threadbare allurements of a career in dental hygiene and rhapsodized at length about an obituary he'd lately read which had presented a Sizemore's violent psychosis as a brand of whimsy.

Otherwise he left me alone to stew in what he'd said of Carol, steep in everything he'd failed to say of Fay. That was my father all over—Tolstoy doomed to live in Dickens's world.

They bought me a handsome valise, my parents did, at the luggage shop in the mall which, given the traditional local distaste for travel, sold soap and scented candles, greeting cards and magazines, and hovered on the brink of insolvency. The clerk threw in a pair of cedar shoe trees as a token of gratitude, and my parents presented the whole bounty to me one night after supper. Even I had to figure that a man with a spanking-new bayberry-scented valise probably had some manner of excursion in his future.

"So where am I going?" I asked my parents, and my mother yielded to tears.

My father had arranged for the job, the shared apartment, had purchased the airline ticket. He provided the explanation as to why it was wholly proper for a grown man to work installing kitchen counters for a living but insupportable for an adult to stay on as his assistant in the capacity of gofer and agreeable sidekick. He even went so far as to suggest Fay had impressed him as the sort who'd find some way to get along without me.

And she did too, that very evening in the wayback of my Civic. Once I'd broken the news, Fay asked me with no air of dewy regret if I'd drop her out the bypass at the motor-hotel lounge. She was a practical girl when it came to men. One unsporting civilian was just about as useful as another.

I flew to La Guardia out of Greensboro on a Saturday afternoon. The woman occupying the seat beside me showed me pictures of a baby whose lineage, as she described it, was so muddied by divorce I couldn't decipher if he was her grandchild or a cousin once removed.

In a bid to avoid construction delays on the Grand Central Parkway, my taxi driver (a turbaned Sikh who talked incessantly on his phone) took a route along secondary roads and residential byways, eventually coming to a halt at Amsterdam and Ninety-first only once he'd put the sort of monstrous fare upon the meter a lesser cabbie would have had to drive to Hartford twice to charge.

I thanked the man. I tipped him and watched him veer out into traffic with my new valise still shut up in his trunk.

LIFE
AND
CASUALTY

THE LIZARDS, APPARENTLY, HAD come with the apartment. It seems a previous tenant had turned them out to prey upon the roaches once the boric acid and the diazinon had failed and then had left them behind with the picture hooks, the stray dust balls and soap scum. Nobody had bothered to inform me we had geckos on the loose before one of the creatures joined me on the sofa. I wailed and levitated and tried to crush it with a bolster which earned me the notice of Do-Ray who shook his head and told me, "Hoss."

Do-Ray hailed from greater Cinnaminson down toward Camden off the turnpike. His given name was Tim, and his casual vocabulary consisted almost exclusively of permutations of "hoss." He would color the word and bend it, had learned to freight it so with inflection that he could make a "hoss" mean virtually anything he pleased. He had his first-beer-of-the-weekend "hoss," his let's-eat-Chinese "hoss," his change-the-channel-because-I'm-not-watching-this-shit "hoss." Do-Ray employed an urgent whispered "hoss" along the street when he'd spied the sort of female he'd be satisfied to service, a scathing "hoss" for girls he'd not lay hands to on a bet.

The "hoss" Do-Ray availed himself of when he was disappointed in you could be as stinging as an exhaustive dressing-down, while the one he preferred when you'd managed to be triumphant in his eyes had a fourteen-karat quality about it. I heard once from Do-Ray a singularly wan pathetic "hoss." We'd just stepped out of the cineplex on Broadway near Lincoln Center, had been discussing across the lobby the cretinous enormity that had been throttling the life out of us for the previous two hours, a movie that had struck even Do-Ray as an affront to decency and a crass assault on rational narrative sense, and this from a man who every evening watched cartoons on purpose.

So we were sharing a moment of cultural disaffection when Do-Ray was stopped beneath the marquee by the sight of a man across the street. He was balding and dumpy and had on his arm the caliber of woman a fellow like him would be obliged to hire. As we watched, he nuzzled her cheek with his nose and moistened it with his tongue. It turned out he was Do-Ray's father, and she wasn't Do-Ray's mom which Do-Ray told me, "Hoss," about with barely muted wretchedness.

I was hardly so close to my other two roommates. I wasn't actually close to Do-Ray, but he was awfully easy to tolerate given his vocabulary. Franklin and Thor were a little spoiled for me by their expansiveness. Franklin most particularly was a burden and a plague. He was gangly and unenticing, had deplorable taste in clothes and took the subway twice a month to Brooklyn for his institutional haircuts. He devoted the bulk of his leisure hours to amateur dermatology, would park himself on the sofa and conscientiously pick at pustules, after which he'd retire to the bathroom and douse himself with aftershave. We could usually hear his shrieks over the TV and the traffic.

Anybody presumptuous enough to dare to call him "Frank" got by way of reply the full account of Franklin's great-grandfather. Franklin's namesake, he'd immigrated penniless from Hungary and (depending entirely on the concentration of Jägermeister in Franklin's system) had either revolutionized the incandescent bulb or mass-produced the flip-flop.

Franklin's parents came to visit him once a month, drove in from Sheepshead Bay. His mother would usually carry with her a couple of quarts of soup, lentil and leek, made with both love and (to taste it) fabric softener. Franklin would brew and serve her coffee which she'd stir but rarely sip because our cups were never clean enough to suit her. Those occasions the geckos chirped and barked, Franklin blamed the poodle upstairs.

Franklin's father was usually occupied checking on his car. He wouldn't park it in one of our local garages, resented the prices they charged, so he'd deposit Franklin's mother just before our building and spend the next three-quarters of an hour circling for a spot. Then he'd join us long enough to enumerate his leading concerns. The blocks he parked on always looked a little lawless to him. He worried about thieves and vandals, was particularly fearful of slashed tires. He had an unnatural dread of scuffs and dings from his fellow drivers, was often closer to a hydrant than he ideally liked to be, and he was given to presentiments (more in the way of baseless hunches) that some fool in a panel truck was about to double-park him in.

They'd been visiting for months, Franklin's parents had, before I finally saw their sedan. I was returning one Sunday from the Laundromat when a beat-up maroon Ford Galaxy slowed to a stop before our building and Franklin's mother climbed from the passenger seat with her jug of soup and her handbag.

The car was spackled and primed most everywhere it wasn't crumpled and rusted. The rear bumper was gone but for the brackets. The tires were desiccated and bald. The vinyl top had erupted and rotted to tatters. The mirror housings held no glass. The lid of the trunk was secured with a couple of loops of insulated clothesline. The license plates, an unmatched set, lay in the sun-baked window well.

As I stepped over to help Franklin's mom with her soup (I was discouraged from touching her handbag), Franklin's father told me, "Hey, you," from beneath the steering wheel. The front-seat beading, I noticed, was held in place with electrical tape. I shut the door, and Franklin's father snorted. He shook his head despondently, said, "Here we go," and rolled off in a cloud of blue exhaust to seek his customary troubling spot along the curb.

I couldn't quite manage to keep myself from owning up later on to the surprise I'd felt upon seeing that Franklin's father's car was a heap. Now, I come from a family of heap drivers. My father never bought a vehicle new, and he'd run them until they'd quit or could no longer clear inspection, when he'd bargain for another sedan somebody had sickened of.

He didn't, however, fret about them. That was the beauty of owning a junker. He didn't care who barked his door against it or rammed it with a buggy. My father assumed that a thief would face a commitment hearing instead of a trial. He never washed his sedans outright, only scoured the windshields maybe quarterly, and he construed the odd tank of high-octane gas responsible upkeep.

So I believed I had the pedigree to inquire of Franklin's father why he worried so over his Galaxy when it was closing hard on scrap. I phrased it politely. I seem to recall I referred to his sedan as "aging," and I chose not to mention the Bondo, the bare bumper brackets, the clothesline, the rust. Even still, Franklin's father took near-bottomless offense, and he raged at me for the quarter hour he had to spare in between double-parking premonitions.

Once he'd run out, Franklin's mother blistered me for a while herself. Like her husband, she behaved as if I'd offered insult to her family, had denigrated her heritage and was a blight upon her son. Franklin, for his part, fell back on his dermatology.

The woman was still simmering as Franklin walked her to the street, and I was taking what comfort I could from Do-Ray's bewildered "hoss" when Thor showed up to air an explanation.

He'd emerged from our only actual bedroom in his cotton briefs. Thor was wiry and looked to be naturally hairless from the earlobes down, so cotton briefs were, in fact, a rather becoming clothing option for him. He was standing in what passed for our kitchen—an electrified alcove crammed with grubby undersize appliances and populated by an unpoisonable expeditionary force of ants. Thor had an arm hooked over the refrigerator door and was drinking eggnog from the carton.

Thor had a weakness for eggnog and had searched the city until he'd found a store downtown that stocked, for some reason, half-gallon cartons of the stuff throughout the year. I stopped in with him once. The place was a near-derelict Lower East Side delicatessen with dusty cans of tomatoes and water chestnuts on the shelves, salt-cod carcasses in the window peppered with boiler soot, some manner of veiny livestock entrail on offer in a cooler and, back in what passed for a dairy case, colorful yuletide cartons of eggnog imported from Argentina but printed, mysteriously, in French.

Thor primarily employed his eggnog as a postcoital supplement. He explained to me once the effect of milk fat and nutmeg on testosterone levels while standing at the refrigerator in his cotton briefs in between greedy slugs straight from his carton. He was offering, I recall, an enlargement on the dietary science when his girlfriend of the moment called out to him from the bedroom to bring her back a juice box from her book bag on the couch.

Thor, you see, had a weakness for schoolgirls as well and tended to run with the juice-box set. They weren't any of them so young and tender as to be, I believe, illegal, but I never knew Thor to romance a female with a college credit to her name. From the wailing he could touch off and the shrieks he would illicit, there was cause to suspect that Thor was one extraordinary swordsman or confined himself to officers of the thespian society.

It was a little dispiriting for me and Do-Ray, particularly for Franklin, to hear through the door of our only bedroom a female making noises we all feared we lacked the job skills and the caliber of equipment to ever hope to drive a girl to make. In the spirit of plucky self-improvement, Franklin once tried an eggnog diet, and he plagued Thor for a week or two on the topic of G-spot orienteering. It turned out, however, that dairy gave Franklin reprehensible vapors and Thor could very nearly groom his eyebrows with his tongue.

Me and Franklin and Do-Ray retired nights to a platform above the main room, a cramped and overheated piece of domestic territory known in Upper West Side real-estate parlance as a sleeping loft. From there we'd occasionally audit and gauge Thor's progress through a schoolgirl (who was staying at a friend's house or whose parents were in Rome), and when Thor would pop out for a rejuvenating dram of eggnog, Do-Ray would rain down on him a hosanna of a "hoss."

Thor's given name was Randle. That's how his mail came anyway, but he was singular and emphatic enough to rate and merit Thor. In addition to his hairless body and his sideshow tongue, Thor had a knack for improvisational persuasive distillation. He could explain away thorny world events and account for human frailties with a brand of pithy economy schoolgirls found seductive, since they were beset otherwise by blossoming womanhood and algebra.

Even I could usually take some comfort in a Thor pronouncement until I'd nosed up at my leisure the rank underlying bunk. I once heard Thor describe to his flame of the moment the history of chicken nuggets. According to him, they'd been developed by members of the electoral college who, throughout nonvoting years, applied themselves to innovations. Thor permitted them text messaging and methanol as well.

That was the beauty of Thor's worldview. Even his conspiratorial agents operated without malice and concocted finger food. Thor was sunny in his way and reliably consoling, and, to judge from the racket he raised, he supplied his stable of schoolgirls with more incisive attention than they'd ever again enjoy from a man.

So I was pleased to have Thor to call upon in the wake of the Galaxy blowup, and he heard me out while swabbing residual eggnog off his upper lip. I touched upon my family history with disreputable sedans and labored to make it square with what I'd lately seen of Franklin's parents' feverish devotion to their shabby Ford. I confessed that I was flummoxed by their sensitivity which spurred from Do-Ray a revival of his bewildered, "Hoss."

Thor heard us out in silence with stark light from our Amana falling across his bare goose-pimply skin. He then folded shut the spout of his eggnog carton and returned the thing to its shelf.

"Car Jews," Thor said at last. He asked if we'd heard of the sorts of Israelis who carried automatic weapons to protect their desolate wasteland homes. We nodded, and Thor informed us both, "Like that. But with sedans."

Then he winked and left us for our only bedroom with a door, and Do-Ray and I lingered before our ant-infested alcove kitchen contemplating, I guess, the troubled history of the Jewish people until Thor had raised a warble from his schoolgirl of the moment when our thoughts lurched to other avenues of anthropology.

It was some six or eight hours later (we were watching the Yankees lose) before I muted the TV to gain Do-Ray's notice and said to him, "Car Jews?"

2

WE WERE ALL WORKING as wretchedly paid trainees at Meridian Life and Casualty. The company held our apartment lease and soundly overcharged us for the privilege of living at no little distance from the Long Island City home office which we could have reached more easily from Trenton on a bus.

We trudged across the park each morning to take two subways and a cab that would drop us off at what we'd been instructed in a memo to call the Meridian Life and Casualty Complex—a half-vacant office tower beside a squat unsightly building boasting two hundred thousand square feet of wholly unlet retail space. There was a parking garage kept closed by inspectors because of stress-fracture issues and a bus shelter that had to be a solid mile off any route.

Meridian occupied seven floors in the upper quarter of the tower, five of actual office space and two of unchecked wayward clutter. Our nearest neighbor was twenty floors below us, some sort of rogue commodities firm that expended considerable corporate energy answering litigants' writs and subpoenas and dodging federal securities warrants. Moreover, they didn't enjoy our unobstructed view of midtown (the monolithic slab of the UN, the blinding glare off the Chrysler Building, the fitful creep of clotted traffic along the FDR) which after a week or two hardly seemed worth commuting clear to Queens to get.

My father, as it turned out, had worked thirty-odd years for a subsidiary of Meridian Life and Casualty, and he proved to be all but legendary for his actuarial skills. He was enough of a wizard anyway to render me a disappointment, and during my stint at the firm, I became exhaustively acquainted with the wide-eyed incredulity and the crestfallen distress that evermore attached to the question "*You're* Louis Benfield's son?"

My father worked in an anonymous sheet-steel building midway between Neely and Greensboro. It was out near what they called at the time the Triad International Airport which, by way of qualification, boasted one flight to Bermuda a week. That structure had been brief home to some kind of tool-and-die fiasco, and a contractor had snatched it up in foreclosure to refit it for office space.

The place had the sort of slit windows you find in your better city jails, carpeted cubicle walls for offices, vinyl accordion closet doors. There was a zinc machinist's sink attached to a wall in the gentlemen's restroom, some type of lathe in the coffee lounge that had proved too cumbersome to move. Sparrows nested in the peak of the roof where the metal had separated, and the contractor had economized so on proper ventilation that the building functioned as a Dutch oven for six months of the year.

There was no sign out front, no reception area, no customers come to call, just a squad of actuaries on duty inside running numbers, figuring every permutation of a probability, cultivating risk assessments, calculating dividends and dispatching results to underwriters from the Rockies east. By way of recreation, they wagered away their lunches like schoolboys, ran office pools on the melt rate of toilet-deodorant blocks, held extemporaneous sparrow rodeos and a bimonthly grand prix that featured tautened rubber bands and spools from calculator tape.

I don't recall that my father even owned a briefcase, just a plastic insulated sack he carried lunches in. It was ruptured at the strap and seized up at the zipper and, to my mother's consternation, a little moldy at the seams. He wouldn't hear of a replacement, but every few months he'd turn it inside out and set it to defungus on the back steps in the sun.

He was happy enough at Meridian Life and Casualty, I suppose. He never struck me as remorseful or tormented. He could run numbers like some people play the piano or pick up French, so he wasn't obliged to expend himself in the course of his employment. He never actively craved a promotion or went ulcerous for a raise, and the only Meridian company outing I ever knew him to attend was a golfing weekend up in Banner Elk where he found in a fairway bunker a raw ruby the size of a plum.

I held out little hope to satisfy as Louis Benfield's son due chiefly to the fact that I was comprehensively ungifted. I had no knack for patter or untapped actuarial talent and a wan and meager strain of personal charm. In six years I'd taken a four-year degree in international studies which is a worthwhile and unified field of academic pursuit in the way the Tater Tot is a wholesome vegetable. I owned two neckties, a cheesy reversible belt, a pair of Nubuck shoes (one of which I'd tried to mend with a bead of caulking), four dingy shirts, one navy blazer and three pairs of corduroys. So I couldn't even look the part of a young executive on the rise while I failed to find my niche and floundered.

Thor and Do-Ray and Franklin got along well enough, but they weren't Louis Benfield's sons and were expected to start as dim undifferentiated youth while there were widespread corporate assumptions I would sparkle from the first which I actively worked to frustrate and to thwart. I could barely calculate my share of the lunch bill every day, much less speak to the tax implications of premature annuity draw-downs which Franklin, oddly enough (while worrying pustules), could hold forth on at some length.

Do-Ray demonstrated a native skill for customer relations. He was capable of fielding telephone inquiries and tamping down complaints with an anesthetic equanimity. Thor succeeded at winning a special friend in our spinster office manager, a large woman named Meg with a Third Reich wardrobe and thinning hennaed hair. She made the mistake of entrusting Thor with his own supply-room key, and he set himself up almost straightaway as a purloined-stationery kingpin. Thor would show up at work one day a week with a clown car of a satchel that he'd fill with Post-its and rollerball pens, notepads, printer paper and binders, highlighters and ink cartridges, pencils and paper clips that he'd haul back to the apartment and distribute to his girlfriends who'd move them at a markdown to their schoolmates.

In a few short months, Thor got so flush that he could pay the son of a neighbor to make weekly trips to the Lower East Side to buy his eggnog for him.

I was not, for my part, as successful and happy at Meridian Life and Casualty as Thor and Franklin and even Do-Ray came to be. At meetings I would stare out the window at the skyline of Manhattan while Farley (he had us call him) would instruct us in company practices, offer grooming tips and explore the subtleties of situational business ethics which generally boiled down to, "Them other guys is shits."

Farley came across as a curious hybrid, a sort of Nassau County cowboy. He wore a bolo, a silver belt buckle about the size of a cocktail coaster, shirts with snaps instead of buttons and a pair of Tony Lama boots. He generally spoke like a dust-bowl hayseed who'd been raised in Levittown—folksy nuggets steeped in marinara.

Every couple of weeks, Farley would summon us singly to his office for a private evaluation in the midst of his rustic bunkhouse decor. I made it my custom to stare at the lone pho-tograph on Farley's desk—a picture of Farley perched on a western saddle draped upon a fence rail. It took him usually about three minutes to shift that photo out of my view and in-form me he was allergic to livestock dander.

I feel sure Meridian Life and Casualty would have cut me loose, was probably right on the cusp of washing me out of their young-executive program, when I made myself a little worthwhile by effecting a repair. One morning the coffeepot wouldn't heat up, and it was my turn to go fetch Hector. He was our super and union accouterment, and he had a room in the subbasement where he kept his tools and his cot and his Wolf-schmidt vodka and his stock of magazines devoted (it appeared to me) to preposterously endowed brunettes.

Hector was not, by any objective measure, capable or handy. He'd show up with a screwdriver usually and a pair of pliers and inspect whatever item he'd been summoned to see after which, without exception, Hector couldn't fix. He'd usually loi-ter about for a half an hour or so contemplating options and looking females in the vicinity frankly in the chest.

The day the coffeepot refused to fire up, all I wanted was hot coffee, not a trip to the subbasement and Hector's leering com-pany after that. So with one of my apartment keys, I unscrewed the coffeepot backing, and I spliced around the charred and desiccated thermostat which had the look of a well-baked aneurysm. I collected a crowd in the process. Coworkers came from adjacent floors for the exotic sight of an amateur non-unionized civilian actually effecting a repair.

City folk are accustomed to calling in tradesmen as a first resort. A sink fixture drips, a rheostat fails, a length of shoe molding splinters, a dishwasher balks, a window lock detaches at the pivot, a smoke detector goes off when there's no smoke to be seen, and the intrepid citizen picks up his phone, dials the appropriate number, and some guy in twills is sent his way in a radio-dispatched van.

What ensues usually is one part repair and two parts calamity. We'd had the experience of calling a plumber to our apartment. The hot-water valve in our shower seized up, and, in the process of replacing it, the plumber fractured a half dozen tiles in the surround. So we engaged a tile man to replace them who caught the shower curtain on fire, not catastrophically but only at a corner. The smoke, however, begrimed the ceiling, and we hired, as a result, a painter who slopped enough Navajo white on the light switch to short it out.

Franklin was ready to call an electrician when I bought a replacement switch that I installed in the bath with the aid of a butter knife.

With its thermostat bypassed and the casing reattached, the office coffeepot came to life, and there was all but carnival rejoicing among my Meridian colleagues. One of the seniorest vice presidents—a gentleman named Mel with office walls that reached the ceiling and an executive assistant—said, "Benfield," and jerked his head in a chummy sort of way which made me feel welcome to join Mel and go with him to his office.

He'd spoken to me previously only once, had told me at the washroom basin, "Move."

Mel draped an arm around my shoulder and ushered me through his office door so as to put in my hands a desk lamp he'd been meaning to have rewired. Consequently, I shortly found myself out on the Meridian grounds (adjacent to the bus stop with no regular bus service, hard by the shopping plaza with no actual retail tenants, across the street from the faulty cement garage condemned to house no cars), where I passed a quarter hour wondering if I were a spool of lamp cord, where in the sprawl of Long Island City I might possibly be.

3

I MIGHT HAVE MISSED out on the actuarial skills, but I was hell with a clawhammer. My father undertook domestic repairs as a point of manly honor, and I was usually conscripted to help him by handing him his tools. So as little more than a toddler, I could identify a basin wrench and match a socket to a bolt head from probably ten or fifteen paces.

My father was usually stuck under a leaky sink or crammed behind the furnace, balanced on top of his five-foot ladder where he was forbidden by OSHA to stand or ensnared between the clapboards and my mother's beloved shrubbery which created the need for an able assistant to hand him the tools he required. I was compensated with the odd outburst of incendiary profanity.

My father could fix anything, more or less. Anything, that is, but his car. He drew a bright unbreachable maintenance line between the house and the car shed and never so much as checked the air in his tires. There was compelling evidence around that the sort of men who worked on their cars—the type to think nothing of a ring job or repacking wheel bearings—were as a rule content to let their houses go to hell. A man who could reassemble a carburetor or overhaul a clutch could never seem to go to the bother to keep glazing in his windows, dredge the leaves out of his gutters or pick the trash off of his lawn.

In my father's view, it was an awfully short trip from a do-it-yourself oil change to a life of unalleviated squalor. So he made it his mission exclusively to keep the house in shape which, given the vintage of it, served as an alternate career. He'd spend his weekdays actuarializing in the sheet-steel building and his weekends staving off dilapidation.

The houses along my parents' street in town had all been built in the thirties except for the one up at the corner where the Sinclair used to be which had been hauled in in two pieces on a truck. The house directly across the street did service as a cautionary item, as a handy practical example of the wages of neglect. Locally it was known still as the Epperson place even though no actual Eppersons had so much as driven by for probably a couple of decades by then.

The Epperson sisters had lived in that house together until they'd lost their bearings. In truth, they'd stayed on for a year or two after they'd all gone hopping mad. We'd hear them screaming at each other in the small hours of the morning, and on holidays they'd wear bed linens and perform ballets in their front yard.

The house was left to the Epperson family which was fractured and far-flung. The only sister who'd ever wed had abandoned her husband and her children, and otherwise they'd been bound to a string of cousins variously removed who were jointly bequeathed in the last sister's will the Eppersons' rambling home place. The cousins, collectively, couldn't decide on anything at all. Some wanted to sell the house. Others preferred to rent it out. A few tried to purchase the place at deep blood-relation discounts which the rest of the cousins elected to object to and resent, and the whole crew of them balkanized at length into churlish unreasonable factions. They thwarted each other as a matter of mindless reflexive course.

One of them even hired a gentleman to set the house alight. That particular cousin had made a number of unfortunate football bets and was hoping to buy himself out of harm's way with his share of the insurance. The fellow he'd paid to burn the place failed to bring enough accelerant to touch off an inferno. He was attempting to fuel his fire with old newspapers from the cellar when he got bit by a copperhead and had to go for help.

The Epperson house sat back in a grove of towering tulip trees which hadn't been pruned in probably thirty years. So the place stayed deeply shaded from April through October, and when the wind was right, the mildew funk overwhelmed our chicken-manure stink. As stick-built structures go, that house was as flammable as a button mushroom.

It did, in fact, get rented out for a while to two fellows from Wisconsin who'd made a career of following hailstorms in the company of their wives. They did paintless repairs to damaged cars with equipment they pulled in a trailer, worked under a white plastic canopy in the Eppersons' front yard. They used fiberglass rods and suction cups to massage the dings away, went at them from top and bottom both at once which required the brand of patience and the manner of delicate touch those fellows sustained with heroic amounts of Old Milwaukee beer.

They drank it all day, pulled can after iced can from a laundry hamper that was moldy enough to declare itself an Epperson artifact. Their wives popped out to the store from time to time to replenish the supply but mostly sunned themselves in their underwear in lounge chairs on the lawn while thumbing through fashion magazines and listening to country music. They supplied us our own little taste of Branson, according to my father. Without, of course, the irreproachable class.

Naturally, he complained. He started with those two couples across the street, tried to inspire them to some measure of neighborly consideration. Being tenants, however, and transients, they claimed to feel entirely free to refuse to give, in fact, a happy goddamn. It was my mother who called in the local police after a high-volume four-hour tribute to Hank Williams Jr. on an AM station out of Burlington. One of Neely's finest stopped in to pass along the complaint and proved pleased to receive a complimentary half hour of instruction in removing dings from the quarter panel of a Celica.

My father worked his way up through the zoning commission to the mayor herself, a devoutly Christian Throckmorton who'd squeaked by in the last election. The woman drove a dingy white Honda and parked it unprotected in front of the town hall. The afternoon of the hailstorm that brought those Wisconsinites to us, the mayor was holding weekly Bible study in the third-floor coffee lounge on city time with city employees where she enlarged upon Leviticus and the law of the burnt offering and set, I imagine, the Founding Fathers spinning in their graves.

The sky went black which the mayor made use of as a visual aid. She touched extemporaneously upon God's wrath and the agonies of damnation and was waxing catastrophic when the hail began to fall. It had shortly beat the chrome entirely off her Honda.

She got an estimate from the dealer, a check from her insurer, and then she took her car to the itinerant dent massagers from Wisconsin who worked on the relative cheap and left her some settlement money to spend which, strictly speaking, was not illegal or decisively unchristian and wouldn't likely have been a problem for a secular town mayor, but that Throckmorton had Jesused the town hall up a bit more than most people could stand. So my father took a Polaroid and had it reproduced, attached a couple of dozen copies to light poles around town. It was a picture of the mayor's Honda in the care of beer-swilling Yankees and their dumpy low-life wives out taking sun in their brassieres.

The mayor saw fit, with her car only half repaired, to shut those Wisconsinites down, and they headed west to fresh unsettled weather in Tennessee. By then a self-serving chink in her holy ethics had been brought to light, and the mayor began to endure fire from the councilman who'd unseat her. He was twice divorced and salty, hadn't been to church in years.

The Epperson house sat vacant thereafter and returned to functioning for my father as a cautionary study in dilapidation and rot. Whenever he felt tempted to forgo paint or stint on a repair, my father would wander over to the Epperson front walk from where he could see the mealy timber sills and the shutters in the shrubbery, brittle windblown shingles littering the lawn. Then back he would come to execute some chore he'd known an impulse to leave for another week or two undone.

Most of my parents' original neighbors had long since given up the fight and sold off their houses to newlyweds with spunk and impeccable credit who took them down to the framing and started, effectively, afresh. They installed skylights and solar collectors, replaced the wall-to-wall with oak, brought in proper tile men from Greensboro, and from Buddy, my former employer, ordered kitchen counters made of polished and authentic stone.

Most significantly, they always paid a bit more for those houses than they were worth and so succeeded at rooting out all of my parents' original neighbors, down to and finally including Mr. and Mrs. Phillip J. King. The Kings had once joined with my parents in an informal after-dinner oath that they'd all be carried lifeless from their homes before they'd sell them. Moreover, the bottom of the Kings' back lot was all but choked with schnauzer remains that Mrs. Phillip J. King had declared repeatedly she would never abandon.

Mr. and Mrs. Phillip J. King had received their first schnauzer as a wedding gift. I remember most clearly the piebald one that went by Itty Bit. She was ill-tempered and excitable and would bounce so when she barked that she used to tumble off the porch and fall into the shrubbery. And not once in a very great while but pretty frequently.

She was almost twenty when she died and even then not by natural causes but more in the way of negligent homicide. Mr. Phillip J. King accidentally trapped her between the storm door and the front door. He wasn't paying proper attention as he locked up late one night and only found that dog come morning when he went out for the paper. She was cold and stiff and more than a little (my father told it) compressed.

So the Kings claimed a special sentimental attachment to the their property which served to cement them there until a couple down from Danville approached Mr. Phillip J. King while he was raking leaves and offered him appreciably more for his house than he would have dared to ask. The talk was initially that Mr. and Mrs. Phillip J. King would travel. They allowed they intended with the money from the sale to see exotic bits of the world, and they did one weekend in December drive to Hatteras and back, but otherwise they hewed to their long-standing custom of going nowhere much.

They moved into a sprawling subdivision on the Burlington Road, what my father insisted on calling Tyvek Acres notwithstanding the masonry gateway with the forged sign bolted to it that identified the place as Shropshire Glen Estates. The property had been a tobacco farm in its previous incarnation and then had sat fallow for, I suppose, a decade or two before a developer from Charlotte had bought it up to execute his vision of (to judge by the results) creeping faux-Tudor blight.

The lots were a quarter acre at best, and the houses came in one of four styles. There were a few semimature trees left from what had been a hedgerow but mostly just saplings and shrubbery and failing sun-baked lawns. Those homes, as a matter of convenience, were wired for emergencies. There was a button in each kitchen intended to summon the county police, one for the fire department and one for the rescue squad, but they never quite functioned the way they were meant to due to some strain of elusive short which called for help all by itself when no help, in fact, was needed. So the cul-de-sacs and lanes of Shropshire Glen Estates were often choked with pump trucks and radio cars and wailing ambulance vans.

Whenever we thought the place was about as big as it could get, new homes would go up on the margins which meant there never was an end to the tradesmen, the mud and the framing, the dazzling-white house wrap.

On occasion my father would drive out to play cribbage with Mr. Phillip J. King. They would sit in what Mrs. Phillip J. King insisted on calling the study which offered a view of the neighbor's half-bath window about twelve feet away. And Mr. Phillip J. King—never much of a gamesman—would miscount his points and play out of turn and speak of far-flung places that he and his wife, it was clear by then, would never actually see.

My father would frequently return from visits to Shropshire Glen Estates and sit for fifteen minutes or more in his car out in the driveway contemplating, I guess, dire turns in this life he never hoped to take. Then he'd come inside and kiss my mother, inform her that he loved her, before taking up a quart of primer or a caulking gun.

4

AFTER A MONTH OR two of working repairs about the Meridian office, I dispensed with my navy blazer, left off bothering with a tie. It was clear my executive prospects had eroded once Farley had carried in a ghastly Conestoga telephone which he'd dropped off at my desk for me to mend. The singletree was fractured, and the ringer didn't sound near as much like a chow-wagon dinner gong as Farley had been promised, so he encouraged me to neglect my meager duties otherwise and tinker with his telephone instead.

Do-Ray and Thor and Franklin still attended the weekly meetings, and Farley continued to summon them into his bunkhouse office for policy chats. Back home at night, they'd thumb through their insurance handbooks, quiz each other on which arcane reprehensible exemptions had been challenged in the courts and in which states, and they frequently indulged in bouts of animated speculation devoted to various plummy Meridian outposts they'd be pleased to man.

So I was regularly privy to tributes to the municipal virtues of Bridgeport, the civic allure of Altoona, of Lynchburg, Akron, Tampa, Hagerstown. To hear them you'd have thought that Thor and Franklin (even Do-Ray on occasion) were cataloging the charms of Byzantium or Augustinian Rome.

For my part I often carried home a little work as well—a balky blender, a toaster oven, the occasional actual office product—which I'd dismantle and diagnose on our front-room

57

floor while Do-Ray and Franklin upon the couch and Thor off by the icebox reveled in the promise of their viable careers. They'd break off once Thor had determined his testosterone refreshed or his schoolgirl of the moment had broadcast from our only actual bedroom the news that her tingling had subsided and she could feel her legs again.

They didn't ignore me exactly but treated me with undue delicacy as if a biopsy had condemned me or my house cat had just died.

Who could blame them? I had purely confounded corporate expectations, starting like I had on high as storied Louis Benfield's son which I'd parlayed south to leisurewear and a reputation among my colleagues for my soldering gifts and inserting the toner cartridge right side up. I was frequently greasy and ripening while they all stayed fragrant and clean, and because he insisted on keeping the tools in his musty subbasement office, I spent contaminating stretches in Hector's company.

Hector had warmed to me after he'd sniffed out how unconniving I was. Early on, in the way of an unavoidable territorial reflex, Hector had threatened to have a couple of union brethren scuff me up. But once I'd proved docile and altogether harmless, content to pop in his office whenever I needed a wrench or channel locks, Hector found it agreeable to think himself my unofficial foreman.

Hector had never met a potable liquid he wouldn't add vodka to. He splashed it into his morning coffee, used it to flavor his soup at lunch, poured it directly into his Shasta cans for a pick-me-up afternoons. By four he was usually pretty well soused and reliably sentimental, and Hector would all too frequently seek me out and wrangle me downstairs to suffer through a misty reminiscence.

Hector was smitten with a woman who went by the name of Divinia DeLuxe. He'd convinced himself he'd known her back in San Juan and bitterly rued he'd lacked the foresight to cultivate and claim her. When profoundly lubricated (usually around four forty-five), he'd declare he should have guessed his little lithesome Barahona playmate would blossom into the fleshy freak of a female she'd become.

Hector had pictures of Ms. DeLuxe taped to the walls of his dank subbasement office which featured, ungirded, her enormous state-fair-quality breasts. They inspired the identical question a fellow might ask of a blue-ribbon pumpkin, namely, "What in the world would you do with one of those?"

So I fell out of the junior-executive orbit and in with the service personnel who had more my look and gave off, I guess, more of my aroma. I got to know the parcel carrier and the bottled-water man, took lunch on occasion with the boys who cleaned the office windows. Skip and Wallace were brothers from College Point, and workaday ammonia fumes had made them, I was inclined to believe, unnaturally high-strung. They listened to sports radio and argued incessantly about the Mets, often indulged in shoving matches high upon their motorized scaffold and would rain window-cleaning equipment onto the Meridian Complex grounds.

By noon they'd usually have to come down to retrieve their squeegees and their sponges, and we'd sometimes have a bite of lunch at the derelict bus stop where Skip and Wallace would enlist me to settle their leading Metropolitan disputes. Seaver versus Gooden. HoJo or Clendenon in the clutch. The Kingman era stacked against the Keith Hernandez years. Then it was back onto their scaffold to clean a few windows and scatter their tools onto the ground.

Mostly I served, between repairs, as a resource for the temporary help. Meridian Life and Casualty employed a regular squadron of hirelings in a bid to economize on salaries and skimp on insurance coverage (which they more or less had lying around to supply). The firm's president and his minions had discovered over time that two temporary workers with presentable clothing and remedial office skills could usually replace about twice their weight in middle managers.

Better still, they were effectively fungible. Once a temp got knocked around, grew resentful and exhausted of goodwill, it was easy enough to swap him out for an unabused replacement. Most of our temps had a shelf life of three or four months, except for Regina in secretarial who'd held on for a couple of years thanks to deplorable self-esteem and an addiction to wild-cherry cough suppressant. So she was either numb to the callous things that people said about her or suspected them already to be true.

Scuttlebutt had it Regina had once bedded Skip and Wallace in sequence over the course of a couple of sultry Indian summer weeks. They'd shown up one day on their scaffold at the window by her desk, and she'd informed them she had previously owned a malamute named Mookie which worked on Skip and Wallace, apparently, like an aphrodisiac. Regina had troubled herself to commit to memory assorted Stengelisms which she used to bait those boys in turn into the unlet minimall for amorous sessions on the cool raw concrete where the food court was to be.

As I free-fell through the ranks of the young executive trainees, even Regina in her wild-cherry narco haze felt exalted enough to shun me.

I chose to supply my parents with a glancing version of the

truth. In the course of my weekly phone calls, I'd assure them I was happy and rather enjoying my Meridian Life and Casualty career which was honest as far as it went if unrevealing and incomplete. I greeted the temps and helped to settle them into their cubicles, showed them how to get an outside line on the telephone, warned them off the falafel cart that haunted the complex grounds at lunchtime and led them to stores of office supplies Thor had not seen clear to plunder yet.

In return they took me into their vinegary confidence and made me privy to the ridicule that they visited on my colleagues for being, on the whole, such irredeemable frumps. The temp service we used provided us mostly with stylish young gay men who dressed smartly and probably paid more for their haircuts than I did each month for food. They were oftentimes nursing floundering careers in dramatic arts or dance, had dreams of opening spas and cafés, designing inaugural gowns, retiring on sitcom residuals to Jamaica.

They'd occasionally invite me to lunch on the vacant floor upstairs where they'd dissect Meridian Lifers on the basis of their footwear or freely speculate as to the psychosexual constipation that had served to make of Farley what he was. There was little they liked better than occasion for a party, and they were evermore bringing in cupcakes in their bids to touch one off. I don't suspect there was much they enjoyed less than authentic office work, so they swanned around and amused themselves, looked busy when they had to and waited for the call to rotate out.

And that remained the general drift of the Life and Casualty experience until pseudo-Romanian royalty paid a call upon the complex and overhauled the way that we did almost everything.

She gave herself out as Cosmina Jaru. I found her one morning down on the bus bench where she was suffering a rather theatrical spot of respiratory distress. She'd propped herself on an elbow, was panting like a terrier, and she summoned me over with her bejeweled fingers once I'd wandered within range. It turned out she'd never visited an outer borough of Manhattan beyond occasional trips to various first-class lounges at Kennedy. She'd not, that is, been on the actual ground in a place like Long Island City, and she was finding the air a bit rowdy, she called it, and troublesome to breathe.

She looked hardly older than I was but far frailer and over-refined, and she requested that I fan her with the paper I was carrying, insisted I employ the Arts and Leisure section alone.

As her anxiety quelled and her breathing deepened, she volunteered an accounting of how a creature with her advantages and conspicuous allure had tumbled all the way from blood ties to a Carpathian czarina to a grimy derelict bus shelter in Queens. Her accent, however, proved so thick and her grasp of English so spotty that I could only decipher the odd scrap and intermittent nugget. As best I could tell, she'd been usurped by a variety of in-law who'd either scrabbled together controlling interest in the family millet business or had systematically had her siblings flayed alive.

Maybe both. Or neither. Cosmina Jaru heaped so many extraneous syllables onto her English that words like "ignominy" required her a quarter minute to say. Everything else she came out with was larded with Romanian which sounded something on the order of Shetland Island French. Lilting, that is, and melodic while entirely unrevealing. So though I nodded and smiled and made whatever necknoise seemed appropriate, I was never quite sure what the woman was saying from one moment to the next.

Certainly the spectacle of her compromised my concentration. She wasn't beautiful exactly but was put together well enough to pass for exiled Bucharesti royalty. When I first saw her, she had on a beaded dress with striking ermine highlights—not remotely your standard Long Island City–derelict-bus-shelter wear. Her stockings were seamed down the back. Her stiletto heels looked sadomasochistic, and she was sporting a platinum tiara with more aristocratic aplomb than most bluebloods reduced to temping could probably muster.

Once I'd helped her to her feet and had pointed out the Life and Casualty tower, Cosmina Jaru groaned with precisely the pitch of contempt that building rated and laid a hand to my forearm by way of charging me to squire her inside. As we crossed the barren Meridian Life and Casualty grounds, Cosmina Jaru acquainted me with my various courtly duties. According to her, she was invested with a regal prerogative that, by law, allowed her to dub or knight or deputize retainers whenever she came across a royal need of one.

As aristocrats go, she didn't insist on terribly much attending. I was instructed to clear out rabble along routes she hoped to take and was schooled in how best to present her. She preferred a simple "Lady Cosmina Jaru of Bucharest" to fussy mention of her lineage's divine right to the throne which she reserved for formal soirées and social calls on peerage.

Almost immediately I was confronted with a functionary crisis. As we entered the lobby, Hector came wheezing out of the stairwell. He often drank coffee and Wolfschmidt while touring the grounds to start his day and frequently spit at the curbing for sport. He was, in short, precisely the manner of beast I should have shunted aside, but he was too well acquainted with me to get shunted.

Hector said to me, "*Hola,*" as he unstoppered a nostril with his thumb.

I told him back gravely, "Lady Cosmina Jaru of Bucharest."

As she was not at all chesty, Hector should have disposed of her with a glance. I watched him consider Lady Cosmina Jaru of Bucharest's sternum, and I awaited Hector's customary acid-reflux sneer, his I'm-afraid-you're-not-up-to-my-fleshy-standards expression. But Cosmina Jaru succeeded somehow with her elegance and bearing in creating for Hector the stirring illusion of pendulosity. Hector bowed and lightly took the fingers Cosmina Jaru extended. He escorted us to the elevator doors and personally called for the car.

Upstairs the girls in reception were a little less won over, but our band of gay temps seemed to sense straightaway in haughty Romanian peerage the human equivalent of cupcakes every day. They bowed and scraped and escorted us into Farley's outer office with as much lively ceremony as Christ inspired from the Nazarenes. The racket brought Farley out before his secretary could call him, and he stood there in his bolo and his alligator boots quite speechless before the beaded dress, the platinum tiara. He couldn't even manage a respectable cattle-drive snort.

I informed Farley, "Lady Cosmina Jaru of Bucharest," as prelude to the extended fingers and the regal dip of the chin. I imagine he was deciding to invite her into his office when she swept past him and, confronted by Farley's bunkhouse decor, loosed the selfsame groan the Life and Casualty tower had solicited from her. Farley motioned for us to scatter. He followed her in and shut his door.

It was the personal grandeur of Lady Cosmina Jaru that made her magnetic, the drama that she gave off like a scent while the rest of us smelled of cooking oil, deodorant soap, Binaca. My mother always liked to believe that her people had some of that about them, helpless resplendence and natural theatrical allure. She found her relations stirring anyway and more than a little dramatic which my father insisted was largely because they tended to be hotheads, were given to showy tantrums and hair-trigger combustive snits.

Cosmina Jaru, on the other hand, was quietly intriguing, and, in her self-possession and her grace, she reminded me, in fact, of one of my father's cousins by marriage—Spencer who, when his mother died, began to wear her dresses which people back home took for an unorthodox display of grief.

In sport coats and wingtips and oxford dress shirts, Spencer had always seemed a bit awkward. Tongue-tied and unforthcoming, not given to meeting a fellow's eye. But in his mother's suits and pleated skirts, even in her jumpers, Spencer had a kind of swagger and an air of self-assurance along with legs that looked to have been all but manufactured for ladies' hose. He wasn't a handsome man, but, under a pillbox hat and a demiveil, Spencer could have passed for Georgian aristocracy.

In her lifetime Spencer's mother primarily wore a cotton housedress, a shapeless sack of a thing with a torn front pocket and a pattern heavy on anemones. Nobody much could remember having seen her in finery before the evening they laid her out for viewing at the mortuary in a blue knit suit with glitter and spangles and an ornate cable weave.

It turned out Spencer's father, who'd passed away some years before, had made his wife regular gifts of clothing, of accouterments, of jewelry in vain hopes, I guess, of tempting her out of her shabby cotton housedress. So the stuff was still new when she'd gone to her Maker, boxed up and packed away, and

Spencer came across it while he was cleaning out the home place. He found cartons from Belk's and Montaldo's, hanging bags from Bergdorf Goodman and (in a cupboard in a guest room) a regular world of preposterous hats with grouse feathers attached and baby's breath, lacquered pyracantha berries.

Now, in my father's view the difference between Spencer and most people was that Spencer didn't puzzle much about the strain of thinking that had caused his mother to prefer her housedress to her better clothes. He didn't seek to have the matter explained to him by a clergyman or counselor, didn't wrestle with it in a public way or hatch plans to write a family memoir, and he failed to gather those dresses up and offer them to the needy but instead removed an Anne Klein suit from one of the Bergdorf bags and held it up for size before his mother's vanity mirror. This was just the sort of unexpected human undertaking to speak to my father's savor for the mysteries of this life.

There are people who thrill to the reach and wonder of a clear night sky, who take for beatific the variety in nature and elect to feel in every breeze the hot breath of their Savior. My father was more a devotee of human vice and folly, an outright connoisseur of foolishness. He nursed an abiding faith (I'll call it) in the proposition that some people are just too goddamned peculiar for words which became his unofficial motto and prevailing sentiment.

For his birthday once, my mother had it stitched onto a pillow, and callers would sometimes read the phrase my father held out as a creed while making themselves comfortable on the couch. Polite bewilderment usually ensued and was quite frequently abetted by the explanation and enlargement my father liked to air.

"Deuteronomy," he'd say, and name a chapter and a verse.

I happened to be in his company when he first ran up on Spencer in one of his mother's tropical-weight suits with a flouncy blouse, a platinum brooch, a pair of navy pumps. We'd been sent by my mother to the Red Apple after vanilla extract. She'd gotten well along in her pound-cake batter before discovering she was out, so we'd been charged to make our purchase and return home double quick which the spectacle of Spencer got entirely in the way of.

Even I'd picked up on the overcharged atmosphere in the grocery mart where a couple of dozen citizens were attempting all at once to keep themselves from dropping their jaws and shrieking, "Sweet Jesus!" which they'd all been raised to know would be considered impolite. So there was a certain frantic traffic in wide-eyed glances and head jerks which my father, of course, proved sensitive to as well. He stopped just inside the door and scoured about for causes until he'd noticed a creature back in produce examining nectarines.

"Would you look at that," my father said to me with wonder in his voice as if he'd spotted a two-headed calf or the Colossus of Rhodes. All I saw was some woman in produce sniffing a piece of fruit, but Frankie the bag boy knew exactly what my father meant, and he left off with his sacking to tell him, "Pretty thing, isn't he?"

Frankie was slow and maybe seventy, and he'd never adjusted to the local practice of refusing to look at those people who were most worth looking at. Not so much the ungainly malformed ones with stunted limbs and wandering eyes but the regular people who'd undergone notable alterations—had gotten fat or sheared or surgically enhanced, had swapped their slacks for shorts, broken out with boils, invested in a hair-replacement system. The two words I'd heard most growing up were assuredly "don't" and "look" which I might have ignored like Frankie if I'd been but slightly dimmer.

We went right over. My father and Spencer were, after all, cousins once removed, and they held for a while a regular sort of confab. My father spoke fondly of Spencer's mother who he'd genuinely liked because she'd disapproved of almost everyone he disapproved of, and they dissected assorted relations who had washed in for the funeral, settled together on which of the potluck dishes had gotten everyone sick.

Because I was in the company of my father alone, I wasn't discouraged from gaping at Spencer who served, at that point in my life, as a pretty singular sight. I'd seen the fire chief in a dress once and a strawberry blond wig, but he was a clownish part of the variety show raising money for the ladies' auxiliary, and I had heard that Horace Venable wore knee-high women's stockings but only to keep his inflamed veins in check. I'd certainly never spied a gentleman, most particularly a relation, out in a woman's dress as a voluntary choice in leisurewear.

Spencer was a curious thing to see, as he'd made no discernible effort to render himself girlish. He'd left alone his thinning cowlicky head of barbered hair. He'd kept his mustache, was wearing his clunky Bulova and his Masonic ring. I could see peeking out from the collar of his blouse a bit of his cotton T-shirt, and I felt certain he had on beneath his skirt his customary briefs. He'd applied no rouge or lip gloss. His nails were ragged and unpainted, and as he talked to my father, he raised by habit his pump-clad feet in turn and buffed his shoe tops against his calves.

Somehow there wasn't anything creepy about Spencer in a dress. First of all, he looked smashing in a way he'd never so much as approached in trousers, and, in his voice and his bearing, he was as manly as he'd ever been. So he gave off no whiff of sexual confusion along with his Skin Bracer, and once he and my father had gotten around to discussing his ensemble, it turned out Spencer's motives were more Scotch-Irish than anything else. He'd simply hated to see his mother's untouched clothing go to waste and was pleased to discover he had the build to make use of her wardrobe.

He twirled once at my father's request, and the patrons about all paused to watch him. He seemed bolder in a dress than he'd ever been in pants, more confident and pluckier, not to mention far more fetching. As Spencer fairly paraded clear of produce toward the checkout lines, he greeted his friends and neighbors, his fellow citizens in the aisles, with the level gaze and ready smile of a man convinced he looked just fine.

Lady Cosmina Jaru impressed me as having something of Spencer about her. She seemed to like the way that tragic Carpathian aristocracy fit. She felt to me from the first to have put it on like Spencer with his dresses because she was fond of the way in which it hung.

She came out, at length, of Farley's office with Farley in close tow. She was teaching him the word for "saddlehorn" in Romanian dialect and holding to his elbow in such a fashion as to make of Farley her squire. He showed her to a desk in a cubicle hard beside a radiator. He tidied her blotter and switched on her lamp, adjusted the height of her chair. He seemed intent upon her happiness and invested in her comfort which was not generally the way with Meridian brass toward temporary personnel.

Ordinarily he would have handed her a ballpoint and supplied her with a lecture devoted to office rights she couldn't claim and privileges she'd be denied, but instead Farley instructed her in the maddening idiosyncrasies of the phone system. When Cosmina Jaru inquired of Farley about the staple puller, wondered of him what such a treacherous-looking item could possibly do, Farley took the thing from her and pocketed it. He made a little bow and assured her she would never need to know.

So while most of the rest of us devoted ourselves to accomplishing next to nothing, Cosmina Jaru got management's blessing to be up to nothing at all. She lounged around the office in her gowns and her tiara (except for Fridays which were casual when she went with gowns alone), and she usually succeeded at tempting some male employee or another to treat her to lunch at the shabby Italian place around the corner where the bread and the Chianti were both younger than the clams.

She even wormed her way into a cut of Thor's office-supply business. After a week or two of watching Thor haul out his freighted duffel, Cosmina Jaru approached him and, in regal broken English, explained to Thor what he would pay to have her unknow what she knew. Thor found her sufficiently comely and brazen to interest him a little until he learned she'd taken a pottery class at a junior college once.

Naturally Franklin plied her with talk of his grandfather, the lightbulb flip-flop king, who'd descended from some diluted strain of Hungarian royalty. Cosmina Jaru, for her part, recommended an astringent to dry up Franklin's pustules. She routinely earned from Do-Ray the variety of "hoss" he reserved for those women who plagued his dreams in our stifling sleeping loft, but I was plainly the one she preferred which only helped to heighten the chafing we were enduring among us already at our apartment nights.

I could, you see, repair a curling iron and load test circuitry, could readily mend a bracelet catch or revive a necklace clasp. I had exhaustive knowledge of toilet works, owned outright a propane torch, could rejuvenate a screw hole with a matchstick and some spit, and Cosmina Jaru—her royal Carpathian blue blood notwithstanding—had to live with the rest of us in this world where things just up and broke. I fixed a floor lamp for her and pronounced her VCR past saving, schooled her one afternoon in spackle finishing and undercoats for paint which impressed me as homely interests for a Bucharesti princess, but I was altogether ignorant of her nation's customs and ways and couldn't be sure Romanian royals weren't required to paint their castles, or their tenement apartments in alphabet city as it actually turned out.

Anymore I suspect if I'd been something less in the way of naive, a little more savvy and probing and attentive to detail, I wouldn't have needed to hear her talking to Stillwater on the phone to know Lady Cosmina Jaru for a rank American mongrel like me.

She frequently lingered late at the office, claimed to have a liveried driver who, given her dip in circumstances, had taken a garment-district job. He could come to fetch her only once he'd gotten off of work, had fought his way through crosstown traffic and over the Queensborough Bridge. Lady Cosmina Jaru insisted on calling him "dear Emile," and she told us he drove a phaeton which (given my ignorance of cars) I was equipped to envision as a low-slung Mercury with fender skirts. I took the fact I'd never seen the thing or run across Emile as a wholesale condemnation of the state of local traffic.

One evening, though, Hector waylaid me, and I stayed around later than normal. Hector had a Zenith radio he listened to all day, only AM and only the all-news station which (given the time it had to fill) defined news rather liberally. One afternoon in his damp subbasement, with his senses Wolf-schmidt-addled, Hector convinced himself he'd heard reported on his tinny Zenith word that Ms. Divinia DeLuxe had been inserted in harm's way.

"*Muerta!*" Hector told me as he pitched over to leave an indelible hair-oil stain upon my shirt.

He implored me to sit in the subbasement with him and await definitive news, so I lingered throughout the afternoon and well into the evening, heard four and a half hours of traffic updates, weather, stock reports and (every twenty-two minutes) a piece about the president's polypy colon. That news station, however, rotated its human-interest stories, those shank-of-the-cycle items that filled the hour after sports—gaudy marital disputes, celebrity snake bites, toupee conflagrations, auto misadventures, house pets stuck in sinkholes, movie-star couplings, Italian octogenarian pregnancies.

It was almost eight o'clock before they mentioned Ms. DeLuxe who, as it turned out, had not been killed or, for that matter, mangled. She'd hired on to wrestle Ms. Paisley Cox, a pornographic starlet, at a longshoremen's retreat in a motor park out by Joshua Tree. There was some sort of pudding involved (as opposed, say, to padded mats or canvas), and Ms. DeLuxe had slipped and fallen, causing one of her implants to burst. The news-radio man had no end of fun pronouncing her "deflated."

Hector, of course, was profoundly relieved to hear she wasn't dead, but he had to come to grips with the fact that she'd been surgically improved. So I was another half hour with him while he labored through the matter and finally accepted Ms. DeLuxe as stirring though saline-enhanced. He capped off the ordeal by licking one of his photos of her cleavage before collapsing onto his musty settee in a senseless heap.

I had to go back up for my socket set, my soldering iron, my hammer, the shorted-out electric skillet I intended to mend at home. When I came out of the elevator, the office looked deserted to me. The overhead lights were mostly off and the cubicle lamps unlit but for a lone one burning by the wall. Once I'd gathered up what I required, I crossed the floor to switch it off, and I only heard her once I'd nearly gained her cubicle proper.

Straightaway I assumed that a cleaning woman was talking on the phone. The crew that came in nights dusted a little and ran their vacuums some but mostly caught up with their relatives in Bangalore and Kiev, in Bratislava, Qingdao, Port-au-Prince, in Veracruz. Farley fumed and railed about it, wrote huffy letters in legalese and got the occasional arid apology from the custodial concern, but nights when the cleaning team showed up to perform their spit and promise, they continued to direct-dial their attachments back at home.

I could hear the casters, the metallic complaint of the desk chair, the scratch and nasal natter of some woman through the handset, and I was hardening up the rake of my jaw in a bid to look severe as I peeked around the half wall to discover Cosmina Jaru.

She didn't see me right away, and I tried to retreat. I assumed she was caught up in royal business, attempting to orchestrate from Long Island City some Carpathian upheaval or chatting maybe with a cousin who'd gone somehow unflayed. In any event, I couldn't imagine it fitting for me to eavesdrop, but she swiveled about and spied me before I could get entirely away.

She spoke as she turned, said into the phone, "I don't much think so, Mama." Then she winked and, in Oklahoma English, told me, "Just a sec."

I was a little stunned. I went and sat in the darkened adjacent cubicle where I reviewed my recent history as a sap and functionary. I relived all the showy presentations of her I had made, acknowledged all the hogwash I had swallowed from a woman, apparently, who'd never been stripped of a royal millet fortune.

Once she'd signed off with a "Hey to Daddy" and attendant Okie endearments, she came around to fetch me back into her cubicle where she sat with her bare feet propped against a corner of her desk, fiddled about with her tiara on the blotter. Her name, as it turned out, was Alice Kay Odom, and she hailed originally from Hallet up toward the Arkansas River and the Osage Reservation. She was an actress and a playwright and a published poetess, and once unhindered by her Romanian accent and brittle regal bearing, she informed me that she doubted dear Emile would pick her up.

We took the subway down to Union Square and walked into the East Village, well past the park and the dog run toward the alphabet avenues. On a grungy block, we stopped before a carcass of a building, just brick and rubbish and vacant sockets where the windows once had been. Alice Kay Odom led me inside and, with only the flame from her lighter, showed me the room where she intended to stage a theatrical production, what she identified as a sort of squatters' drama-circle event.

She'd written a play about a listless motorman on the IRT who allowed his train to dawdle between stations, and all she needed to mount the thing was a cast and a set and a ream of handbills along with a modest stream of alternating current. On the way outside, we detoured by a crack in a sidewall which gave onto a view of the neighbor's service panel. Alice Kay Odom wondered if a man with talent for it could find a way to splice a harness up.

Then she permitted her lighter flame to die and took me by the hand, held to it as I saw her down the block to her building where she kissed me on the landing with more warm breath and humidity than a fellow might enjoy in a lifetime of pecks and busses from Romanian royalty.

She was just another couple of weeks at Meridian Life and Casualty before fresh unembittered temps rolled in, and she got transferred out. She stayed a czarina's distant regal descendant the entire time, and we failed to discuss her listless-motorman production or the evening we had passed together off the complex grounds. We had a cupcake-and-sangria party on Cosmina Jaru's last day, and she allowed me to escort her down to wait for dear Emile who showed up in the form of a Lebanese gypsy cabbie in a Lincoln. When Alice Kay Odom leaned in to kiss me good-bye, she nipped my ear.

If I'd been the sort to organize, to scheme, plan and connive, I would have known what I would be about before I was about it. But instead not two weeks later, having walked across the park, I stood in the Sixty-eighth Street station waiting for the local on my way to the Meridian complex where I had no itch to go.

As the 6 rolled in, the crowd pressed forward on the platform, and I handed to Do-Ray the juicer I was carrying in a sack, told him whose it was and held my ground as the doors slid shut. I watched the train pull out and lingered long enough to hear in full a medley performed on the ocarina by a man on the northbound platform who demonstrated far more fervor than technique. "Abide with Me" (I think it was) gave way to "Spinning Wheel" which yielded at the last to "Summer Wind."

METHUSELAH'S CHARIOT

1

SHE HAD MAYBE TWO dozen boyfriends. Or rather we thought of ourselves as such while Alice Kay Odom considered us more in the way of a labor pool. Looking back I can see that we all boasted skills and talents and resources, but at the time with my nose to the glass, I sorted my rivals by fit and finish—hair and teeth and wardrobe, cash flow, native wit and muscle tone. I was convinced I could rise in the standings with the proper renovations, so I peroxided my uppers, restyled my coif, defined my flexor carpi when all Alice Kay Odom required of me was a couple of spools of Romex, a sack of wire nuts, a gross of utility lights.

I didn't share with her straightaway that I'd quit my insurance job, although I made a fairly honest attempt to tell her. I walked down to her apartment from the Sixty-eighth Street station, hoping to cobble up some sort of declaration along the way, a spot of talk largely devoted to my affection for Alice Kay Odom with built-in lulls for her to own up to an appetite for me.

She wasn't home, so it hardly mattered what I'd failed to decide to say. She was off, as it turned out, being a Huguenot at a software concern which left me free to walk back uptown and consider what I'd done. I'd not resigned exactly from Meridian outright, had only declined to make the morning commute which, when Thor and Do-Ray and Franklin had all returned from work, I would be expected somehow to explain. So I had to decide if I would acquaint them with my professional misgivings, reveal that the life-and-casualty game was manifestly not for me due to my native sensitivity and pronounced artistic streak which, no matter how I put the thing together in my head, qualified for a devastating "Hoss!"

Instead I allowed them to find me on the couch under Aunt Sister's afghan which was composed of more puce and aquamarine than the average retina could stand. My mother had shipped it to me although I'd pleaded with her not to, had accused her of merely trying to get the thing out of her house. We'd only had it a couple of days when the exterminator came, a Pakistani gentleman with a reeking sprayer full of ant poison. When he saw that afghan on the sofa back and said abruptly, "Yikes!"

So I used it in the manner of an invalid's distraction once Do-Ray and Thor and Franklin had collected at the couch. They squinted at me while I spoke of my intestinal complaint which I laid to the moo shoo pork that had been stewing in the icebox for the better part of a month and a half by then. They were entirely sympathetic, not suspicious or surprised since we depended, as a group, on explosive diarrhea instead of solid culinary judgment and expiration dates.

I went back to work, at least for a while, because I'm not decisive. I made my tortured self-pitying way around the Life and Casualty grounds, waited to be approached and hoped to get interrogated by a colleague keen to hear why I'd become so glum. I even passed an hour one forenoon underneath the scaffold where Skip and Wallace were cleaning windows on the eastern building face. I was half hoping they'd drop something onto my head to disqualify me from service while I waited for them to motor down for lunch. Implementa rained about me. A soggy chamois splashed my shoe, but otherwise I came through untouched and undebilitated. Though Skip and Wallace, in fact, recognized that I was uncommonly gloomy, they laid it off to the weak-hitting shortstop the Mets had traded a closer to get.

If anybody had asked me, I was primed to reveal exactly what I'd rather be about, was prepared to make the case for a young gentleman like myself indulging (while he had the chance) his latent artistic impulses. Anybody, that is, but for my mother who sniffed out my distress. Over the phone line, she detected that I was plagued and troubled, could distinguish simple respiration from freighted moans and sighs. Since I assumed at the time my father was proud of his Meridian service, I couldn't bring myself to tell her that my ambition was to quit and devote myself to lighting a theatrical production by plundering voltage from a Korean laundry through a crack in a masonry wall. It was easier just to claim that I was homesick for her cooking.

She shipped up frozen Tetrazzini that we let spoil behind the milk.

Alice Kay Odom couldn't be bothered to buck me up herself. She was hard at the time securing the fealty of a metalworker, a fellow with the know-how to construct her subway set and licensed access to the butylene he would require to do it. By way of complication, though, he had an actual fiancée and so was equipped to frustrate Alice Kay Odom and throw up fair resistance to her wiles and charms, her coy allure, the promise of her love. Naturally she managed to wear him down and win him in the end, held out for that welder the specter of lifelong union drudgery spiced with domestic chafing in a Nutley fixer-upper as compared to the romance of theater work for no discernible pay which Alice Kay Odom (and this was her gift) could make seem a heady prize. Even still, that fellow held out against her overtures. His fiancée was a hothead, and he had cause to fear her wrath which meant he required from Alice Kay Odom intense applied persuasion, and he monopolized her notice for that interval of time when I had need myself of bucking up and baseless flattery.

As a consequence I ended up stalking Alice Kay Odom a little. I told myself I was merely trying to orchestrate a coincidence, intended to loiter in her vicinity until I could manage to run across her which called for a healthy bit of misdemeanor skulking. All day she was a Huguenot in Chelsea, and come evening she had a welder to detach from his intended, so I had trouble finding a chink in her schedule when she was reliably on offer for getting, after a fashion, run across.

Of course, I had misgivings to nurse as well and doubts to entertain which held me back those few occasions I did spy her out alone. My personal history with women was sparse, all but bordering on pathetic for a hardy young man who'd not spent his teen years institutionalized. In addition to Fay, I'd had one girlfriend the bulk of my adolescence—from the time I was twelve until I was seventeen—but we'd observed between us a strain of makeshift chastity due to the fact that she'd been raised a fundamentalist Moravian and I was pretty poorly versed in precisely what went where.

So I had no experience with Alice Kay Odom's brand of creature, hardly any useful knowledge of females in the wild at all which made me, I guess, available for near-bottomless ill use, most particularly from a prodigy like the pride of Hallet who'd won me with a brief and slightly lubricated kiss. The rest of her boyfriends seemed to require of her more in the way of loving persuasion. They expected from Alice Kay Odom phone calls and exclusive evenings out, probably intimacies (I was pained to imagine) in the way of upkeep while all I got was the odd message she would leave for me at work. Mostly squatters' drama-circle talk, though once, via Farley's fax, a wildcat wiring schematic she had sketched out freehand. I carried it folded in my pocket until the thing had frayed and torn.

Naturally I plagued her with invitations to movies, to dinner, to brunch, but she'd evermore put me off and forestall me with excuses, leave me messages explaining why it was wise we stay apart. Ours, according to Alice Kay Odom, was a combustible attraction, perilously magnetic and devastatingly intense. She proposed anyway that, if we did join up romantically, a kind of interpersonal fission would ensue. Feverish. Consuming. Destructive in the end, leaving us seared and broken casualties of catastrophic desire.

I believe anyway that's what she said. She phoned the apartment while I was out and left the message with Do-Ray who jotted down the high points on a scrap of envelope that he filled up front and back. Do-Ray passed it on to Franklin who gave it presently to me. I'd been busy, in fact, lurking down by Alice Kay's apartment and came home to have Franklin offer me that scrap of envelope, not immediately but after we'd been sitting for some hours on the sofa watching the Rangers on TV.

Franklin picked up his beer with that piece of envelope stuck to the bottom of it. "Oh, yeah," he said. "Some girl called." And he gave me the soggy thing.

So I was obliged to decipher, extrapolate, manufacture a little. Then I sat down at our dinette and composed a reply to Alice Kay Odom, two pages of prose doggerel on the topic of my love which I hand-delivered, slipped anyway beneath her building's security door and loitered across the street until she'd come along to claim it. I suppose once she'd read it, she realized that she'd snared me full and proper, concluded the time was ripe for her to employ me the best way that she could.

Alice Kay Odom summoned me down to meet her by Cooper Union, out on the street where (she'd suggested) we'd likely keep our passions in check. I was hoping we'd confess our love, have Thai maybe for lunch, and then retire to her place for a spot of consummating. I'd bought for the occasion new underpants, had worn clean and unpilled socks. Instead, however, we walked along the Bowery arm in arm while Alice Kay Odom rhapsodized over the artful prose in my letter. She congratulated me on my ear, the aptness of my phrasing, and she wondered how a fellow with my native gift for words could tolerate a life bereft of daily composition.

Of course, she had no way of knowing of the work I did for Hector, of my regular libidinous dispatches to Divinia DeLuxe. They often opened with a couple of benevolent observations before degenerating into salacious proposals and scandalous commentary which was the approach to pendulous females Hector endorsed and preferred. It seemed to work well enough. He'd get glossy autographed photos in reply with Ms. Divinia DeLuxe's cleavage on conspicuous display.

As a wordsmith herself, Alice Kay boasted a keen nose for her colleagues, and she all but berated me as we walked for holding my talent close. Though I wasn't at the time aware of it, Alice Kay Odom insisted her boyfriends—particularly the ones she'd cultivated largely for their trade-school skills—pursue some sort of Alice Kay Odom–sanctioned artistic endeavor. That way she could speak of her plumber, her welder, her carpenter, her mason's apprentice, her electrician (for that matter) as evolved and engaged.

I was to write a novel, she informed me, of ideas. She already had in her stable a sculptor, a sonneteer, a fusion drummer, a collagist, a plasterer by day who made pornographic shadow boxes from herring cans at night. But they were all, she told me, dabblers after a fashion and dilettantes while I impressed her more in the way of a steady long-form sort of guy. I suspect she meant plodding and dogged, probably grindingly relentless, but the way Alice Kay Odom intoned it, it came out a compliment.

By then we were in a cluttered building-supply store toward Canal where Alice Kay Odom had effectively taken possession of a clerk, a swarthy young man with a reptile tattoo and a rather arresting haircut, a Mohawk with more sprawl and ambition than most Mohawks demonstrate. She kept his attention by laying her fingers upon his bare forearm while she quizzed me on the items a girl was likely to require to electrify a squatters' drama-circle production.

As I listed them for her, she'd turn to the clerk and repeat what I'd just said before dispatching him into the bowels of the store with a fond pat on the shoulder. Once he'd collected everything and had tallied up the price, Alice Kay Odom allowed me occasion for chivalry. I paid with the credit card my father had instructed me to use only in the event of a ransom demand or an appendectomy. It was a full two months before he got the bill and finally wondered of me what a young insurance professional footloose up in Gotham might do with a 150-foot spool of twelve-gauge electrical wire.

2

I HAD A LINE. Well, a word really, but I got to repeat it throughout the course of the evening to changeable effect. Comic often but wrenching occasionally and, every now and again, surreal. I'd stir from fitful sleep. I'd interrupt a bout of scratching. I'd leave off with the bath-soap jingle I'd been humming maniacally, and usually I would rise to my feet in my grimy topcoat to deliver myself of my only article of dialogue.

"Hobgoblin," I'd say, and sit again. I'd claw my privates and doze.

By the time we'd finished with the set ("we" being Alice Kay Odom's squad of eager boyfriends), it bore a remarkable resemblance to a New York subway car. Perched like it was in a derelict tenement awash in filth and vermin, it was no chore to imagine that cutaway car lingering between stations. Garbled announcements from an unseen conductor completed the effect.

Naturally Alice Kay Odom claimed the starring role of Eustacia for herself, a talkative Lincolnshire nanny-without-portfolio who, during the course of the evening, made a piecemeal scattershot confession of having buried her brother in a peaty hole out on the wolds. The boy had been left in Eustacia's care while their parents were away, and, in the spirit of wholly regrettable scientific inquiry, Eustacia had slipped up behind him and brained him experimentally with a stone. Her brother had recovered, at least for a while. He'd awakened anyway and screamed and might well have survived with a spot of minor neurosurgery which had impressed Eustacia as far more trouble than the boy was worth, so she'd hit him again. Harder this time and with a larger stone.

She told the constable he'd been taken by an uncommonly hairy man who'd come into their house through a breach in the basement wall behind the boiler. The man had smelled of turnips and vulcanized rubber and had tied Eustacia to the hall tree. He'd informed her she should probably not expect her brother back. Eustacia claimed to have seen in a waking vision the place where her brother was buried, and she led officials to him, stood by as they dug him up. The boy was wearing a pebble-grained cowhide belt Eustacia had long admired, and she badgered the constable for it once her brother was unearthed.

Most everybody suspected her, especially her mother and father who had intimate knowledge between them of what a frightful ghoul she was which had served to make Eustacia's life in Cleethorpes on the Humber more of a trial than she'd known the starch to bear. So Eustacia had traveled to New York City for a fresh beginning. She was seeking a position and had come by papers from an agency certifying her a suitable au pair. Holding forth, she even made herself seem fitting for the job provided no rocks of any heft much came to hand.

As plays go, Alice Kay Odom's was a sort of monologue with intermittent interruptions and philosophical commentary in addition to the "Hobgoblin!"'s I would stand up and uncork. And some way or another, Alice Kay Odom lured people to come and see it. Not just the available East Village types with their pierced lobes and their boots but legitimate citizens with a full range of entertainment options. Young Upper West Side professionals and Montclair suburbanites, Park Slopers and

Tribecaneers, the occasional Murray Hill matron, and even one night (I was told anyway) an Astor once removed who swept in with her silver-haired husband and claimed two seats down front for an evening of cutting-edge drama which included the threat of tetanus and an unrelenting rat-urine bouquet.

Alice Kay Odom had previously cultivated a theater critic who wrote for one of the weekly magazines. He attended on opening night which went well enough except for a technical glitch that allowed us to hear through the speakers exactly what the conductor was saying and so lent the proceedings an air of whimsy and wishful fantasy. Though he had his complaints, that critic chose to pass a fair chunk of his notice in marveling over Alice Kay Odom's Lincolnshire accent.

He knew Alice Kay Odom as a transplanted Portuguese waterman's widow who had filled in at the photo lab where he got his film processed.

Alice Kay's drama-critic buddy brought us both a paying audience and the scrutiny of the housing authority, so we were sold out right up to the night the city shut us down. I even got Do-Ray and Franklin and Thor to sit through a performance since, after all, I'd endured countless evenings of their insurance talk. Thor brought a date who lasted to intermission before her asthma kicked in, but Franklin and Do-Ray stayed on to what passed for a final curtain when Eustacia, after a spot of palaver with a straphanging cleric, recognized the evil inherent in braining a sibling with a stone.

She'd break down nightly and throw a rather comprehensive Lincolnshire fit—with keening and howling and wailing and a showy bit of weeping—while our motorman slowed us on the tracks to loiter in the dark.

As dramas go, Alice Kay Odom's play wasn't terribly effective. It tended to lurch from one bombastic bit of business to the next with ample opportunity for Eustacia (most particularly) to gnaw on the plastic, chrome and brushed-aluminum scenery. Do-Ray, I thought, penetrated to the failings of the enterprise when, after the performance, I met up with him and Franklin on the street and asked them what they'd made of the production. Franklin confessed he would hardly have guessed Eustacia was Romanian. Do-Ray chose instead to wince and shrug. He shook his head and told me, "Hoss."

Alice Kay Odom, understandably, capitalized on the exposure, and, since she'd been spread already fairly thin among her various men friends, the demands of being a playwright and leading lady about town who rated the notice of a weekly magazine took her entirely from us for a while. She didn't require mere tradesmen just then but had need instead of publicists, investors and producers and the companionship, it turned out, of a tabloid columnist who (to judge by his work) backbit for a living, sniped and carped and goaded, except those occasions he took for his topic the unrivaled glory of himself.

If I'd had just Meridian Life and Casualty duties to fall back on—afternoons with Hector in the dank subbasement, nights at home with my soldering iron—I would have surely found Alice Kay Odom's neglect impossibly tormenting, but I was enjoying the spoils of theatrical triumph a little bit on my own. Mine came in the form of Salvatore "Little Pony" Delgado who'd sought me out after a performance near the end of our squatters'-circle run. He was wide and short, barely five feet tall with jacket sleeves that reached to his knuckles. He poked me with his knobby foremost finger, left (I later discovered) a bruise.

"You've got it," he said, "and I ought to know." He shoved a business card my way. "Tomorrow. Lunch. Cooty's. Know it?" I'd almost mustered the breath for "No, sir" before he told me, "Good," and vanished into a knot of full-size people.

His business card was an unfortunate color, a pale erratic dusty rose that looked to have been accidentally mottled and bleached. It had the head of an animal embossed on it, possibly a pony or a flop-eared rabbit, a wildebeest in repose. Sal Delgado's office address was given simply as "Water at Jay." His telephone number had a 718 exchange.

At the bottom of the card in very nearly illegible cursive script were the words "Actor's Agent *** Talent, Wall to Wall."

Naturally I permitted myself to be flattered there at first, pleased that my performance as a degraded sociopath with a half-empty pint of Mr. Boston and one word of dialogue had captured the notice of a legitimate theater professional, even one with a Brooklyn number and a chemically faded business card. I'd seen, however, respectable talent agents courting Alice Kay Odom, and they didn't dress or look or sound like Salvatore Delgado had. I studied his card on my subway ride home and decided "Talent, Wall to Wall" probably meant that Sal Delgado ran a floor-covering concern and kept guys with one line in off-Broadway productions staged in derelict buildings gamely employed in the daylight hours putting carpet down. So I probably wouldn't have shown for lunch if I'd been happier in insurance, if I'd not been handy and keen to hear what New York carpet laying paid.

Cooty's proved to be a dive in Brooklyn under a ramp to the Manhattan Bridge. I found the number in the phone book and called for directions, first got some knucklehead on the line who asked me, "You want I should draw you a map?" Then he tossed, by the sound of it, the telephone handset out into the street where it was snatched up by a fellow pleased to inform me chiefly in Spanish how I might arrive at Cooty's (coming from Staten Island, I think).

I found the place anyway. It was Saturday, and everything else in the area was closed—warehouses mostly with grubby truck bays, a plumbing-supply wholesaler, a marine outfitter with cleats and winches and three cats in the window, a salvage yard which appeared to specialize in coil springs and panel doors with, for variety, the odd ornamental iron railing, the occasional restaurant range.

Cooty's occupied the corner of a block of otherwise abandoned buildings, buildings empty so long that obscenities written in grime on the ground-floor windows had half filled in with soot and been replaced by fresh smut over time. Cooty's seemed by comparison tidy, or at least marginally filth-free. The place was so dark—even on a sunny Saturday afternoon—that I was obliged to pause inside the doorway to let my eyes adjust. I eventually saw a bar lit by neon beer signs, a television tuned to billiards, the cigarette coals of the trio of patrons who'd fallen silent and turned my way.

They'd been screaming at each other before I'd stepped inside. I'd heard them well enough out front debating the merits of overland shortcuts to Canarsie as opposed to the clotted Shore Parkway. One guy was a decided Flatbush-to-Eastern-to-Rockaway man. Another preferred Atlantic to Pennsylvania, and the third had tried to claim he could see the advantages of each, and he was taking abuse from his companions when I'd entered.

"I'm meeting Sal Delgado," I announced for general consumption.

"Ain't seen him." I immediately recognized the voice. Did I

want he should draw me a map? The bartender. His back was to me, partially illuminated by a cream-ale sign. He was watching a game of nine ball on television.

"This is Cooty's, right?"

"Pony ain't here," the bartender told me.

"I guess I'll wait for him."

I mounted a barstool with tattered vinyl on the seat and tufts of pestilential stuffing leaking out.

"You drinking or what?"

I requested the Belgian pilsner I routinely ordered at our favorite watering hole uptown. The bartender jabbed his thumb at six dusty beer cans on a shelf between the straight rye and the rum. I settled on the blue one which tasted like effervescent aquarium fill.

"He said lunch." I smiled at the bartender who was massive and unkempt. He had on a Giants sweatshirt which was stained and speckled with culinary encrustations.

"Pony ain't here," he told me, and turned back toward the television screen. My fellow patrons set in debating the location of a clam house. They agreed it was no fit place for decent humans to eat, but that hardly stopped them quarreling over the shortest route to reach it. I determined at length I'd try the beer in the silver can for a change which proved tepid and brackish and tasted vaguely of steeped athletic socks.

I was about to leave by the time Sal Delgado finally showed up. It being Saturday, he was wearing (I guess) his usual leisure ensemble—a sport coat over a V-neck T-shirt and husky-junior jeans. He slapped me on the back, around about my lumbar which was as far up on me as Little Pony could reach. "I like a man who's on time," he said.

"So do I," I told him back with but the merest hint of bile.

He laughed. "HA!" It turned out anyway to be laughter but could just as easily have been Little Pony's response to an impromptu colon exam. It was loud and sharp and not, by any normal measure, jolly. "Come on," he said, and led me to a table in a corner which, by the time we reached it, I could even very nearly see.

Little Pony was one of those guys who required no partner for conversation, preferred to orchestrate exchanges entirely by himself. "You'll eat a burger, won't you? Of course you will," he said once we'd sat down, and then he called out to the bartender his order and mine both. "And, Jimmy," he added once he'd relieved me of my silver beer can. He displayed it with squeamish distaste as if it were a dead raccoon. "A couple of Mount Gays, huh?"

"Hey, Pony." One of the guys at the bar had swiveled around to speak. "How do you figure you'd get to Canarsie from here?"

"Why the hell would I go to Canarsie?"

"Say you had people . . . or something."

"I don't." And Sal Delgado shifted about to train his attention on me in such a fashion as to let it be known to the quarreling patrons of Cooty's that he was not available for conflict resolution. Then for a quarter hour, he lavished me with entirely unwarranted praise, asked me about my theatrical instincts and supplied me with responses, admired how I knocked back my rum and Pepsi (to rinse the sock taste from my mouth), and, once our burgers came, he allowed me relish and ketchup and nothing else. He even went so far as to summon Jimmy to take away my fries.

"Probably cooked," he informed me, "in the oil they greased Methuselah's chariot with."

I managed once when his mouth was full to put to him a question. He responded by explaining that his Nonna (he called her) who'd grown potatoes in Suffolk had bought him a pony that was even by Long Island equine standards slight. I'd also begun to tell him that I'd previously laid linoleum and had taken up my share of carpet but had never put any down when he squinted at me and asked me, "What?"

It turned out, you see, Sal was only in talent and not in floor coverings at all. The "wall to wall" on his business card referred to his theory of acting which he ordered two more Mount Gays and revealed to me at some length. There were stars, Sal explained, with looks and presence, awash in magnetism, and largely unmagnetic supporting actors who helped to make the stars shine. Sal was partial to a packing-peanut analogy. He claimed to represent excelsior and gave it out as the job of his clients to insulate delicate treasures, to keep them snug and safe.

Sal "Little Pony" Delgado, you see, hadn't much cared for my "Hobgoblin!"s and the way I'd gestured and declaimed them. He'd far preferred me lolling grubbily on my subway seat while Eustacia prattled on about her brother.

"She was all right," Sal told me. He shrugged. He sipped. He didn't seem to mean it. "But you," he said, and pointed my way. "You I believed."

He had a stable of glorified extras. Sal preferred "backgrounders," and he promised nearly enough work for a paltry second career. Sal even had something that afternoon if I had need of fifty dollars, and I made a show of sorting through my schedule in my mind as if there were more on my plate than Farley's secretary's immersion blender with its seared resistors and its racked drive shaft. Sal had stood and burped and dropped cash on the check before I'd managed, "I'm free."

He took me across the Brooklyn Bridge on the upper pedestrian walkway with its perilous blend of Eurotourists and kamikaze cyclers. Some Bavarian was evermore drifting into the bike lane with his camera and running the risk of death by Cannondale. Along the way Sal informed me I'd be working down on Broad Street milling around behind a correspondent for the network news. I recognized the name, had seen the man on television usually standing in front of the Stock Exchange or the steps of Federal Hall. He had a decided way with baleful economic tidings, was prone to speak of grave reversals and deteriorating prospects with the faintest undertone of glee.

The man wore, Sal informed me, a hairpiece he'd once suffered to be removed by an intoxicated civilian during a stand-up on the street. Some fellow had come rolling out of a bar at Bowling Green, had seen the video crew and recognized the correspondent and had blundered up behind the man in order to inquire if he wasn't some sort of big shot on the news. He'd tripped as he'd approached and, in falling, had grabbed on to the toupee which was hardly so well attached to hold a drunk civilian up. That correspondent was left with an uncovered pate, splotches of hairpiece cement and an unrelenting distaste for the general population which bordered, Sal informed me, on psychosis.

Ever since, those people milling around behind that correspondent when he savored a market downturn or lethargic housing starts were acting professionals who'd been paid to mill. I appeared twice in a four-minute piece, first in an executive topcoat strolling with my briefcase past the Federal Reserve and then later in a ball cap at a shoeshine stand hard by Trinity Church. My mother was pleased to learn I was pursuing an artistic hobby provided it didn't, she cautioned me, interfere with my underwriting career, and my father attempted to tape the nightly news show I appeared on, but he proved helpless against the technocratic demands of the VCR and ended up instead with half an episode of *Matlock*.

3

THEY LET HECTOR DO it. Hector. They didn't even call me to Farley's office, failed to permit me the usual grim walk to the bunkhouse for my severance but calculated (I guess) I was closer in the basement to the street. So they authorized Hector to give me my check—two weeks' worth of FICA detritus—and inform me that my services were not any longer required. First he directed me to drop a line to Divinia DeLuxe. Hector had come up with a novel use to put her hotbox to (he called it) which he charged me to describe in the usual clinical detail after a jolly salutation and some courtly overtures.

Once I'd polished the thing and had made up a proper copy for Hector to sign, he dispatched me to a bodega a couple of blocks off for some stamps, had me pick him up a bear claw and a copy of the *Post*. I found him in the lobby upon my return in the company of Claude, our guard, which should have clued me in to what Hector was up to before he, in fact, got up to it. Claude was Caribbean and so religious as to make Cromwell seem a slouch, and he and Hector hardly ever passed a civil word between them. Hector would frequently visit on Claude some godless sneering profanity and provoke thereby description of the agonies of hell which, delivered in Claude's lilting basso profundo island accent, sounded often like the features of a summer on St. Croix.

They never just stood around together the way I came across them when I returned with Hector's postage stamps, his pastry and his paper, and I was full across the lobby when Hector broke the news.

"Hey, *chico*," he said, and dragged his index finger across his throat. Then he smiled. The morning sunlight glinted off his platinum bridgework. Aside from the magnitude of cleavage a fellow could mire in to his ears, there was precious little Hector preferred to another man's hard luck.

Only then did I notice the packing box sitting at Claude's feet with the contents of my desk drawers tumbled in it. I could see my hammer handle, a portion of my coping saw, a corner of my daily planner, the spout of my epoxy tube. I stopped where I was to digest the situation. From across the lobby, Hector indulged in an interlude of counseling. He sucked (as was his custom) an audible dollop of spit through a tooth gap. Then he shrugged and asked me philosophically, "What are you going to do?"

At that moment my dream was to work for Meridian Life and Casualty, and I found myself swamped by unjustified nostalgia for the place. The sour smell of the elevator shaft. The warbling of the phones. The spectacle from the upper floors of stalled traffic in Manhattan. The mysterious stains on the carpet. The pencil holes in the ceiling tiles. Regina's dull narcotic glare and viscous syncopated cough. Farley's alarming seafoam pallor during his snuff experiments. The fluffy coat of boiler soot along the waste drain in the basement. Hector's moldering stack of rat-chewed pornographic magazines.

I felt betrayed and wounded, bereft over the loss of a job I'd detested, and I mounted the only show of displeasure I could think to mount. I wound up and fired Hector's bear claw high against the lobby glass where it stuck for a moment before it began to slide down the window, leaving a trail of glaze, cinnamon and pastry scraps.

I believe I said by way of enlargement and commentary, "Shit."

By the time Hector and Claude had joined me, I was sensible again, settled enough anyway to apologize for destroying Hector's breakfast which Hector responded to by shifting phlegm, relieving me of his *Post* and stamps while Claude delivered himself of a scrap of ungermane calypso Scripture, something about the lamb of Moab and Jehu's judgment against Baal. Then Claude gave me my packing box and walked me out onto the landing where he assured me of the glorious everlasting love of Christ and warned me not to try to come back in.

In a show of efficiency rarely in evidence at the office, there was a gentleman waiting for me in our apartment when I got home. I found him improving his time by making sporting use of one of our geckos, chasing the larger of our specimens around the front room with a broom. Kyle, his name was, and he'd shifted the sofa well away from the wall, had overturned a table lamp and scattered magazines, and he was attempting to drive that lizard out from under a radiator with a combination of broom straw and combustive profanity.

It finally darted out between his legs which sent Kyle into spasm. He leapt and twitched and shrieked, convulsed, in fact, so violently as to bust a window light with the handle of the broom.

I sat my box down on the dinette table and asked him, "Who are you?"

He fished a card from his jacket pocket and shoved it at me on his way to our Pullman kitchen. Kyle jerked open the door of our Amana and examined the scant contents, plucked out at length Thor's carton of eggnog and drank directly from the spout. To judge from the noise Kyle made and the violence with which he spit into the sink, I had to guess he'd been expecting ordinary 2 percent.

"Security consultant?" I asked him. That was his title on his card.

Kyle nodded and wiped his mouth with his sleeve. "They want you out of here in a week." One of our geckos scuttled across the raw brick wall beneath the loft, and Kyle shivered with disgust and pointed. He told me shrilly, "Look! Look! Look!"

I beat him to the broom and withdrew it from his reach. "They eat the roaches," I explained.

This stunned Kyle a little. He dropped heavily onto one of our dinette chairs. "They're here on purpose?"

I nodded, and Kyle lapsed into sober study. He appeared hard-pressed to imagine a New York apartment so overrun with vermin that the tenants would give up on boric acid and choose to let lizards loose instead. Eventually Kyle shook in my direction the carton in his hand. "What is this?" he asked me.

"Eggnog."

"Christ, it's awful."

"I know," I said.

We ended up having a leisurely brunch together around the corner at a tidy little diner I'd never previously gone in. Kyle proved pleased to speak to me of his employment at some length. He turned out to specialize in a brand of freelance corporate menacing, was sort of a hulking gray-flannel thug for hire. The way Kyle explained it, he usually followed hard upon the pink slips—the zeroing-outs, redundancies, divisional constrictions—and it was his responsibility to impress upon the firelings that they had been quite authentically let go.

"People," he said, and shook his head. "They'll just keep coming to work."

So Kyle had concocted a sort of career for himself out of being emphatic for hire. The germ of the enterprise lay with a favor he'd done once for a cousin who ran a machine shop out in darkest Queens. The man was having trouble shaking a terminated employee, a Guatemalan who wasn't content to stay fired but kept riding the bus in from Great Neck and trying to operate his lathe. It turned out he was fluent only in some exotic mountain dialect that none of his Puerto Rican colleagues could speak. So though he smiled and said, *"Sí,"* whenever they explained he'd been discharged, he couldn't seem to understand that a firing in Queens held over from day to day. So he'd go home and ride the bus back to work the following morning when he'd get fired afresh and explained at in island Spanish all over again.

Kyle said he'd merely dropped by to see his cousin about a loan, was hoping to start up some sort of interborough car-detailing service, when he'd found him exasperated and threatening to brain a swarthy little man in dungarees.

"So I got the story and talked to the guy."

"The Guatemalan?" I asked him.

Kyle nodded. "He went home to Great Neck. He didn't ever come back."

"What did you tell him?"

Kyle made an experiment of spooning marmalade onto his hash, tasted a forkful and discharged it into his napkin. Once he'd swabbed his tongue on his shirt cuff, he re-created the spot of talk he'd visited on his cousin's Guatemalan.

"Adiós," he said while glaring out from underneath his brow. After a bit of a lull, he added behind it, *"Capisce?"*

"He understood that?"

Kyle shrugged and told me, "I've got a way with people."

And the genuine truth of the matter was, he did. Kyle took

pains, once he'd determined I felt victimized and wounded, to tell me of various Meridian Life and Casualty employees he'd rousted out of their cubicles and their company-owned apartments. "Just business," Kyle told me, and shrugged in a way to make me understand that he meant callous and frosty and almost never properly justified.

"It's a rare day," Kyle assured me, "when a fellow's got it coming."

So Kyle comforted me and bucked me up enough to inquire of him if I could maybe have an extra week in the company apartment. To Kyle's everlasting credit as a hooligan for hire, he told me without hesitation, "No."

Of course, I immediately dialed up Alice Kay Odom and left a plaintive message, hoping pity might drive her to me the way affection never had. I'd left in her foyer three full chapters of my novel of ideas (if the story of venomous skinks on the loose could qualify as thoughtful), which she'd not acknowledged or responded to in any way. She was busy, I had to figure, with her latest squad of boyfriends, and I had clipped and saved an item from an entertainment weekly about the staging of Alice Kay Odom's existential motorman play by a repertory company in Providence. They'd induced Alice Kay Odom to star which meant, when she wasn't in town romancing, she'd be up the road two entire states away.

Do-Ray and Franklin and Thor treated me to a farewell party at our usual watering hole on Amsterdam. We were joined by Thor's most recent addition to his bevy of schoolgirls, a lanky blonde with braided hair, about a baker's dozen ear studs, a tattoo of a dolphin on her collarbone and a catatonic manner. In social situations she'd sit glassy-eyed in unperforated silence until somebody had asked her, "Are you all right?" when usually she'd say, "Huh?" Evenings with Thor, however, in our only proper bedroom, she would frequently howl and yelp like she was being vivisected.

Thor and Franklin and Do-Ray did me the service of not discussing work even though they were just two weeks away from completing the Meridian trainee program and fanning out into the rust belt to their trophy destinations. Instead they commiserated with me over the sorry turn in my fortunes, and after a quarter hour of peeling his label off his beer bottle, Thor graced us with the theory he'd seen fit to cultivate to explain why I'd been chosen for ill use.

"Cracker guilt," he said, and laid out for us his take on southern karma, his view that the lily-white descendants of the old Confederacy were obliged to pay in soured luck and foreclosed personal prospects for the grievous moral failings of their kin, and this from a man who'd never traveled south of Atlantic City. Thor goaded me to act upon a theory of my own. I'd reasoned that maybe a half cup or so of cider vinegar added to a carton of eggnog would ferment it into a witches' brew of curds and slimy whey and thereby constitute a grim surprise for a hairless guy in briefs out to give a postorgasmic boost to his testosterone.

Sal bailed me out. He resisted me at first, but I proved able to do him a turn, and he helped me by way of compensation. He'd landed me by then a half dozen jobs at respectable guild wages which called usually for me to mill around behind a speaking actor, in back of a topcoat model, in the vicinity of a child. I'd proven myself reliable and, for a client, uncomplaining even after a night spent eating tepid chowder in a restaurant two tables back from a lantern-jawed actor bewitching his companion partly with his repartee but mostly with his dazzling smile.

Once she would reach to take his fingers, he'd turn toward the camera lens. He would grin and say, "Thank you, Laser Bright," with something shy of the bubbly persuasion the director thought a painless space age whitening system rightly deserved. So he would say it again and say it again and say it one more time while I spooned my chowder and pretended to talk to a pixieish brunette who made, in my professional opinion, a pretty poor show of pretending to listen.

I had no gnawing actorly ambitions and so didn't fret that I was being underutilized. I was wholly content to think myself flocked wallpaper in pants, happy to sit or stroll in the middle distance and indulge in faux palaver in exchange not just for wages (usually counted out in cash) but catered food and imported bottled water and reliably on each job at least one monumental snit. Ordinarily some slumming theatrical type would quarrel about the lighting or joust with the director over the reading of a line, usually the sort who'd played Benvolio at the Tampa Civic Center and so guessed he knew how best to phrase his irritable bowel distress. Those disputes could be relied upon to go incendiary given the caliber of psychoses invariably at play, so a fellow could sit with his bottle of Badoit and citrus-honeydew salad and watch two grown men (most usually) engage in a shrieking fit.

Sal represented his fair share of Bard-in-Podunk types who'd been expecting chiefly Broadway with stray cinematic detours but had ended up on cruise-ship stages and in dinner theater instead on their way to doing stints for Sal as advertising flotsam. Most proved content to confine themselves to the odd outburst, but Sal was having a more persistent problem with a former client along about the time he signed me up. I met the fellow once. He was going just then by Monsanto Duarte-Jones and shopping himself as a Latin-Afro actor and slam poet. His real name was Tod. He'd moved east from Indiana and had made a pretty substantial bust of being blond and white.

Unadulterated Tod had played waiters and clerks in a slew of failed cable pilots while Monsanto had landed a minor role in a feature film. He'd won the part of the leading lady's former boyfriend's older brother, a comprehensively tattooed plot device doing life at Ossining who delivered his solitary line from behind smudged security glass over an intercom in sneering Spanglish. It was just the sort of turn, Sal told me, that might have done Monsanto some good if it hadn't been edited out of the finished film.

Monsanto Duarte-Jones, you see, presented a color-balance problem. He'd gone ethnic by way of a tidy goatee and the liberal use of bronzer which had left him about the hue of adolescent copperplate. So he didn't look Hispanic exactly but more in the way of Mercurochromed, an effect that was heightened whenever he stood next to naturally tinted actors. It got to where Monsanto couldn't hope to land a part since he showed up burnt sienna through the lens.

He tried to go back to Caucasian, but the bronzer wouldn't fade, not sufficiently to make him look again like Tod from Indiana but just enough so that casting directors would see him and ask, "Are you all right?" His previous authentic talent agent had passed him on to Sal once word had begun to spread that his condition was infectious, that he could make his colleagues orange too. Naturally enough, I felt for the guy. The arc of my underwriting career pretty closely resembled the general course of his prospects as an actor, from the giddy heights of middling down to "Thanks for coming in."

We ran across him on the street one day. I'd been summoned

to Brooklyn by Sal who was having problems with the Taiwanese scanner I'd warned him not to buy. It had seemed to me folly to purchase office equipment on the street from a man selling chiefly tube socks, knockoff sunglasses and wallets. I thought it a wonder that scanner had failed to ignite as soon as Sal plugged it in. Instead it sat blinking for three full hours before the circuits melted.

Sal had called to ask if acrid smoke from Taiwanese resistors had much chance of being carcinogenic.

I'd made the mistake of improving once an idle quarter hour by repairing Sal's office-window fan while he was on the phone. The wiring harness had rotted through where the cord joined to the motor, and I'd used Sal's letter opener to improvise a splice. Through the cloud of boiler soot I'd raised once I had toggled the thing on, I'd watched Sal cut his phone call short and train his gaze upon me with the brand of wonderstruck expression I'd run across before, back when I'd made my inaugural Long Island City repair.

Sal, as it turned out, was far too thrifty to hire a proper tradesman, so a man who could fix a window fan with just a letter opener was precisely his variety of guy. We worked out a barter system. I'd build up points with Sal by making repairs and doing maintenance for him, and he'd throw me, when acting jobs came up, the choicest of the gigs.

Once I'd drawn out the screws and cracked the case open there on Sal's office floor, we discovered that Taiwanese scanner had been manufactured to blink and burn, was packed with cardboard instead of circuitry and pertinent electronics. Sal helped me carry the smoldering carcass down into the street where he lit one of his stubby foul Canary Island cigars which even Sal couldn't tolerate the stink of in his office.

Often when I'd visit Sal, we'd climb up to the roof so he could enjoy a rank robusto out in the open air. Sal bought his cigars through an uncle in Bronxville, and they looked like German shepherd leavings, smelled more than a little digested and processed as well. Apparently, though, mild and flavorful smoke came out the punctured end, and I could hardly hope to stop by Sal's without a half an hour passed among the vent pipes on the filthy membrane roof.

I didn't much like it up there myself. The parapet was so very low that a sudden stiff wind or aggressive pigeon might send a fellow over, and there was always evidence scattered about of potential death from above. Sal's building was situated directly under the Manhattan Bridge, and the roof was covered with items that had dropped from the motorway. Tailpipe clamps and lug nuts, chunks of plastic undercladding, bits of rotted muffler, twisted sheet steel off of semi trailers, scraps of tires and mirror housings, the occasional fractured spring or strut. Then, of course, there were the actual pieces of the bridge itself—bolts and straps and rivets, loose strands of suspension cable, rust-eaten hunks of roadway grid, bits of rebar and cement.

At least on the street I wasn't terribly likely to plunge my death, so I was pleased to help Sal carry his smoldering scanner toward the harbor where a neighbor of his was renovating a tumbledown waterfront building. Or rather he'd brought in a Dumpster the size of a freight car, had posted construction permits and had put up a sign that held out the promise of luxury apartments, but I can't say I ever saw anybody actually do a lick of work.

That Dumpster functioned locally as a flea market and godsend. People pitched into it items they were reluctant to set by the curb. Disassembled boilers, washer-dryers, ruptured sofa beds, fissile material, expired house cats, water pipes and body parts, and then pickers would descend to sift and sort and haul off the choice stuff. A fellow, in fact, intercepted us before we'd reached that Dumpster proper, a man collecting rubbish in his Key Food shopping cart who didn't seem to care our scanner was disassembled and smoking still. He took the thing from us, extinguished it in a milky curbside puddle and tossed it into his buggy with the rest of his junk.

We were almost back to Sal's block when we came upon Monsanto. He was standing at a corner that afforded him a view of Sal's grimy office window three floors up. I doubt I'd have noticed him if Sal hadn't veered across the cobbled street so that he might give Monsanto Duarte-Jones a violent shove. Sal knocked him directly to the ground and then stood over him a moment, appeared to visit upon that fellow a spot of incendiary abuse.

He looked oddly unperturbed. He was a shade of burnt sienna. I couldn't help but ask of Sal, "Is he all right?"

I got the particulars once we'd returned together to Sal's office where we stood at the window and watched Monsanto glare at us from the street. There had been a misunderstanding, Sal informed me, about a commission. Sal had withheld forty dollars his client felt Sal wasn't due, and, as a result, Monsanto Duarte-Jones had fixated on Sal, had condemned him as a chiseler and a faithless advocate, the root cause of Monsanto's disappointments and professional reversals which he preferred to facing up to the wages of being tangerine. He'd decided to haunt Sal as a brand of thespiannic protest.

"So give him forty bucks," I suggested.

"I did," Sal told me. "Twice."

We'd passed a good half minute in silence watching Monsanto Duarte-Jones stand on his corner and watch us devotedly back before Sal floated a theory to explain the man's behavior. "Bronzer poisoning," he said which impressed me as altogether worthy of Thor.

Sal, of course, was not without resources in such matters, but everybody he knew in personnel (that's what Sal elected to call it) was sure to be more thoroughgoing and comprehensive than he'd like. To his credit, Sal wasn't remotely convinced Monsanto Duarte-Jones had earned a trip to Bayonne in the trunk of a sedan. Sal wanted the fellow shaken up, but Sal's associates shook too hard, so Sal was frustrated and stymied and invited from me a suggestion. I fished out my wallet and put into Sal's hand a business card.

"Security consultant?"

I nodded and informed Sal, "An *adiós*-ist," which Sal gnawed on in silence while I tried to raise Kyle on the phone.

He was in between jobs, had been out at La Guardia meeting the flight of a former CFO so as to separate him from his corporate Visa card. When I reached Kyle, he was motoring southbound on the BQE en route to a junior vice presidents' bloodbath on Whitehall at Bowling Green. So he was convenient to us and proved ever so pleased to work Monsanto in, came rolling through in his Civic not a quarter hour later.

Sal and I looked on as Kyle climbed from his car and located the solitary orange civilian about. Kyle stepped over and joined Monsanto on his plot of corner sidewalk, and we watched him share with Monsanto what seemed a genial piece of news. Kyle smiled as he spoke and leaned in. He rested a hand on Monsanto's shoulder and then winked (it appeared) and withdrew a half stride to let Monsanto digest what he'd heard.

From Sal's office it didn't look like awfully much of a confrontation, and Sal exhaled and made what I took for a rather snide noise in his throat. He impressed me as verging on giving voice to his withering disappointment when we saw Monsanto Duarte-Jones shrug and depart. He twitched at the shoulders and shook his head, stepped off the curb and abandoned his corner, wandered north up Front Street until he'd strayed entirely out of sight.

"He's got a way with people," I informed Sal. "He said you could mail him a check."

Almost immediately Sal told me, "Come on," and led me up the gloomy stairwell, two flights to an apartment he kept for his troubled friends. Relatives mostly dodging the wages of felonious misadventures. Of course, Sal was well acquainted with my Meridian situation. I'd brought myself to make a few oblique pathetic overtures in hopes that Sal would advance me money or let me sleep in his office foyer. Instead he'd walked me up to the roof where he'd smoked a foul robusto while apprising me of the bright line that he never crossed with clients, the services he never rendered, the personal loans he never made. But that was all before I'd called in Kyle to rout Monsanto Duarte-Jones with hardly more than a brief word and a wink which had overhauled my standing and had qualified me for special privileges and welcome considerations.

"It's yours if you want it," Sal told me, and then bucked against the door which swung open to reveal a studio apartment a Realtor would have advertised as "a secluded pied-à-terre" or "a snug Brooklyn hideaway." It was, in fact, a glorified closet with a Murphy bed and built-ins and enough accumulated grime on the windows to obscure the air shaft wall three feet away.

The kitchen boasted a refrigerator hardly larger than a hatbox and enough counter space to nearly rest a dinner plate upon. The bathtub was littered with expired roaches and chips of ceiling paint, and I pulled down the bed to reveal a mattress peppered with mouse droppings.

Even still, I was delighted, was equipped to construe that apartment my salvation, and I was busy being actively pleased I wouldn't need yet to go home when my father called to deliver a piece of sobering family news. My phone rang, or rather it began to play "Greensleeves" at quadruple time. I'd lost my instruction manual and didn't know how to change the setting so that my phone would vibrate or warble instead, even strike up the *Godfather* theme, so I tended to answer it in a flash in hopes of staving off the usual who's-playing-a-madrigal? glances.

My father detested cellular technology. He preferred the phones he called to be attached still to a wall, seemed to feel he had a right to know just where he might be dialing. Consequently he asked me invariably the same question straightaway.

I said, "Hello," just as I reached to open a kitchen-sink tap and loosed a silty stream of what appeared branch water. I heard my father say, "Well," the way he always said, "Well," when he called me. I heard my father inquire, "Just where the hell might you be?"

BACK HOME AGAIN
IN
INDIANA

I'D BEEN IN WEBELOS with her doctor, had known him as Buddy. He'd worn loafers when nobody wore loafers much, and he'd smelled of cling-peach juice and cheese. His mother had worked in the principal's office at the middle school, and she'd once circulated among Buddy's classmates a thermofaxed announcement declaring her wish that we would, in future, refer to Buddy as "Charles." I believe for a while we did call him Charles but not in the spirit she'd hoped for.

I once slept over at Buddy's house before they moved into the county, before his parents enrolled him in the private day school up in Eden. Buddy showed an unnatural interest in their beagle's undercarriage which I persuaded myself at length was probably just premedical. Buddy's mother fed us rye crisps and meatless sausage links for breakfast that even Buddy's molested canine couldn't bring himself to eat.

We met in a corridor of the Amos Collins Wing of the Neely hospital which had itself once been the Martha Penn Memorial Wellness Center before the Penn family fortune had dissipated in a business reversal and the heirs had declined to pony up the balance of the endowment. They claimed cash was tight, and Martha was hardly in a position to care. The Amos Collins Wing was spanking new and (I guess) entirely paid for. With its paneling and Berber carpet, watercolors and recessed lighting, the place had the look of an interstate-junction primary-care motel. The nurses' uniforms were a shade of white I'd have to

117

call bone or cream, and Buddy's sage green lab coat had enough embroidery about the sleeve cuffs to suggest he'd made admiral or, at the least, was bucking for bell captain. Buddy still smelled, I noticed, of treacly peach juice and overprocessed cheese.

"Louis," he said, and offered the hand he'd used on his beagle's scrotum. I let on to be pleased to take it. I smiled and told him, "Charles."

He was grim and insensitive and unconsoling, abrupt and humorless which is as common among doctors, I've noticed, as icy stethoscopes and third wives. I've yet to meet the medical professional fit for social intercourse, equipped with the grace to reveal an unfortunate diagnosis to a loved one without sounding like a service manager down on a sedan. While Buddy could boast an uncommon aroma and a lab coat approaching teal, they hardly compensated for his arid disquisition on ischemic cascades and bothersome subarachnoid hemorrhages.

He kept calling Aunt Sister "Matilda" which I'd never even called her, so he managed to come off as callous and familiar both at once, and I probably would have gotten ill and exercised about it if I'd not been accustomed by then to thinking Aunt Sister already deceased. Now my ordinary practice is to fail to recall that the dead have passed away, and I have more than once inquired after the health of friends and relations who I've seen boxed and lowered into the ground. I once ran across a cousin at a Calabash clam house and poisoned, I imagine, a fair chunk of her vacation by asking how exactly her late father was getting on. I could hardly conceive of Aunt Sister, however, upright and unembalmed.

She'd lived in the same overheated apartment for probably fifteen years. It was located in Neely's first and (mercifully) only retirement village, a welter of poorly constructed board-and-batten vaguely Cape Cod buildings perched atop a buried county landfill. I believe the place was originally designated Muscovy Falls, notwithstanding a paucity of ducks and no flowing water to speak of. Early on, though, the van the seniors rode out to the Rexall in clipped the ornate sign at the entranceway and knocked it into a thicket where it was left for several years to rot and lie, long enough for locals to come by a preference for Methane Estates instead.

Aunt Sister had lived the bulk of her life in the sprawling family home place, had stayed on there taking in boarders after my grandparents had both died which had provided her with an income and almost limitless aggravation since she was altogether capable of renting a fellow a room while deploring the shiftless and profligate ways that had made of him a tenant. Her boarders aggravated her. They were a little too free with the water. They let the storm door slam no matter how often she cautioned them against it. They shared among them a goading indifference to the extravagant price of fuel oil. They snuck cigarettes on the landing and watched their TVs way too loud. They drank fortified wine and rained saltine crumbs pretty much all over the place.

Aunt Sister was evermore threatening to clear the house of her boarders and sell it, but in truth she had a native preference for irritation and upset and couldn't hope to be happy unless somebody was getting under her skin. My grandfather, Aunt Sister's brother-in-law, had plagued her while he'd lasted. He'd enjoyed a senseless argument about as much as she did. They'd quarrel over almost anything, agreed on virtually nothing, and I can clearly recall a morning I was on their kitchen floor rolling a metal milk truck along a join in the linoleum while

Aunt Sister and Grandpa Buck elected to differ with each other over the proper use of a handbrake when parking on a hill.

They refused to be stymied by the fact that neither of them drove. Aunt Sister had never sought a license and far preferred to control a car from the passenger seat with a stream of admonitions to the driver while a general fear of surgery and an aversion to hospitals had prevented my grandfather from having his cataracts removed. So my grandmother carted the pair of them wherever they needed carting which my father calculated took a decade off her life. He'd driven them some himself until the grousing and the squabbling had provoked him one day into trying to tempt one of them into the trunk which had served to touch off between them a lively uninformed disagreement over the human chemistry of suffocation.

My father was out in the county on the Burlington Road at the time, and he pulled into a graveled turnout with a picnic table where he succeeded at putting the pair of them entirely out of his car and drove off leaving them to argue over when he might be back. He came home and read the paper, watched the early-evening news and was in the middle with me and my mother of a perfectly commonplace supper when my grandmother pulled into our drive in her lumbering Monterey. She left her engine running, let herself into the house and found us in the breakfast room sitting at the table. My grandmother circled around to my father's end and kissed him on the cheek before retiring to her car and driving off.

"What was that about?" my mother asked, and my father shrugged and shook his head as if he couldn't possibly imagine.

The potato-chip guy had picked them up and ridden them home in his step van where they'd been chastened and blessedly silent for almost an hour and a half.

My milk truck was from Coble Dairy. Since its axles didn't turn, I can't authentically say I rolled it but rather skidded it down the seam and scuffed, I recall, my grandmother's yellow linoleum. She was washing the breakfast dishes, stood in her apron at the sink singing as was her custom a spiritual or perhaps an Irish ballad. Her personal repertoire boasted probably six or eight of each. Aunt Sister and Grandpa Buck were sitting on opposite ends of the dinette plaguing each other with talk of handbrake mechanics and practical vehicular motion when my grandmother, without dropping a note or breaking her melody, turned and threw a coffee cup in the direction of the dinette. It shattered against the plaster between Aunt Sister and Grandpa Buck.

Now my grandmother's coffee cups were from the Hotel Belvedere. The place had gone out of business and sold off all its furnishings and fixtures, so citizens throughout Neely slept on metal hotel bedsteads, lit their parlors with hotel ginger-jar lamps, ate with engraved hotel flatware from Belvedere dining-room tables (some of them) on Belvedere upholstered chairs. My grandmother had bought a couple of kitchen knives and a dozen hotel coffee mugs which were white and stout and embossed with the Belvedere coat of arms and weighed empty about a couple of pounds apiece. They held maybe four ounces of coffee and were so thick about the rim that what didn't go down your gullet tended to dribble off your chin.

So they were hardly fine crockery and not remotely cherished, and until my grandmother finally shattered one against the kitchen wall, we'd all assumed that they were indestructible. Naturally Aunt Sister and Grandpa Buck were silenced by the impact while my grandmother, who'd never stopped singing, turned back to the sink and returned to washing up the breakfast dishes.

If a saucer or tumbler had come to hand and she'd thrown one of them instead, she might well have produced a lasting punctuational effect since saucers and tumblers break, as a rule, against a plaster wall. So Aunt Sister and Grandpa Buck might both have felt compelled to notice the irritation that had served to launch the thing. Instead they marveled over the fact that a Belvedere mug had broken, studied the ding that cup had made in the wall and then proceeded to disagree about the actual year and season the Belvedere Hotel had given up the ghost and closed.

My grandmother stepped onto the back-porch landing to die just a bit, I assume.

Boarders, of course, could never suitably substitute for family since they could hardly afford to argue with Aunt Sister to her face, tended as a group to prefer a roof and a bed to debating points and so were evermore choking back their bile and staying their objections which rendered them unfit for sporting use. Consequently, after both of my grandparents had passed away, Aunt Sister had nobody to bicker with and agitate her. My mother was by nature the placating sort, and she kept a tight rein on my father, refused to allow him to bait Aunt Sister and devastate her with wry remarks. I, of course, had been raised to agree politely with my elders, so Aunt Sister began to waste away from want of acrimony.

She lost both her zeal for quarrelsome living and about eighty actual pounds, became withdrawn and quiet, a little feeble and noticeably addled, and when she almost burned the home place down with a citronella candle one night when the power failed and she caught the wallpaper alight, my mother and father persuaded her to move to an apartment and sold her somehow on the dubious virtues of a unit at Methane Estates.

So she was not the Aunt Sister I'd always known by the time she'd relocated, and I would catch myself occasionally thinking of her as deceased.

We'd fetch her over for Thanksgiving dinner and bring her out for Christmas Day, and my parents would drop by and sit with Aunt Sister every other Sunday, would read the Greensboro paper in her sweltering apartment while drinking her watery coffee, and they'd refresh Aunt Sister on names she'd forgotten and events she couldn't place. I'd swing by maybe twice a year and stay for half an hour, would usually know the chance to watch Aunt Sister dozing in her chair.

She went for a while talking about the funeral that she wanted—the music she favored, the text she preferred, the flowers she detested, the location in her closet of the dress she hoped to wear—until her neighbor in the adjacent unit had a coronary and went off to be a burden to his son in Wilmington. The place got let instead to a transplant, a woman originally from Milford, Connecticut, who had a granddaughter in the air force, a collection of Depression glass and a constitutional inability to withhold an opinion, most particularly on topics she had no working knowledge of. She was, in short, the second coming of my mother's father, a squabbling partner for Aunt Sister ever handy for a quarrel.

Death suddenly must have seemed to Aunt Sister less of an escape and more like an undignified concession which helped, we decided, to bring the woman back to chafing life. She and Louise, her Milford neighbor, could snipe and argue all day long. They shared a common wall which permitted them to hear each other's voice through the flimsy drywall and along the heat return, so they weren't obliged to put on clothes and step out for a bicker but could snipe in their quilted housecoats from the comfort of their homes. They seemed to truly dislike each other and genuinely disagree, so there was nothing the least bit sentimental about the bond between them, no danger they would reconcile and swap out strife for peace, give over at length the primal joy of raw antipathy which appeared to renovate Aunt Sister's appetite for life.

It got to where she rose each morning with a vitriolic purpose and could expect to be sustained by irritation through the day. Moreover, since she and her neighbor, Louise, had met so late in life, they found they had a lot of disagreeing to catch up on. Aunt Sister, consequently, was not so free for social calls as she'd been before her former neighbor had his coronary. So my parents went back to reading their Sunday Greensboro paper at home, and I spoke to Aunt Sister only occasionally on the telephone, dropped in with Fay once to see her before I moved up to the city, but she was busy with a quarrel about space travel at the time.

Fay, I recall, exchanged her tube top for an armchair antimacassar and lured me into Aunt Sister's spare back room for a tumble on the rug. We could hear Aunt Sister acquainting Louise with her theory of ion propulsion. We could hear Louise insisting there was no such item back.

Charles led us into the ward where they confined their direst cases, six beds of semiconscious intubated geriatrics and one nurse at a station reading a *Southern Living* magazine. Aunt Sister had lain on the floor of her Methane Estates apartment for hardly half an hour before Louise became alarmed, Louise who was making provocative comments about the postal service which ordinarily would have earned her an uncharitable rebuttal, at the very least an irritated snort. When she met instead with twenty minutes of unembellished silence, she called in the county police and the paramedics.

Charles went to some lengths to acquaint us with just how lucky Matilda had been as we stood at her bedside soaking in the sight of her. She was ashen and waxy-looking and harnessed variously to equipment which allowed her to breathe and hydrate, thinned her blood to circulate it and kept her in a docile narcotic haze. Charles informed us Matilda would likely be challenged to regain function (he called it) and would be faced with months of arduous therapy. Then he rested upon her shoulder his beagle-fondling hand and assured us nonetheless Matilda was a fortunate patient—and here Charles went severe and doctorly—given the alternative.

Aunt Sister waited a couple of hours before she chose to disagree. A nurse called around midnight with news of her death in the Amos Collins Wing.

Louise from Milford showed up at the viewing to object to Aunt Sister's casket, to call into question Aunt Sister's taste in lying-in-state attire, to deplore the perfumy stink of the lilies among the wreaths and sprays and to wonder of me if wasn't I the rascal of a nephew who'd despoiled his girlfriend on Aunt Sister's deep-pile spare-room rug. Then she lit a Raleigh, and before the funeral director could come scold her, Alice Covens-Llewellyn stormed over and plucked the thing from her mouth. Alice had given up smoking. She'd lately turned to Jesus and carbohydrates, had married a Baptist minister who was very nearly twice her age and had gained a parsonage, a hyphen and probably forty pounds.

She snuffed out Louise's cigarette in a pot of baby's breath. Then Alice sneered and was about to stalk away in triumph when Louise fished out a fresh butt while informing Alice, "Cunt."

Viewings in Neely aren't, as a rule, terribly entertaining. The family is ordinarily too wrought up for receiving company. The corpse tends to be a bit of an imposition. There's rarely any food, so people are left to just bromides and subdued pleasantries. I do recall one instance of an ex-wife, a mistress and a freshly minted fiancée contending for real estate in the vicinity of an embalmed Jessup and promoting, each of them, their claim on his affections, but I'd never seen the pall of a funeral home put so utterly to rout as Louise from Milford managed with one word of commentary.

Alice Covens-Llewellyn stopped short and inhaled with noticeable violence. The rest of us were more than a little stunned ourselves, but ours was shock (I have to think) touched with delight and wonder. It was as if we'd been touring a cow lot and had spied among the Herefords a woolly mammoth or the Princess Anastasia. We all dispensed at once with assuring each other Aunt Sister had led a full life and turned our collective attention on Alice Covens-Llewellyn who was widely detested but never to her face.

She'd failed to outgrow the bossiness best suited to a child and so was evermore acquainting people about with her frank opinion of them. You couldn't hope to run up on Alice around town and escape without suffering her appraisal of your leading flaws which she was evermore pleased to tell you, uninvited, how to mend. So if your ankles were chunky or your hair was unkempt, if your clothes were dowdy and unbeguiling, if your skin was discolored and wrinkled, if you had a child in jail, if you'd lost your job or painted your house, if you'd been diagnosed with an illness, if there was anything much at all in your life you didn't hope to discuss, Alice Covens-Llewellyn was sure to sniff it out and lay it bare.

"Here," she'd say, "is what you ought to do."

So it was pleasing to hear a spot of commentary inflicted on her instead. Alice managed at last to ask of Louise from Milford, "What did you say!?"

Louise was good enough to spell the word for her, proved delighted for the chance to repeat it, and Alice could only summon her husband with a gurgle by way of response. The silver-haired Reverend Llewellyn rushed over to support his wife, and he looked keen to uncork a spot of Old Testament insolence on Louise, but she advised him before he could make a remark, "Shut up."

In a way this was all just a modest local instance of globalization. Not much trace of the wide world had actually penetrated Neely. We had an altogether deplorable Chinese restaurant on the bypass where they tried to compensate with cornstarch for what they lacked in cooking skill, and there was a sort of a taco shack out near the public pool which got by on corrupted adaptations like pulled-pork enchiladas, dirty chowchow and refried black-eyed peas. We had no actual overseas foreigners but for a Greek and a pair of Koreans who a few of our veterans insisted on vilifying as Japanese.

What we did have by way of exotica was relocated Yankees who were steadily chiseling away at our Confederate filigree. They'd introduced us to brisket and whitefish salad, intemperate car-horn blowing, ladies' mohair sweaters littered with unsightly rhinestone studs. They'd made of our vacant Congregationalist church a Catholic sanctuary, had helped send an unregenerate liberal to the Raleigh legislature, had risen up in righteous anger when the alcohol-control board tried to close our only liquor store. They'd put lamb shanks in our butcher case and Vic Damone on the Q Lite playlist, had joined our theater troupe in numbers enough to break the monotony of nasally mid-South faux-Shakespearean accents. And they'd injected into our normal intercourse an untraditional pitch of irritation.

We'd all been raised to be nice, especially when we weren't feeling kindly disposed, had been brought up to resist uncharitable urges and deflect confrontation with a ready laugh and counterfeit conviviality. What we got for our bother was a chummy municipal veneer undershot with galloping dyspepsia. But our friends from the North were making inroads with obscenities, the odd fit of rage, the occasional colorful gesture.

So what we were witness to there at the viewing was a cultural exchange, and once Alice Covens-Llewellyn had abandoned the room in tears, we responded with a spontaneous ovation. My father anyway began to clap, and the rest of us joined in. Louise, for her part, wondered if someone would get her a goddamned ashtray.

We buried Aunt Sister in the memorial park on the hillside studded with cedars which, with its mausoleums and ornate headstones (heavenly angels, lambs of Christ), looked a bit more like a cemetery and seemed far preferable for repose to the unshaded lower pasture—what my father called God's own Dutch oven—with its flush-cut granite markers, its brown scalped fescue, its wind-upended funeral wreaths and sprays. She was laid in next to Grandpa Buck who got trapped in the everlasting between the sister he'd married and the sister he'd battled, pretty much like in life.

The Reverend Mr. Shelton performed the graveside service at my mother's request as Aunt Sister had been a wholly unaffiliated heathen. She'd failed in her lifetime to locate the variety of faith that preferred, like she did, strife and debate to unprovocative cheek turning. The reverend opened with a joke about Paul's revelation on the road to Damascus that Aunt Sister, who lacked a sense of humor, would have tolerated poorly, and then he declaimed from memory a poem about a spunky geriatric which gave way to a nugget of Scripture that functioned as preamble to a fond remembrance of Aunt Sister the reverend visited on us before inviting testimony from the assembled mourners. The reverend was fishing for any little spot of chatter to help to pass the time.

Mrs. Vestal was late, you see, and we couldn't really lower Aunt Sister without her. She'd not been a particular friend of Aunt Sister's and had no anointed holy calling, but Mrs. Vestal had provided for years an unofficial benediction that we'd come locally to think of as a sort of sacrament. Mrs. Vestal had burial services instead of needlepoint or gardening, in place of bridge club or ballroom dancing, rather than baking or bus tours. As a younger woman, graveside ceremonies had (I imagine) authentically stirred her, but in her dotage her enthusiasm for showy grief had ebbed.

For years she'd blessed our local burials with a sense of tragedy. A citizen could fail and falter and know with each waning breath that Mrs. Vestal was sure to send him off with a proper show of anguish. She'd rarely show up at a viewing or a sanctified church funeral but spared her grief for the moment when the casket was dropped into the ground. She'd charge to the lip of the open grave. She'd wail, "Farewell, brave soul!" and then fling her linen handkerchief onto the casket lid. Anywhere else that sort of eruption would have been frowned upon, but a burial service fairly cries out for the spice of melodrama. So we didn't just tolerate Mrs. Vestal but grew to count on her in time.

At length, however, she appeared to weary of her graveside obligations. She was like a pop star who'd had a hit recording in

1962 and was still, even forty years later, expected to sing it wherever she went. Mrs. Vestal was old and frail and got around with the aid of a practical nurse and a walker, and I suspect she'd reasoned she'd spend enough time in the graveyard soon enough which naturally served to dampen her appetite for recreational visits. So while she still came out to oversee the flinging of her nose rags, Mrs. Vestal rarely troubled herself to climb entirely out of her car. She'd gotten to where she'd dispatch an emissary and perform her duties by proxy.

Ordinarily Mrs. Vestal's daughter functioned in her mother's place. Kimberly Ann was a capable wailer, and she could usually approximate passable anguish, but she was kind of a tramp with a tattooed ankle and a taste for luminescent eye shadow, so she couldn't much help but seem cheap and easy while also seeming sad. People buried near a cemetery roadway got the original Vestal still. With her practical nurse and her walker, she'd usually venture to the curbing, from where she'd declaim her sentiment and fling her handkerchief. Kimberly Ann would have reliably tied a rock inside the thing, so it would usually sail at least within the vicinity of a mourner in a position to redirect it into the grave.

Aunt Sister, as it turned out, didn't get mother or daughter either one. She was too far into the cemetery for a curbside toss, and Kimberly Ann was off with her married boyfriend of the moment in a beachfront motel near Kitty Hawk. So Mrs. Vestal's son, Jack, was doing temporary duty as his mother's driver and stand-in. Jack had always been a little embarrassed by his mother's calling, and he'd tried to shift her off onto canasta and macramé, but his mother had proved dogged and entrenched. Jack was a bottling-plant executive with a wife and a son and a Westie, a Tudor house on a quarter-acre lot in

Shropshire Glen Estates. He drove a wagon and wore short-sleeved Orlon shirts under his blazers. He had not the faintest residue of melodrama about him.

Jack came racing up in his Taurus with his mother beside him and her keeper in the back. He rolled out and lumbered toward us across the intervening grave sites, past the markers and around the mausoleums. All the while he was struggling with the cellophane linen handkerchief wrapper. His mother bought the things by the gross and tossed them stiffly creased and fresh. Jack had no fingernails to pick the cellophane open with and was chewing at it as he gained our canopy.

The Reverend Mr. Shelton toggled on the casket-lowering motor, and Aunt Sister began to sink into the ground before Jack was prepared to send her off the way his mother would have wished. He ended up tossing that handkerchief into the grave still wrapped and slightly spit-moistened, and Jack managed to shrug and shake his head before he turned to go which we decided to take for his wordless rendering of "Farewell, brave soul!"

We cleaned out Aunt Sister's apartment, packed her furniture into our car shed, gave her clothes to the Christian Mission and sifted through her pertinent papers. She had warranty certificates for every electrical item she'd ever bought, a welter of receipts and grocery-store coupons, outdated insurance forms and several half-spent bags of rotted rubber bands. She also had a letter from a man named Gerald dated 1938, Gerald who called Aunt Sister "Mattie" and besieged her with endearments. His obituary from the *News and Record* was pasted to the envelope. He'd died from his wounds at Cassino in 1944.

I kept intending to tell my parents I'd left Meridian Life and Casualty. I'd been improving my leisure by sifting through squirrelly language in my head, had passed almost an entire week at home searching for some way to make getting fired sound like career advancement. I'd settled on "parted company" which could be taken for divorce, and I'd worked up a little airy palaver about my acting prospects and my natural inclination toward the arts. Then I'd kept it all to myself until the day I was to leave. We were sitting out on the front porch killing the final half an hour before my father was due to carry me to the airport in Greensboro when I discovered the nerve to uncork everything that I'd rehearsed.

My mother and father sat and listened and then mulled for a moment in silence before my father told me, "Funny. The way we heard it, you got canned."

It seems he'd called for me at the office and had spoken directly with Hector. "Who exactly," my father asked me, "is Divinia DeLuxe?"

I was spared from having to tell him by a woman on the walk who was wearing Aunt Sister's belted violet raincoat. We all recognized it immediately from the ink stain on the hem, and when that woman approached the front porch steps to ask us for a handout, my father and I went groping for our wallets while my mother buried her face in her apron and wept.

2

I HAD SILVERFISH ON the bathroom floor and ants in the kitchen cabinets. I had what looked to me like ladybugs in the overhead light fixtures, tiny beetles in the flatware drawer and roaches most everywhere else. Mice snacked on my bar of hand soap nights and chewed my oven mitt to tatters. Weevils infested every scrap of food I troubled to bring home, and I'd only been ensconced a week when I found a dead rat in the toilet which I'd half persuaded myself had probably drifted up the waste drain until I'd failed with aid of my fireplace poker to flush the thing back down.

It probably goes without saying my apartment didn't boast an actual fireplace. I'd bought that poker in a junk store on Atlantic Avenue once Sal had declined to sell me a revolver. He kept a quartet of .38s in the bottom drawer of his desk, insisted he was holding them for dear friends and relations who'd discharged those guns in the commission of various lawless enterprises. Sal allowed he didn't want me putting rounds in an intruder only to have ballistics tie me to some homicide in Queens. Now while I fully appreciated Sal's species of thoughtfulness, starting awake in the dark of night and reaching for a pistol shores up a man like reaching for a fireplace tool just can't.

And I did a fair bit of starting awake on account of my transient neighbors, friends of Sal's who used the apartment just below my own for drunken disputes and riotous assignations if not (and this was commonplace) a blend of both at once. Sal's friends were given to mistresses and bottomless libidos, manicures and marginally convincing toupees, Eurosuits and Cadillacs, while their nieces (they evermore called them) went in for heels and ringlets, navel studs and diamond bangles, Frenchtipped nails and gum. Those girls shrieked and warbled in a way I knew for counterfeit since I'd heard the racket Thor could manufacture with his tongue.

Worse still, my only permanent neighbors directly across the hall raised all sorts of clamor on their own. The husband, Faysal, was from Yemen, and his wife, Safwah-Yusriyya, was a former Episcopalian from Dutchess County who seemed intent on antagonizing her white-bread parents into their graves. Her given name was Monica. She was fair and blond beneath her burka, and she'd taken up the Muslim faith with dogged fanaticism.

Religious custom, apparently, didn't permit her to speak to me, but I got her story one Sunday afternoon from her father on the street. He and his wife had driven down for a visit at his wife's insistence, and he'd elected to linger out on the sidewalk in front of our building and stew. There was nobody else about but him. Sundays under the Manhattan Bridge tended to be sooty and sun-shafted studies in urban desolation. He was smoking an Upmann, a stout one about the size of a pepperoni, was wearing a monogrammed powder blue oxford shirt and jeans with creases ironed in. I was on my way for a paper when I happened on him, and he quizzed me without bothering to take his cigar from his mouth.

"How do you live down here?"

"Excuse me?"

Then he gestured to suggest he thought our immediate neighborhood hell on earth. An obliging chunk of bridge detritus dropped nearby onto the pavement to emphatic confirmational effect.

I hardly felt like explaining my wretched life choices to a fellow who'd wear creased jeans, and I would have gone about my business and left the man to smoke and wonder if he'd not started in unprompted on the story of his daughter who I still only knew at the time as Safwah-Yusriyya across the hall. Monica's father had worked up a theory on the course her life had taken. He'd decided to blame a religion professor his daughter had fallen in with, a gentleman of Persian extraction with an appetite for coeds and charm enough to tempt a child of Dutchess County from her own.

"Poisoned her," he told me, by which I think he meant (at bottom) deflowered.

"They seem happy enough." They didn't actually, but I felt like I ought to say something. Faysal and Monica rarely missed a chance to bellow at each other. They fought about Faysal's Western habits—his Members Only leisurewear, his appetite for pizza and lo mein, his enthusiasm for the Yankees, his willingness to allow their son to watch the TV nights which flew in the face of Safwah-Yusriyya's sense of Muslim duty that she hewed to, being a convert, grimly like a convert would. Their son was seven when I moved in, and his given name was Omar, but Faysal was angling for a Yemeni shortstop and called him faithfully Derek instead.

"Teddy," I told him, "seems like a nice enough guy."

He glared in such a way as to cause me to know he wasn't acquainted with Teddy.

"Faysal," I said, and added, "Your son-in-law."

His friends called him Teddy. He worked for a car service over on Henry Street. It was pretty much a Yemeni operation top to bottom with Yemeni drivers and Yemeni dispatchers and only the odd Egyptian for variety and relief. Faysal owned at the time a Town Car that he had dented and barked up. He was a bad one for drifting between lanes and pulling heedlessly into traffic. He parked with violence and had a notorious history of knocking meters down. Faysal had scraped off both of his sideview mirrors in spatial miscalculations and used the rearview on the windshield just for watching passengers. He liked to see fares when he talked to them, and he talked to them quite a lot as Faysal had a tireless cultural curiosity, a wealth of political opinions and a passion for all professional team sports but hockey, most everything he required to serve as diverting company except, perhaps, for some appreciation of the rules of the road along, of course, with a lawful driver's license.

A Yemeni friend of Faysal's who'd resembled Faysal a little had made a gift of his license once his deportation order came through.

As it turned out, Faysal was such a relentless menace on the roadways that the wags among his colleagues took to calling Faysal Teddy after the Kennedy he reminded them most of behind the wheel.

Monica's father from Dutchess County studied our building for a moment and then snorted in such a way as to prompt me to understand that Monica's husband couldn't possibly hope to be nice enough to deserve her because Faysal was not (I extrapolated) Episcopalian and white. Monica's father went on to assure me he was fair and open-minded. He mentioned a pair of Cambodians he had sponsored and educated, spoke at length of a Guatemalan woman who slept in a room off his kitchen and who enjoyed the benefits of Dutchess County living when she was not occupied with cooking and cleaning and creasing (I gathered) his jeans.

"Where," he asked me at length, "can a guy get a cup of coffee in this pit?"

I took pains to give Teddy's father-in-law meticulous directions north through four blocks of warehouses and shuttered derelict factories and then west down toward the river on a grubby cul-de-sac I knew to be no coffee and all pit.

Teddy thanked me with a mizmar serenade at two-thirty in the morning. He'd get, I'd noticed, on mizmar jags and take to his fire escape where he'd play what I'd decided were traditional Yemeni folk songs until I'd awakened one night to endure in exotic three-quarter time what sounded to me distinctly like "Back Home Again in Indiana." Teddy's mizmar was ancient. It looked essentially like a rosewood clarinet, darkened by hand grease and worn smooth at the finger holes with use. And it sounded, most particularly in the small hours when Teddy chose to play it, like a frantic waterfowl in the throes of operatic death.

I actually met Teddy to speak to him while complaining about his music. He'd rousted me just after midnight. He was waiting to call his mother once she'd gotten home from the market in Sanaa, and he'd decided to improve his leisure with a mizmar medley that commenced with "Ave Maria," lapsed for a few bars into "My Way" which yielded to what impressed me as some brand of Yemeni polka that itself gave way to a strident rendition of "Total Eclipse of the Heart." So when I stalked to the window and began to manhandle the sash, I was probably driven less by the racket and more by the repertoire.

Teddy's fire escape attached to mine, so I could see him from my window, but the sash was hindered in the slides by a dozen coats of paint. It proved, consequently, a lengthy chore for me to get that window open wide enough to stick my head through the gap and say to Teddy, "Hey!"

He was well into "Muskrat Love" by then, was playing with his eyes shut and seemed intoxicated by the tune. Teddy only turned to acknowledge me once he had finished with three verses. He smiled my way and told me, "Hello, friend."

Teddy was not the sort of guy you could stay mad at, even when he was playing his mizmar in the middle of the night. He was gentle and good-natured and thought well enough of people to assume that music held for me the charm it held for him, so instead of troubling himself to wonder what I might want of him, Teddy asked me to name a tune I'd like to hear. He wasn't acquainted with "Too Late Now," though Teddy promised me he'd learn it. He did play a bewitching rendition of "Stardust" to help me back to sleep.

Teddy used entirely too much cologne, was partial to shiny shirts with patterns. He had a pair of burgundy slippers he preferred to regular shoes. Teddy wore one of his wife's cast-off scarves in the winter under his leatherette coat which had snaps and buttons and zippers instead of an insulated lining. Teddy smoked Pall Malls though not with any savor and never more than halfway down. He was infatuated with one of the women on the Weather Channel who he seemed to believe was speaking directly to him. Teddy insisted evenings on playing catch with Omar down in the street. Omar was passable at it, but Teddy was a thoroughgoing menace. The ball never seemed to go remotely where he hoped it might, and Teddy was evermore bouncing it off parked cars, quite frequently his Lincoln.

A few weeks after I'd spoken to Teddy out the window, he knocked on my door and asked if I would do him a small favor. Once I'd agreed, he gave me a GameBoy that he'd bought on impulse for Omar but had lost his nerve and couldn't quite see clear to take it home.

"She's strict," Teddy said, and then he glanced at his door in such a way as to conjure for me the rigors of life with a Dutchess County convert.

I kept the thing in a drawer, and Omar would tap on my door some afternoons and come in and even play with it a little, but he preferred to ask me questions about whatever popped into his head. We'd frequently walk, me and Omar, west to the Heights and along the promenade, down to the pier out over the harbor directly under the Brooklyn Bridge where I'd reveal in stages my abiding ignorance of American history and physics, of biology, structural engineering, constitutional politics. Omar tolerated me anyway and suffered through my regurgitations of bastardized bits of flotsam I had soaked up from the *Times*.

I came to find out that Omar didn't have any use for baseball, was blessed with a knack for mathematics and was uncommonly fond of clementines. He had one friend at the grade school he attended on Middagh Street, a Korean girl named Yon-Min who had no friends but him. Omar fretted about his stature, had designs on being six-three. He intended to own a motorcycle and fully expected to win a patent for a contraption he had in mind that sounded like a golf cart with wings. He had no key to his apartment, so whenever we came home, Omar would knock to raise his mother who'd refuse to look at me.

3

SAL PROVED AS GOOD as his word. He kept me regularly employed both as an on-camera background professional and an all-purpose repairman. I did a topcoat add for a discount store's fall sale at their Weehawken warehouse, poached a cab from a woman in a public-service spot for the MTA and appeared in a series of jolly up-with-Broadway advertisements which called upon me to stand in toothy rapture out on Forty-fourth Street while the cast of one musical or another danced and sang in the road. I was even on the network news again for several evenings running once tech stocks dipped and the Dow Jones took a plunge. I milled behind the semipsychotic financial correspondent for what I recall as the better part of a week until I happened, during a break in taping, to jostle him and got dismissed.

It didn't really matter since Sal was in a position to compensate with the sort of steady repair work that paid a living wage in cash. The way Sal explained it, he had acquaintances with a native distaste for record keeping, no love of vouchers and work orders and trade-union regulations, no wish for me to supply them a proper receipt. What they preferred was for me to show up and do their little bits of business and then put from my mind just what I'd been about. Sal had assured me he wouldn't send me out on anything illegal, but most of what I did for his friends impressed me as marginal at best.

I helped them circumvent housing codes and fire-safety reg-

141

ulations, bring in premium cable without the bother of a proper account. I installed safes and strongboxes in walls and closet floors, discreet surveillance equipment in social clubs and family rooms. I once in a hideous Neapolitan restaurant in Bay Ridge made a successful weld to the boiler of an ancient espresso machine that so delighted the owner—an octogenarian with an eye patch—that he saw fit to kiss me flush upon the mouth.

They always paid me in cash, most usually in wrinkled exhaustively handled twenties, and almost without fail they'd lay to their lips a vertical index finger and tell me by way of parting instruction, "Shhhhh."

The work, then, was a little shady but not alarmingly so until Sal got word to deliver me to a Staten Island grandee, a gentleman I only ever knew as Bunny. I was a victim, essentially, of my own competence and reliability. I was capable and quick and circumspect, polite and presentable, and Bunny decided to try me once his long-standing fix-it guy had gone plump and gouty and emphysemic on him. Word came in the form of Bunny's driver behind the wheel of Bunny's Fleetwood, and I could tell by the way that Sal behaved when he came upstairs to fetch me that Bunny was not the sort of guy congenial to "no."

Sal came with me that first trip out. We met Bunny at Wolfe's Pond Park on a little walkway there above the ocean. Bunny had ideas about the healthful qualities of sea air which he expounded on at length. Bunny had a lovely manicure and a handsome cashmere topcoat, not remotely a discount Weehawken warehouse item. He had a gentle winning manner, a ready laugh and a relentless tidy streak. He picked lint as we walked off Sal's tweed jacket, ushered us around boggy patches and buffed clean his eyeglass lenses with a handkerchief three or four times. I didn't offer to speak, and Sal only made the odd trifling remark. I'd never before heard Sal call anyone "sir."

We were followed by a rather portly associate of Bunny's who wheezed along in audible respirational distress. He approached only once Bunny had snapped his fingers as he told me, "I've got a little problem. Maybe you can help me out."

Bunny's associate produced a booklet from his jacket pocket which he gave over to Bunny who handed it to me. It proved be to the owner's manual for a Frigidaire chest freezer.

"It was working just fine," Bunny told me. "But now . . ." He shook his head. "It just won't freeze."

I ran in my mind through everything I routinely would have said. Suggestions about the power supply, the thermostat setting, the warranty, but Bunny had hardly brought me out to a vacant park on Staten Island to hear from me generic appliance fix-it advice. I flipped through that booklet, perused the schematic, had repaired a compressor once before, and I told Bunny the only thing I sensed he'd probably tolerate from me. I said I'd be pleased to see what I could do.

Bunny sent Sal back to Brooklyn in the Fleetwood we'd arrived in. I joined Bunny in a newer model, and as we rode out of the park and headed north on Hylan Boulevard, Bunny handed me a sleep mask. It was violet, I'd call it, and had a girlish ruffle around the rim. It reeked of what I figured to be Mrs. Bunny's night oils and powders. I put it on and sat in overly fragrant darkness in that Caddy while Bunny explained to me the nature of his faith in people which involved his colleagues knowing as little as they had need to know.

Accordingly I can't say exactly where we ended up, though we hardly drove for long enough to get off the island proper, and once we'd stopped and I was helped from the car by

Bunny's portly associate, he ushered me up what I took to be the sidewalk of a house. Inside, the place smelled of fry grease, cigarette smoke and cat box, and I could hear the tinny sound of a radio tuned to a sports-talk station. A caller was discussing Tom Seaver's lifetime statistics with the host, a caller who sounded to me like Wallace on his motorized Meridian platform.

Bunny's portly associate escorted me into the basement, or rather grabbed me by the jacket collar and wrangled me down the stairs. That cellar was dank and stank of a mixture of laundry detergent and waste-drain gases, and we stopped under a powerful light which I felt heating the top of my head.

Bunny removed the mask, and I found myself standing before a freezer, a standard white chest model that had been shifted away from the wall. It was illuminated by halogen work lamps clipped to the overhead floor joists, and I could see that somebody had removed the back panel and pawed at the wiring harness. The freezer lid had a hasp and a closer attached, secured with a stout key lock.

"The patient," Bunny said, and directed me toward the open freezer panel, and only once I'd circled around to squat and eye the compressor works did my eyes adjust enough to let me take in the onlookers who stood in the murky darkness just beyond the wash of the work lamps which lit their lower trouser legs, their shoes. There were maybe a half dozen of them altogether, excluding Bunny and his portly aide, and they offered no comment and made no useful contribution beyond the occasional robust hacking cough.

For tools I had the few that were lying on the cement floor. A screwdriver, a pair of channel locks, what looked an upholstery hammer and a crescent wrench too large to be of practical freezer-repair use. There was an illegible mildewed wiring diagram stuck to the back of the freezer, a spiderweb in the cavity where the freezer works were housed with an occupant clinging to it about the size of a fifty-cent piece.

I managed to say, "Let's see," in a tone that sounded almost natural. Unmortified. Calm and businesslike. I was just then in the process of realizing that not eight inches from me, just beyond a piece of thin sheet metal and rigid freezer foam, a disassembled colleague of Bunny's was very likely thawing out.

Fortunately for me, there were only a couple of items that could have failed. I checked the connections and made a hopeful assumption about the compressor which left me with just a relay to suspect. I detached the thing and gave it to Bunny who handed it to his associate who wheezed his way out of the cellar and across (I could hear him) the upstairs floor. Bunny, as it turned out, had an interest in a parts distributorship, so his portly associate knew just where to go for the replacement.

In the interim Bunny and all of his colleagues in the basement smoked. Nobody, not even Bunny, bothered to say anything to me, but they talked lowly among themselves while dipping ashes onto the floor. For my part I kept my eye on the spider in the freezer hollow, and inasmuch as I could guess where its eyes were, it seemed to be watching me back. Bunny's portly associate returned to us in maybe twenty minutes with a brand-new relay in a pasteboard box. He presented the box to Bunny who handed the thing to me.

I dithered a bit while I installed it to allow me to cobble up an alternative diagnosis if that relay happened to fail me. But once I'd attached the thing and had reinserted the plug into the outlet, the compressor kicked on and the freezer began to operate again. A general murmur of approval filled that murky cellar, and Bunny glanced at his portly aide in what proved an instructional sort of way. That gentleman reached into his jacket pocket and withdrew an envelope. He removed from it and dealt to the freezer lid five pristine one-hundred-dollar bills. Bunny winked at me, and once I'd thanked him and scooped the money up, he handed me the frilly violet eye mask.

I was in Brooklyn on the Gowanus alone in the back of Bunny's Fleetwood before the portly associate behind the wheel told me to take the thing off.

Sal was sitting at his office desk when I showed up at his door. "Did Bunny treat you right?" he asked me.

I nodded and failed to offer a commission.

"Good man to know," Sal said, and I was but half prepared to believe him since Bunny had seemed the sort who might make as well for a fairly treacherous chum.

"What exactly does he do?" I asked of Sal.

"You know," he said eventually. "This and that."

Bunny, as it turned out, owned a chain of day-old-bread stores. One in Bayonne. One in New Dorp on Staten Island. One across the narrows in Bay Ridge. They were the most bedraggled uninviting retail operations I ever in my lifetime hope to see. I worked on equipment in each of those stores at one point or another, and the shelves were never more than half stocked with stale overripened baked goods, moldy bread and damaged dinner rolls, the odd forlorn pound cake. There was reliably one employee in each store, some guy on a stool at the front counter where he smoked and talked on his cell phone, read the *Daily News*, the *Post*.

I only saw once what I would call an authentic certified customer. She was a woman in a grubby quilted topcoat who was wearing a plastic head scarf, the sort with the accordion folds that had once, by the look of it, actually been transparent. She was filling a handbasket with packs of what appeared to me desiccated doughnut holes, and as Bunny and I passed by her on the way to the back room, she caught sight of him and all but genuflected. In her alarm she dropped a package that Bunny kicked out of his way.

Every so often Bunny would greet me with a "How are we doing, Marty?" when he had equipment for me to work on in the back rooms of his stores, items that had nothing at all to do with his day-old retail business but looked instead to have been violently removed from wherever they had been. Generators from construction sites. Coin-operated drink machines. Cash registers and computer terminals. Jukeboxes and Fry-O-Lators. The odd digital telephone system panel and countless ATMs. Clearly the stuff was all stolen, and with every repair I was leaving myself exposed to some sort of facilitation or accessory indictment, but Bunny was not the manner of fellow it seemed sensible to resist. It didn't hurt that I was being comprehensively overpaid and carted around in one of Bunny's Fleetwoods, and I consoled myself with the fact that he didn't seem to know my name.

4

HE LIKED ME. I was polite and tidy and effective as far as it went, and I probably would have stayed on doing trifling work for Bunny, commuting in his Fleetwood to Staten Island those occasions Bunny's men had plundered stuff for me to fix. But Bunny got into his head I'd make a fine match for his daughter and persuaded himself in some benighted portion of his brain that she would feel the same. So he invited me to dinner at his house in West New Brighton which he shared with his wife and daughter and his daughter's Lhasa, Dom.

Bunny's back veranda offered a stunning view of New York Harbor. His house was built on the order of a split-level château with plush wall-to-wall carpet and heavily gilded tomb-of-the-pharaohs décor. Bunny's wife was decidedly matronly from about her collarbones down and looked otherwise like she sat for cosmetological target practice. Her hair, in incandescent light, looked ever so slightly pink.

Bunny's daughter, Carlina, was about my age, and she was a bit of a looker. As criminal empires go, Bunny's was modest and provincial, but he certainly took in sufficient plunder to keep his only child in gym memberships and elective surgery. She didn't resemble her father or mother, not physically anyway. Her nose was so small and her face so symmetrical, her cheeks so prominent, that I couldn't help but believe that Carlina had been effectively rebuilt. At dinner she sat on a special cushion and spoke in clinical detail of the procedure she'd lately undergone to reshape her derriere.

149

We ate some sort of pasta in thin tomato sauce with incendiary sausage on the side. It was served by the family domestic, a woman named Ruth in a sweater and tights who gave the impression of being sullen and exasperated. She never said anything exactly but dropped our plates before us from height, and I noticed when Bunny politely (I thought) requested the saltcellar, Ruth muttered and rolled her eyes like she'd been asked to rebuild his transmission. When she came to clear plates and I told her how very much I'd enjoyed my dinner, Ruth snapped that she'd bought the stuff already prepared from the IGA.

Bunny, like any conniving father, kept trying to point out to Carlina my beguiling virtues which Carlina tolerated him at while she picked first at her pasta, then at her salad and at what tasted like a day-old sponge cake. She'd occasionally pipe in with mention of shoes she'd seen and hoped to buy, would repeat some uncharitable piece of talk from the lips of her girlfriend Wendy or would contradict most everything her mother had ventured to say.

For my part I sat and smiled and vented the odd convivial necknoise while Dom, the Lhasa, lavished upon me what I took for affection. I could feel him rubbing against my ankle underneath the table and hear his labored respiration through his abbreviated snout. He'd been at it for a while before I shifted the tablecloth to discover that Dom was rubbing his eye chum onto my pant legs.

At Bunny's insistence Carlina and I retired to the veranda for vin santo, and Carlina spoke ever so frankly about her feelings for me. While she confessed that she didn't know me well and suspected I had my charms, she assured me she would rather suffer agonizing death than find herself condemned to be my girlfriend. As a grace note, she added, "Don't take it personal, Marty."

She went on to speak at excruciating length of a gentleman named Pino, a Brazilian she'd been seeing for months without her parents' knowledge. He was somehow attached to the fashion industry as a consultant or importer. Carlina didn't seem to much care which. She was far more interested in the fact that he was a splendid dancer, had access to an inexhaustible narcotic supply and was hung (Carlina informed me) like a gelding. I have to think that's not quite what she meant.

Carlina shared with her mother the sort of voice that could penetrate cement or, if applied and directed, pulverize kidney stones to a harmless powder. Even there on the veranda where Carlina was making a bid to be discreet, I couldn't help but imagine that the barge crews in the harbor channel could hear her, maybe even some keen-eared citizens of Queens. I can't begin to explain how Bunny hadn't come by word of Pino.

Bunny drove me home himself, and there on the Brooklyn-Queens Expressway, he laid out for me the sort of dowry a girl like Carlina would bring to a holy union with, for example, a deserving husband like me. I tried to discourage Bunny while I complimented his daughter, and when I suggested she didn't much like me, Bunny assured me that she would, and in the tone of a man with a rival or two packed away securely in freezers. Accordingly, I changed tactics and began to run me into the ground. I claimed to be divorced and matrimonially shiftless, suggested I was vaguely alcoholic with a trashy string of repos and foreclosures in my past.

Once Bunny had scoffed and assured me of his unerring sense of people, I didn't see that I could help but bring Brazilian Pino up. I told Bunny about his business. I told Bunny about his dancing. I described Pino's swarthy South American good looks, and then I imagined the brand of rage that Bunny might rain down upon him and decided to insist that Pino and I were godless sodomites.

Bunny sucked air audibly and lapsed into a gloomy study. He stood on his accelerator as he whipped onto the shoulder and raced to the nearest exit where he told me to get out.

It was Sal's considered opinion that Bunny would probably do me no harm, was unlikely to visit upon me any severe disfiguring damage and might even employ me a little as evidence of his open mind. And Sal was the one, as it turned out, with an unerring sense of people, since Bunny continued to call me in to perform for him the odd repair, though not so frequently, certainly, as he had called me in before.

So my income suffered, but I knew that Sal wouldn't pitch me out. Consequently I didn't go scouring for actual salaried employment or sign up with a temporary service. I made repairs for Sal and, occasionally, Bunny and took all the background work that came my way, most especially TV spots with their union rules and buffet tables. I played on a freeze-dried-tastes-like-roasted-coffee commercial an actual restaurant patron with a line of dialogue, a word, really, which I like to think I delivered with some bravura. I was called upon to sip from a cup of a pretty unspeakable brew and say on "hidden camera" to my wife across the table, "Wow!"

Sal parlayed my performance into a job on a thirty-second lozenge spot where I was called upon to shovel snow and cough. And we were both half persuaded that I was primed to move into the foreground when I got involved in a snit on the set of a shoe-insert commercial. The actor playing the podiatrist accused me of eating far more than my fair share of melon off what was, in fact, a pretty skimpy catering table. He was probably right, and I imagine I might have even apologized to him if he'd not, by way of emphasis, poked me with his tongue depressor and been more haughty than a featured shoe-insert player had cause to be.

I asked him what sort of self-respecting podiatrist would use a tongue depressor. Then I grabbed the thing and poked him back which prompted from him a recitation of his résumé. In his very best preening orotund House of Windsor baritone, he announced the professional triumphs he had known which included what sounded like the entire Arthur Miller repertoire performed in every county seat along the Ohio River Valley. I shoved him once he'd mentioned his repeating character on *Trapper John, M.D.* and earned for it a nagging reputation as a troublesome hothead which cost me for no few months thereafter bits of paying work.

So I happened to be at professional loose ends on the weekend that Teddy and Omar and Monica-Safwah-Yusriyya came suddenly into a seaside rental down at Brigantine. A buddy of Teddy's had signed a lease on an oceanfront house some months before but had since run afoul of the INS and gone into detention. On short notice, Teddy got invited to share the place with a Yemeni workmate who insisted (for their safety) that Teddy and his family ride with him to the shore which would have left Teddy's battered Lincoln idle for the weekend if he'd not popped over to jangle the keys and ask me to drive in his stead.

"Win-win," Teddy told me. It was possibly Teddy's favorite Western expression. He was given to baseless optimism in the storied American fashion and could sniff out the good in virtually every option that came his way.

I chose to fix instead on the fact that Teddy had allowed his insurance to lapse, that I'd not been behind the wheel of a car in almost a year by then, that Teddy's tires were bald and his starter required the odd loving tap from a hammer, that it cost Teddy two hundred dollars each spring to pass the state inspection. So I was busy picturing the wreck I would have and imagining the passenger I would mangle when Teddy tossed his keys my way like he threw a baseball in the street. They sailed over my head and struck the blinds, clattered to the floor.

Teddy lingered there in the doorway favoring me with his best toothy grin, and I told him back the only thing I could bring myself to tell him. I nodded and smiled and said to Teddy, "Win-win."

I knew the dispatcher a little. He played some manner of sub-Saharan lute that he'd bought off the street on the Lower East Side from a luckless Tanzanian who'd decided, instead of strumming the thing, he would prefer to eat. That lute appeared to have been fashioned out of a gourd and hand-planed ebony, but while it was lovely to look at, it was pitched at such an elevated tone that it did reliable service as a musical irritant. Teddy and Azal, the dispatcher's name was, would take to the fire escape nights and put me on edge with overly lively renditions of classic eighties rock, hair-band stuff for the most part, with intolerable quack and twang. I'd stick my head out my window and strike up a conversation to make them stop.

Azal sounded delighted to hear from me over Teddy's radio. I'd been sitting for probably a half an hour by the curb in front of our building before I'd mustered the nerve to take up the radio handset and call in. I'd adjusted the seat and the only mirror Teddy had yet to scrape away, had removed Teddy's essence-of-lilac car freshener to a pasteboard box in the trunk and had opened the windows to dissipate the aroma. I'd practiced assorted car-service-driver conversational strategies which boiled down to three or four different ways to ask a fare, "Where to?" Then I passed a good ten minutes trying to figure how a fellow, if he so wished, might switch Teddy's radio on.

Once I'd located the proper toggle, I got just low-level static at first but soon enough bursts of sullen Arabic between Azal and his drivers. I keyed the mike and, acting on my sole scrap of instruction from Teddy, said as officially as I could manage the number of Teddy's car. "Twenty-nine. Twenty-nine."

I could hear Azal laughing through the static. "Loose!" he shouted which was as close as he could come to saying my name. It was followed hard on by a chorus of "Loose!"es from my far-flung Yemeni colleagues.

Azal had what he assured me would be a simple job to start. A fare in Cobble Hill just on the south side of Atlantic Avenue was flying out of La Guardia on Northwest. Azal gave me the street and the number which, through the static and his accent, I could almost understand. I went, consequently, on a bit of a tour of greater Cobble Hill before I spied in front of a brownstone a man with an overnight bag who appeared to be in a remarkably poor mood. He was my guy, as it turned out, and he was late for his flight to Memphis. In his view it was all my goddamn fault, and he was still actively debating as I reached Grand Central Parkway whether he'd prefer to sue me for the full price of his ticket or absorb the loss for the satisfaction of strangling me outright.

In truth, I wasn't even all that late, but he'd had trouble getting a ride, and he proved to be pretty much the norm for Yemeni-car-service fares. People, as a rule, preferred the Lebanese outfit on Montague Street. Their drivers all wore coats and ties and kept their Town Cars impeccably clean. They were prompt and polite and seemed to know all the shortcuts and sly alternative routes around rush-hour bottlenecks and construction projects. As a result they were usually in high demand and couldn't often handle the volume which left customers to make do, by way of second option, with the local Egyptian car service instead.

They had a shabby office at the bottom of Atlantic Avenue where it ran into the shipyards, and to a man they all drove ivory Lincolns with velour upholstery, so you couldn't help but feel as a passenger like you were off to the prom. The drivers were polite and serious and, usually, overqualified for guiding ivory Lincolns through the boroughs of New York. One of them once recommended an ointment for my rash—a bit of inflamed bother on my forehead—as we were inching in clotted traffic down the Bowery toward the bridge. He'd been, as it turned out, a dermatologist in Port Said.

People only phoned up the Yemeni service when nobody else would come, when they'd exhausted their options otherwise and had gone to the Yellow Pages where Azal had taken out a half-page ad which was both eye-catching and riddled with deceit. The cars were not new, the drivers not liveried, the response hardly immediate, the pricing erratic, the passenger airbags a wholesale fiction. But the ad was big, the phone numbers bold, the customers without sound recourse which seemed to ensure they'd be ill humored by the time we picked them up. It was appropriate, then, that the employees were by nature the sorts of people who'd play airy mizmar and lute selections from the Def Leppard songbook on a fire escape in the middle of the night.

Not being carefree and Yemeni, I was a little shaken at first. My initial fare abused me all of the way out to La Guardia, both directly and to the friends he dialed en route on his cell phone which didn't, I noticed, prevent him from tipping me above the charge. I laid the gratuity off to the fact that I'd been scrupulously unantagonizing, even a little meek, but I learned in time that nothing I did had much effect on tipping. Fifteen percent, as it turned out, was the local going rate for abuse.

At Azal's direction I picked up an irate woman at Continental arrivals, and she screamed at me all the way in through the Midtown Tunnel to Manhattan. She was full of vodka, had missed her connection by mere minutes in Kansas City, repeatedly wished aloud that she had taken a taxi instead. But once she'd directed me onto her street and had pointed out her apartment building—or had shrieked anyway, "Stop for fuck's sake!" once I was in front of the place—she pitched money at me, including an extra ten dollars for my trouble. It wasn't Bunny wages exactly, but the work was legal and oddly relaxing, like driving peevish children who were obliged to pay their own way.

My leading problem was that I didn't know how to get anywhere in a car, wasn't acquainted with the best overland routes or mindful of detours and shortcuts since I ordinarily rode the subway and only occasionally hailed a cab. So I was doomed my first two nights behind the wheel of Teddy's Lincoln to function for my customers as a further provocation. I took wrong turns and preferred main arteries more than anybody liked, was altogether too polite and defensive when obliged to merge into traffic, and I frustrated my fares from indulging in a handy class of insult by being (selfishly, they seemed to think) homegrown and American-born.

Even still, there was something deeply appealing to me about the work. It combined a few of my favorite ungainful pursuits into a source of paying employment. I got to ride around and eavesdrop, chat and psychoanalyze, visit advice upon perfect strangers once they'd beseeched me for it and present the unoffending back of my head to drunken groping couples while surveying their progress with the odd glance in the rearview mirror. When I'd reach a destination, I'd call to Azal for the charge which left him, in effect, to the commerce and me to the acrimonious fun.

I'd gotten it backward, you see. I'd assumed that Teddy and his Yemeni colleagues, being placid and calm by nature, were well suited for their work when, in fact, the work proved soothing and unexpectedly therapeutic. My passengers seemed to function as a sort of collective poultice. With their impatience and their chafing, their reliable ill will, they drew out my native poisons and put them thoroughly to rout.

I tried on one occasion to explain the phenomenon to Sal. We were up on the roof where Sal was enjoying a Canary Island robusto, and for whatever reason it was a treacherous day for bridge detritus. We seemed to be getting a Dodge van piecemeal from the motorway. First a chunk of belted retread. Then a fractured tailpipe clamp. A brake caliper followed hard upon by a piece of transmission housing that just barely missed our building and shattered on the cobbled street. Ordinarily I would have been flinching and agitating to go inside, but I was still operating on residual inner peace and so just stood there while vehicular nuggets rained down all around me.

Sal was enduring just then a problem with a producer he detested, an unreliable skinflint I'd worked for a time or two. Once in a mouthwash commercial where I'd played a tollbooth clerk tasked to enjoy the minty-fresh breath of a lithe brunette commuter and once in a foot-fungus ad where I was finishing concrete when my brogans (as an emblem of keen discomfort) burst into flames. That producer—his name was Rubin, though everybody called him Jack—was evermore trying to squeeze shooting schedules and chisel down payrolls, wasn't above cheese food and pickle-pimiento loaf on his craft tables or in-laws filling in for union hands.

Sal stayed convinced that Jack was always chiseling him a little, and every now and then he'd catch Jack skimping on a fee which, Sal informed me, was the cause of his foul mood up on the rooftop. By turns he chewed and puffed his reeking cigar. Sal was invariably torn between suing Jack or simply having him pummeled senseless, and he was actively debating his options as a portion of heat shield sailed down from above and clattered off the parapet beside us. When I failed to shriek and twitch, Sal asked me, "You okay?"

So I told him about my weekend of carting furious civilians, acquainted Sal with my newfound peace of mind and equanimity and generally oversold my theory of car-service empowerment to the extent that Sal perused me in grim silence for a moment before he snorted and, through a cloud of blue cigar smoke, told me, "Right."

MARTY
ON
STATEN ISLAND

1

LIKE THE VAST MAJORITY of aimless unindustrious people on earth, Teddy preferred to think himself enterprising. He was evermore floating half-baked schemes for raking riches in, favoring me with impractical business advice and ideas for the sorts of products that routinely held out the promise of inadvertent fatalities. Spring-loaded kitchenware. Battery-operated clothing. Dual-use tools for the handy homeowner (the nail gun / saber saw comes to mind) and a panoply of self-defense items for imperiled urbanites, from exploding wallets to cell phones with taser capabilities.

Once I'd owned up to the pleasure I'd taken from driving fares in Teddy's car, Teddy set about calculating how he could turn the sensation to profit. He preferred to believe that I was a representative American, that my fellow citizens would endorse most anything I liked, so once I'd acquainted Teddy with the soothing spa effect of carrying irate strangers through the city, Teddy decided my fellow citizens might be keen on it as well.

Teddy arrived in time at the notion of a strain of urban dude ranch. He figured if otherwise sensible people would jet out to Montana and pay for a week in a flyblown pasture mucking around with cows, why wouldn't they come to the queen of cities to motor carping civilians about? In retrospect I imagine I oversold the therapeutic value of traveling the avenues and the parkways, negotiating the river crossings with unbridled peevishness wafting from the backseat of the car. I tried to retrench, volunteered provisos, indicated what impressed me as glaring flaws in Teddy's thinking, but Teddy was generally immune to misgivings once he'd embraced an idea.

He hoped to put tourists behind the wheel of a car-service sedan, open up to them the blue-collar / immigrant metropolitan experience which had the benefit of being prickly and spiritually cleansing both at once. Without intending to, I'd succeeded in selling Teddy on the notion of recreational hired-car driving as something like Canyon Ranch on wheels.

I peppered Teddy with tough questions and trotted out calamities. I tried to infect him with my native fear of baleful consequence, and I wondered of him as my trump complaint how he expected out-of-towners to possibly know how to get anywhere they'd been instructed by fares to go.

"Satellites," Teddy told me. "Right?" he said to Omar who withdrew from his GameBoy the penknife he was using to dissect it so as to shrug and inform me, "Satellites," as well.

Naturally I assumed that Teddy's enthusiasm would flag. I knew how I was with a personal pledge. I'd yet to master Italian or realize stark abdominal definition, hadn't succeeded at learning the tango or winning back Alice Kay Odom by graduating to TV drama and intoxicating the creature with my chops. I'd set aside my venomous-lizard novel after only a handful of chapters, walked for exercise merely up to the Thai take-out place and back, and when it came to sacred personal oaths and abiding core convictions, I suspected Teddy was probably as unreliable as me.

He certainly seemed to be. After a couple of weeks of urban-dude-ranch chatter, Teddy dropped the topic entirely, went back to mizmar serenades, played wayward catch with Omar on the street before our building, drove his shifts and bickered with his zealous convert of a wife. He tried out on me his idea for a personal-security ensemble—a jogging outfit that unzipped into a hazmat suit—and sulked for a night or two on my couch once the spunky blonde he adored had shown up on the Weather Channel in maternity wear.

So I had ample cause to believe that Teddy had moved on to other interests by the time I mentioned the late-model Crown Victoria I could get for him cheap. I'd noticed that Teddy's Town Car was in a pretty wretched state, not just from the cosmetic damage inflicted by his brand of driving, but I'd heard bearing roar and fierce spark knock, unsettling suspension racket throughout the two nights that I'd driven in Teddy's stead.

Bunny, of all people, had offered that Crown Vic to me. He'd undergone a change of heart. One evening a few weeks before, he had met with a rival in SoHo. They'd get together every couple of months to iron out disagreements, carve up new territory, condemn offending associates to death. They'd invariably meet at a Sicilian restaurant on Spring Street where the chef made a lobster fra diavolo specifically to Bunny's order. I'd had it once at Bunny's insistence. It was far too spicy for a human to eat.

So Bunny and his rival, I imagined, had sat there and outcayenned each other until they'd tidied up their differences, polished off their Nebbiolo and stepped out to exchange the usual feudal blandishments on the street. That's when Bunny happened to glance across and catch sight of his daughter. Carlina was walking along the opposite sidewalk clinging to a wiry Latin with an open shirt and a tousled head of hair. A goatee. A concave chest. A syncopated strut. My Pino.

The way I heard it from Bunny, he charged across the road and demanded an introduction and thereby learned for a fact his only child had poached my sodomite. So he was mad at Carlina and disgusted with Pino for going either way, but mostly Bunny was sympathetic to my romantic situation. Men of Bunny's profession share among them a vile opinion of betrayal.

Bunny had Danny fetch me to his shop in Richmondtown, Danny who made vague reference to a problem with the boiler and then busied himself, as was his custom, swearing at his fellow motorists as we raced south along the Brooklyn-Queens Expressway. Danny would follow offending drivers for some miles if necessary so as to enjoy occasion to threaten them with his nickel-plated gun. On this particular trip I noticed that Danny was kinder to me than normal. He troubled himself anyway to ply me with odd scraps of trifling talk when customarily Danny was only good for interludes of phlegmwork and curdled glances my way in the mirror. This day he pursued an erratic Pontiac down the Fort Hamilton Parkway ramp, caught up with it on Sixty-fifth Street and bestowed on me the honor of showing the Lubavitcher behind the wheel his shiny PPK.

I discovered straightaway when I got to the basement of Bunny's day-old-bread store that there wasn't anything the matter with the boiler. The water in it was hot. The pilot was burning. The thermostat worked just fine. Naturally, then, I feared that Bunny had brought me there to do me in, and I do believe I was piecing together a case for my survival (something along the lines that I was too inconsequential to kill) when Bunny informed me with more delicacy than he could usually muster that his daughter had tempted away my "special friend."

This was not the sort of news I was equipped to make immediate rational sense of, so my initial reaction was bewilderment which must have looked to Bunny like grief because he laid one of his princely manicured hands upon my shoulder as he apologized for his part in producing the sort of child who, with no end of manly men about, had set her sights on my life partner.

Bunny shook his head as he inflicted on me a fond squeeze. "Sorry, Marty," he told me.

Bunny offered the car in consolation for my plundered sodomite which was entirely in keeping with the antique standards of Bunny's way of life. It was as if he'd filched my mule and was compensating me in chickens, had family honor to consider and tribal elders to appease. Bunny had calculated that a low-mileage sedan was just about a fair exchange for the loss of one healthy fey Latino boyfriend, was in fact a little richer a bargain than even I deserved. So Bunny offered me the Crown Victoria for fifteen hundred cash and enlisted Danny to assure me that he was taking a beating on it.

We went outside to look at the thing. It was sitting behind the Dumpster. The title in the glove box had been signed over by a gentleman named Art who, Bunny informed me, had moved to Florida in a bit of a rush. I learned later from Danny that Art had relocated against his will and not to Florida exactly, though given the drift and warp of the ocean currents, there was a chance that some of Art would get to Florida in time. Even by the Dumpster while Art was still (as far as I knew) in Boca, I got the feeling Art's was a discount Ford I couldn't choose not to take.

In the spirit of enterprise corruption, I sold the car that very evening, offered it to Teddy for two thousand dollars and change.

I'd assumed Teddy would dump his Lincoln and go with the finer specimen, but instead Art's sludge-brown Crown Victoria served as an omen for him, a sign that the time was, in fact, ripe for his car-service rodeo, and I do believe that Teddy might even have gotten an actual franchise going if his mother hadn't fallen ill and summoned him back home. She was suffering through complications from a botched female procedure, was expected to live but wanted her children to gather nonetheless and see up close the misery that birthing them had caused her. To hear it from Teddy, his mother was a tireless scold and a relentless shrew. He hoped to stay two weeks at the most, and I was happy to drive in his stead.

Just then Sal didn't have much for me. I was weathering still the fallout from my spat with the podiatrist, so it was nice to have a little paying work to see me through. I elected to drive Art's Ford, and I paid daily rental to Safwah-Yusriyya for it. Or rather I paid it to Omar who his mother always sent to answer the door since she was far too devout and holy for commerce with the likes of me.

That Ford still smelled new. The seats were stiff. The carpet was pristine. I couldn't help but occasionally think about Art barking along the sea floor, but I managed nonetheless to enjoy my shifts behind the wheel. There was little I liked better than slipping into that Crown Vic, announcing myself on the two-way and hearing from my colleagues, "Loose!"

In the mornings I carried geriatrics to their doctors' appointments, double-parked on East Side cross streets and waited for them to come out, helped them into the back and heard at length about their diagnoses, their diet restrictions, their profligate children, their insensitive neighbors, their cats. Afternoons I drove business professionals, men usually who called me "pal." They were late, of course, and irritated and talked incessantly on their phones. They wore tailored shirts and smelled of leather, were evermore heading for squash or drinks and tended to spice their conversation with the sorts of raw obscenities that would have given pause to a merchant marine. Nights were mostly for couples and evolving intoxication from slightly beery to snoring and dead drunk.

I was in and out of the airports, all over the five boroughs, saw parts of the Bronx and Nassau County I'd not in this life expected to see. And by the second week, I was so thoroughly at my ease behind the wheel that I hardly noticed the vehicular chaos swarming all around me, took no personal offense when cabbies and unmedallioned urbanites failed to yield and cut me off or tailgated maniacally. I had fares to study, a regular pageant of personalities to plumb, strife and tribulation to decipher and account for, romances to parse and justify, personal narratives to filter, biographies to cobble up from evidence at hand. It was usually all I could do to recollect where I was going.

Driving for Teddy was just the sort of thing my father would have loved, he of the exhaustive and (oftentimes) demoralizing philosophical inquiry. Ordinarily he was put upon to seek his victims out. He had to suffer through dinner parties, attend weddings and receptions, wander the aisles of the megacenter out on the Danville Road in hopes of chancing across a candidate for penetrating study, some hapless soul with his sills bug-eaten and his framing out of true. In Teddy's sludge-brown Crown Victoria, the victims came essentially to you.

So I could readily picture my father behind the wheel of Teddy's sedan, a newer vehicle than he would have sprung for himself but agreeably stout and American-made. I could imagine him sizing up passengers, enduring from them their complaints, subjecting them to his usual manner of inquisition and perusal and acquainting them with his assessment once they'd arrived at their destination so as to supply his passengers something to be "gratified" about.

Understandably, though, I couldn't confess to my father what I was doing, own up to the fact that I was driving a sort of glorified cab, that I'd tussled with the ilk of podiatrist who would use a tongue depressor and was working off my unsavory reputation behind the wheel of a Ford for hire. I couldn't think of a way to say it and not come off compromised, not suggest that I was, very probably, a bit of a disappointment. So instead when I talked to my mother and father and they asked me how I was doing, I'd pause as if thinking the matter over before I told them, "Fine."

I was midway through my second week of filling in for Teddy when, one afternoon during a rainstorm, a fellow hailed me on the street. I was strictly forbidden from stopping for passengers I'd not been dispatched to fetch, and I would have ignored this guy if he'd not thrown his house keys at me. I heard them hit the fender panel and skip across the trunk.

He yelled at me, "Hey!" By then I was lurching to a stop already, had instinctively decided that unprovoked key throwing was something I couldn't tolerate with grace.

I threw open my door and engaged that gentleman in the prevailing brand of local Socratic inquiry. I asked him, "What the fuck is wrong with you!?"

He was balding and dumpy and a little drunk, had that double-bourbon-at-lunch glaze to his expression, and he growled something I couldn't understand as he pitched off the curb and wandered out into Broadway to pluck his keys from the pavement. That's along about when I heard her say, "No cabs."

She was back under an apartment-house awning, standing protected from the weather, and she stepped forward apologizing for her friend's stripe of gallantry. I was as good as helpless against her well before she'd finished talking as she was better put together than practically any woman I'd ever seen. She had gloriously shiny copper hair that fell about her shoulders, green eyes and what even I knew to be a naturally perfect nose. She was six feet tall in heels and sleek and voluptuous both at once, revealed sinews and muscular hollows along with mesmerizing cleavage, and she was striking enough to seem to have no use for being coy.

"Where are you going?" I asked her.

She pointed south and was just about to tell me when her companion jerked open the near back door and instructed her, "Get in."

She troubled herself to pause at the curb and provide me occasion to stop her, but if she'd been bound for Havana, I'd have offered to drive her there. Her friend rolled in behind her and left the door for me to shut.

We were up in the Eighties, and I decided to take Broadway all the way down once the gentleman in the backseat had insisted I head west toward the highway. I offered politely to pull to the curb and let him, if he would prefer it, out. He kicked my seat back and was unburdening himself of a string of salty modifiers when she laid a hand upon him and stifled him by saying, "Don." She had no polish on her nails, a ring on her thumb, a persuasive talent for suggestion. Don flopped against the seat back and grumbled a little but effectively shut up.

He began to look familiar to me in the lower Seventies, but I didn't recognize him until just south of Lincoln Center when we were stopped at a light by the cineplex where I recalled having seen him before. He'd been squiring a blonde. Shorter, I remembered. Not nearly so finely boned. We were drifting into the roil and chaos of Columbus Circle when I snared his glance in the mirror and asked him, "You're Do-Ray's dad. Right?"

She leaned in and asked him, "Who?"

When he didn't answer, I said, "Do-Ray." After a moment I dredged up, "Tim."

He groaned and neglected still to speak, so I smiled at him in the mirror. I said to Do-Ray's father, "Small world, huh?"

He sulked all through the Forties, was plagued (I guess) by a residual sense of shame, and he and his friend engaged in a low murmuring conversation which ended with him directing me curbside at Thirty-fourth Street where he got out to catch, I figured, a Cinnaminson train.

"Harrison at Greenwich," she told me. "Know it?"

I nodded and eased into traffic. I said, "Sorry," but she just shrugged and waved me off.

The usual afternoon clotting had taken hold, so we crept along Broadway until I could cut west to Seventh where we reached the Village before we got stymied again. Since she was lounging against the far door, I had to adjust the mirror to see her, and I watched her between interludes of abject vehicular peril, expected to get caught at it but ended up catching her instead. I found her subjecting me to clinical study. Rather than shifting her gaze, she pitched herself forward to pinch up a tuft of my sport coat, sampled the material between her finger and her thumb.

I also had on a tie and a pressed and laundered shirt, dress slacks and decent shoes which pretty well set me apart from the bulk of my car-service colleagues who were given to homely sweaters with argyle patterns in the weave, leatherette jackets, Pacific basin jeans. As she turned me loose, she asked me, "Where'd you come from anyway?"

"Brooklyn," I told her.

"Got a card?" she asked me.

I reached into the ashtray where Teddy kept them and handed one back to her. It was more poorly conceived and even less well executed than Sal's. The design boasted an unsuccessful blend of Eastern filigree and General Motors luxury sedan.

"Faysal?"

I shook my head. "It's Teddy's car."

"Teddy?"

"Faysal. I'm Louis. Marty on Staten Island."

"We're not on Staten Island." She fished a pen out of her pocketbook and wrote my name on the card. "Just ask for you?"

I meant to tell her that I was only filling in for Teddy. I intended to acquaint her with my acting career, make mention of my venomous-lizard novel, have her to understand that I was interrupting artistic pursuits in order to follow my nature and do a selfless favor for a friend. I wanted to cause her somehow to know that I was sensitive and witty, convey to her that Do-Ray's dad had impressed me as a bit of a lout. I hoped to assure her that she smelled better than any girl I'd been downwind of, that I was strictly heterosexual and entirely unattached.

Instead I nodded and told her, "Yeah," by which I meant, "Just ask for me."

She'd directed me to pull to the curb where Harrison met Greenwich, had opened the door before she paused to tap her sternum and introduce herself. "Rachel," she said and winked as she got out.

She was standing on the sidewalk fishing for her purse when I told her, "Forget about it," and apologized again for driving Do-Ray's father off.

She shrugged and assured me, "He'll be back," and she'd

hardly finished speaking when the telephone in her handbag began to chirp. Rachel left it to ring where it was and told me, "See?"

I made lascivious use of her in my head as she entered her building. I begrudged her doorman the gentle way she touched him, in passing, on his sleeve.

And the hell of it was that she did call me, and almost straightaway. Two nights later I got directed by Azal to an East Village cross street to pick up a fare in front of a boutique, and there was Rachel with a shopping bag, Rachel wearing a mink.

"Marty," she said, slipping into the back.

"Still Manhattan," I told her, and she reached up to touch my shoulder pretty much like she'd touched her doorman's sleeve.

I carried her to the Pierre on Fifth opposite the park where two gentlemen waited for her on the sidewalk before the hotel. One was monstrous and swarthy, a pile of a man who turned out to be Samoan and who was clearly in the devoted employ of the fellow he was with who was trim and black and nattily dressed. His suit was impeccably tailored, his shirt a crisp unwrinkled white, his tie knot slender and snug. He relieved Rachel of her shopping bag as she joined him on the sidewalk.

She nodded as he spoke until, at length, he turned to gaze my way while Rachel apprised him of my pedigree.

He gave her money, neatly folded cash, passed it to her discreetly as if he were lubricating a maître d' or making a street cop blind, and then he kissed her on each cheek in the European fashion, walked her to the hotel entranceway and held for Rachel the door. Afterward he stepped directly curbside and submitted me to study, peered at me long enough in silence to cause me to ask him, "Sir?"

"You work for Bunny, right?"

The question chilled me a little. I had no cause at the time to be aware he was the sort of fellow who made it his habit to know most everything he could possibly know. I nodded at length and saw fit to tell him, "Sometimes."

He smiled. He had an extraordinary and disarming way with a smile. There was a general air of threat and menace that seemed to hang about him which was only partly hulking-Samoan-associate-inspired. He had a purely clinical gaze, came off as pitiless and decisive, not a man it would pay to cross or even dream of trifling with. But when he parted his lips and showed his teeth, he could almost get taken for harmless.

"Tell him Giles said hey."

"Just Giles?"

He nodded. "He'll know."

And boy did Bunny know. When I finally met occasion to pass the greeting to him, he glanced at Danny who reached instinctively under his coat and felt for his gun.

"Should I wait for her?"

Giles shook his head and offered me a plugget of currency which turned out to be five freshly minted twenty-dollar bills. "Tomorrow morning? Say eight? Right here?"

"Yes, sir," I told him. "Eight," I said.

He handed Rachel's sack in through the window and asked me to keep it for her. Then he gave me a parting intoxicating smile and said to me, "Good man."

I watched him and his associate claim the midnight blue Town Car at the head of the block. They disappeared in a veritable sea of taxis while I lingered by the curb, peeked at the blouse in Rachel's sack and wondered what exactly Rachel might see clear to do for money in a fine hotel with views of the park for something like twelve hours. Then I went on to wonder if I could afford to hire her to do it with me.

2

I HAD NEED OF a girl just then and couldn't seem to attract one with charm. I'd lately flown home for a weekend visit and had claimed to be attached, had boasted I had met a woman, gave her out to be a sculptress, a creature who worked with a maul and chisels and had a decided possessive streak. Mrs. Phillip J. King was hoping to inflict me on her niece, and I was trying to stave her off with the threat of a jealous bludgeoning. Unfortunately, though, that niece was strapping and a little hotheaded herself, woman enough (I was assured) to make short work of a Yankee sculptress which served to fire the libidinous imagination of Mr. Phillip J. King who announced that he'd about pay money to see it.

He was seated across from his wife at the time at our walnut dining table, so Mrs. Phillip J. King had to rise from her chair and circulate to smack him. She informed him on her way around he was a filthy rascal, and Mr. Phillip J. King kept spooning pudding all through her approach. He failed even to twitch once she'd drawn back and swatted the side of his head.

My mother had insisted on having them over. When the Kings used to live next door, my parents and them would dine together probably twice a month, most particularly while my mother and Mrs. Phillip J. King were suffering through their simultaneous menopausal indifference to cooking. For a string of months there, they could hardly be bothered between them to make a meal and tolerated poorly even idle and innocent talk of supper such as "What might we hope to dine on?" or "Will we ever eat again?"

Those were the hamburger-shortcake months. A recipe had run in *Redbook* for a manner of no-fuss stovetop enormity which called for ground chuck with tomato paste, chili powder and chopped bell pepper to be stewed up together and spooned over buttered toast. It was dead simple as entrées go and quite reliably indigestible, and my mother would make enough at a throw to last us nearly a week.

My parents had fallen largely out of touch with the Kings once they'd picked up and moved to their flimsy tract home in Shropshire Glen Estates, and I have to think anymore my mother and Mrs. Phillip J. King got together just to conspire to set me up with the strapping niece.

The girl needed, as it turned out, a date for a wedding the following day, and Mrs. Phillip J. King and my mother declared in an orchestrated fashion that it would be ever so kind of me to offer myself up. When I tried to let on that I wished I could but didn't have a suit, my mother fetched one of my father's double-breasteds from the bedroom so quickly that I couldn't help but think she'd laid it out. The thing was probably twenty-odd years old and was an unfortunate shade of blue. The trousers were both cuffed and flared. The jacket had enameled buttons. The pockets were piped, the shoulders padded, and the lapels were a half foot wide apiece.

My father and Mr. Phillip J. King, I noticed, were both uncommonly silent, content to let me draw fire on my own. I objected and complained and indulged in a rather forceful disquisition on the topic of my sculptress with her passions and her mallets, but my mother and Mrs. Phillip J. King merely herded me from the table and drove me into the front bedroom to try that blue suit on. It fit me which is to say it was cinched and snug and unbecoming, and I wore it out into the dining room to general applause.

As strapping hotheaded nieces go, Mrs. Phillip J. King's wasn't so bad. Her name was Adele, and she disliked me almost instantly. I assumed it was the suit, and I made straightaway explanations and apologies for it notwithstanding that she was too beefy a girl for the sleeveless thing she had on. She didn't care, she up and told me, for the way I wore my hair, had heard from friends of hers who knew me that I was dull and self-important, and now that she'd met me on her own, she could confirm that they were right. She didn't at all approve of the way I drove, was snide in conversation and took pains to acquaint me with the virtues of her former boyfriend who'd been kinder than me and cuter than me but got thrown over nonetheless. She hated where I chose to park, and as we walked to the sanctuary, she instructed me not to touch her the remainder of the day.

I prefer anymore to believe that she was being self-defensive, had maybe suffered enough in romance to make her churlish preemptively, but at the time the abuse she ladled on had a completely different effect. She disliked me quite enough to cause me to itch to have her. In the part of my brain the testosterone couldn't reach, I knew we were a poor match. She was a scold with Republican leanings, an eye-shadow devotee, an unregenerate Baptist who would have been content on a quarter acre in Shropshire Glen Estates. But that was all trumped by the fact that she found me detestable which obliged me (as was my custom) to think her desirable back.

The wedding was to be held in the Methodist church, the original one downtown which consisted of a gloomy sanctuary, a linoleumed fellowship hall, and a half dozen mildewed Sunday-school classrooms downstairs. The membership skewed geriatric because the younger upwardly mobile Methodists had split off to build their own church adjacent to a bypass junction. It had a nursery and a gymnasium, a sheltered barbecue and a cavernous sanctuary of modern design that was finished in varnished teak and looked like a schooner stateroom crossed with a hospital chapel. The new church had a pastor from Oregon who ate macrobiotic and conducted the sort of lite-mix service that frequently called for acoustic guitar.

The old Methodist church had managed to hold to the Reverend Shelton who still each Sunday took a scrap of Scripture for his lesson and proceeded for twenty minutes or so to flog it half to death. The reverend had taken to writing a column in the local paper, about four hundred words every other week that ran under the boldfaced headline "Glad News of the Natural World." He was given in print to turning up some sweet trace of the Savior in even the homeliest human endeavor or trifling earthly enterprise.

Adele didn't approve of Methodists, and she occupied herself at first belittling the hymnal and riffling through the book of responsive readings to something of a less-than-charitable effect. She kept scooting away from me along the pew, so I was obliged to pursue her until more friends of the groom boxed her in and effectively chocked her in place. I tried to make myself agreeable, inquired after her interests and let on to find most everything she told me stimulating.

Then I asked a question that served to throttle and undo my affection. "Who's getting married anyway?"

She shoved her embossed ivory invitation at me and said, "Doug."

I could barely read the thing. The script was so ornate and florid that I could hardly tell where the words left off and the squiggly border set in. There looked to be a raft of confectionary palaver on the front mostly concerning the blessed presence of the congeries and the joyful bonds of holy matrimony. I was a while locating the principals and was asking Adele after Doug when I saw a name I recognized. It was Fay's.

"He drives a gas truck," Adele told me. "Used to coach at the junior college."

"Linebacker?" I asked her.

Defensive backfield as it turned out, not a specialist per se, and he'd been cut a few years previously from three arena football teams. Doug delivered propane. It seems he'd met Fay on his route. I recalled that Fay's aunt's tank was in the backyard by her pool, and I could pretty readily picture Doug trudging around the house with his hose to discover Fay greased and topless and tattooed upon her chaise lounge.

I was all but interrogating Adele as the organ began to play. It turned out she'd gone steady with Doug when they were in high school, and she seemed to think a little more poorly of him than she did of me. She'd been on the drill team, and he'd been a cornerback, and she professed to be happy that Doug had finally found a woman who would have him. Adele appeared even for a moment there a bit vulnerable and misty, but she shortly recovered and gave me shove.

She huffed and told me, "You're breathing on me!"

Doug came out from behind the altar with his brother for best man. They were both shoulders and bloated torsos under seven-dollar haircuts, and their tuxedos were uglier even than my double-breasted suit. The bridesmaids' gowns were off-the-shoulder and conspicuously revealing, but Fay had called into service the sort of girls I could readily picture popping out of cakes. Compared to Fay, though, they were conservatively dressed because her gown (in white organza) appeared to have been tube-top-inspired. She had a veil and a train and a bouquet and her silver-haired daddy on her arm, so at first glance Fay suggested a standard-issue bride, but her bodice left off where her rib cage stopped and revealed her bare midriff which was toned and tan and ornamented with, what looked to me, the scaly scarlet hind part of some variety of serpent Fay'd had inked upon her abdomen since I'd seen her last.

Of course, since Fay was on her way up the aisle to be joined in holy wedlock, I couldn't help but hunger for her and rue the day I'd let her go. I was busy conjuring the sight of Fay in my Honda wayback when Adele leaned in and muttered, "She looks like a whore."

I understand now that Adele was grappling with her regrets about Doug, probably was pining for him a little, but at the time I was blind with indignation, and Adele and I traded obscenities and very nearly came to blows.

Up by the altar, Doug and his brother watched the bride approach them with the glassy-eyed slack-jawed expression common to patrons of topless bars. What with all of the skin on display, there was a hint of unsanctified sexual tension in the air, and I wouldn't have been much surprised if Doug and his assorted groomsmen had made wanton use on the riser of whichever females came to hand.

Loudly and with plodding primary-school deliberation, the reverend set about describing the duties and obligations of marriage. He sounded like he was reciting the boilerplate on a car-rental agreement, emphasizing the collisions without much mention of the carefree driving. He gave out a holy union to be a sort of tandem marathon, rife with peril and disappointment but blessed, he added gaily, by God.

Quite naturally the reverend couldn't help but compliment Fay on her outfit, and I doubt anyone failed to notice he was speaking to her navel when he told her what a lovely bride she made.

The reverend read through the service, and when he invited commentary from the crowd, when he presented the friends of the bride and the groom the chance to raise objections, Adele muttered, "She's got some hell of a nerve in white," which carried a little farther than I have to think she intended. Even Fay's mother up in the front pew heard her, to judge by how she jerked around.

The Reverend Mr. Shelton elected to marry the pair of them anyway. He pronounced them man and wife and took a half step back as they fell into an embrace and kissed like a couple on a daytime TV drama—all breathy murmurings and plunging tongues.

The organist struck in the recessional, and the bridal party fled the church. An usher came back to fetch Fay's mother who glared so at me that I pointed at Adele in a bid to identify her as the culprit. Adele caught me at it and seethed and so revived her magnetism.

The reception was held at the country club, the old one down along the branch on the north end of town. The place had been seeping off members and failing to prosper for decades. A new country club had opened a few years back on the Greensboro Road which offered eighteen championship holes of golf, a dozen tennis courts, condominiums and faux-baronial houses along the fairways, a restaurant with a chef recruited from Charleston who assuaged (I have to think) his regret by providing the members nightly an almost maniacally spicy cuisine.

The golf at the old country club was lousy. The pool was pestilential. The composition tennis courts were weedy and out of true, and there was never money enough in the physical account to keep the moldering pile of a clubhouse in even passably decent repair. The roof leaked, and the north-facing windows were insulated year-round with plastic. The place smelled of socks and vegetable oil with a hint of cherry deodorant block. The chairs were all ruptured and head-grease-stained. The carpet was worn down to the backing. The club pro was so old and arthritic he could barely hold a putter, and even back when he was able, he'd been a hacker and a cheat. There was no chef to speak of for the dining room and no concerted attempt at cuisine, just moonlighting cooks and whatever was marked down out at the Red Apple.

I had to think Fay was stuck at the old country club through neglect on her part. She'd probably been casting around for an alternate groom even after she'd taken Doug's ring, was loath to resign herself to him when, on any given day, she might stray across better defensive-backfield material than Doug. Fay was a bit of a cockeyed optimist when it came to football players, an up-with-people-who-can-tackle-in-the-open-field sort of girl. Her mother must have badgered her to settle on her plans, firm up her venues and her reservations, because she sported a look of triumph as she greeted guests in the dowdy clubhouse foyer.

She'd say, "Thanks for coming," and glance balefully around as if to add, "I told her this was what she'd get."

Fay had contracted for the warm hors d'oeuvres and the champagne fountain, but the champagne pump kept overloading the circuit and tripping the breaker, so we were left with more in the way of a champagne dipping trough. As for the food, it was not warm exactly due to alcohol-burner problems. The chafing dishes, like everything else at the old country club, were old and in poor repair, and the wicks on the burners proved a little too charred to hold a flame.

Fortunately, Fay had hired a band, so we had music to distract us. Or rather she'd hired a guy with an electric keyboard who could sound like a quartet. He could very nearly sing well enough to carry an authentic tune, and he was given to portentous anthemlike noodlings on his keyboard between songs. The thing had an ancient sticker on it, faded and peeling, with almost illegible ghostly Gothic letters that spelled out "Mötley Crüe."

As I dipped my plastic champagne flute into the champagne trough and brought up my first brimming measure of what proved to be cold duck, Fay and Doug were already having a spat over by the terrace doors. They sounded to be at variance on reception protocol. From what I could hear, Fay felt a hostess's obligation to her guests while Doug was agitating for a tumble in his pickup. They settled on a sort of compromise and retired to the country-club pantry for about a minute and a half where, knowing Fay, I have to imagine their honeymoon commenced.

I was standing by the buffet table eating a cube of cheddar and wondering if that wretched excuse for a party could get worse when the one-man band struck up what sounded like a medley of "Smoke on the Water" and "Horse with No Name" played together at once. Adele swept by sneering at me and swilling champagne from a go cup just as Fay slipped up behind me and took my hand in hers.

"Let's dance," she said, and tugged me. I tried to wriggle free because I didn't want to dance and I felt like I knew just where her hand had been lately, but she was determined and succeeded at dragging me out onto the parquet where she pressed her chest against me and left me to try to discover the beat. We waltzed essentially. It was the best I could manage. Fay was no help whatsoever because, as it turned out, she'd taken three Valium—two for her nuptial nerves and another just in case they didn't work.

She asked me what I thought of the groom, and while I was cobbling up a response, Fay pressed her lips to my ear and said, "Me too." I can't say I detected any pride of ownership to speak of.

She'd heard I was living in New York, and she asked me to pass along her greeting to a free safety who returned punts and played in the third-down package for the Jets. Then she laid against me full on and reached around and groped my backside as if she intended to give my lower intestine a massage. Adele saw her from across the room and stalked over to confront Fay. She asked Fay just how many men exactly she intended to pilfer and poach. To Adele's way of thinking, Fay had already succeeded at stealing Doug who had armed Fay, it turned out, with personal information about Adele that Fay began to unfreight herself of in a voice that projected and carried.

We all heard from Fay an approximation of Adele's avian orgasmic shriek. We were told of Adele's weakness for Kit Kat bars, fruit skins and canned fried onions, were informed of merchandise that she'd shoplifted from the Rexall, magazines she used to steal from her next-door-neighbor's mailbox, damage she'd caused to a fellow's truck in the shopping-plaza lot and then had fled without informing him who'd caused it. Fay recited lies Adele had told, ambitions she'd not realized, just every little thing she could dredge up that Adele had confided to Doug and Doug, for whatever reason, had seen fit to reveal to Fay.

For her part Adele was equipped with information of her own, and once she'd recognized precisely the line of bile that Fay was up to, Adele chimed in with a spot of stinging counter-commentary. She proved to be well acquainted with Fay's numerous affairs of the heart which Adele was pleased to catalog at encyclopedic length.

Now I happened to be standing between them, no sensible place for a human to be, and once Fay had let go of my sphincter, I tried to sidle out of harm's way without seeming to be in headlong retreat. I'd even put a little daylight between me and Fay before the best man showed up. He was functioning as an emissary for his brother, the groom, who'd gotten temporarily drained in the pantry of his enthusiasm for women and couldn't seem to muster interest enough to handle the matter himself. So he'd dispatched his best man who, instead of tangling with the woman, elected to simply shove me to the floor.

That was all it took. Straightaway the entire banquet room was in an unholy uproar. Fay and Adele were locked together in a spitting rage above me, and most of the other guests had enough sparkling wine and resentment under their belts to welcome mayhem as a substitute for tepid appetizers. The guests erupted into quarrels that eroded into grappling while I crawled for protection under the keyboard player's Yamaha. A semiprofessional to the end, he never quit the music. That room was wrecked to the strains of "Kickstart My Heart," "Whole Lotta Love" and "Slow Ride."

3

"Undesirable" was hardly a word that suited Teddy. I made Omar spell it for me after he'd said it already twice, and even still I couldn't figure exactly what he was getting at, so he resorted to offering to me the scrap of paper he'd consulted. His mother had written on it in her girlish private-day-school hand.

"Right," I said. "Undesirable." And I saw underneath the word the telephone number for the Manhattan branch of the Immigration service.

I ushered Omar back across the hall and into his apartment where his mother was standing eating Cheez-Its in their kitchenette. At the sight of me, she pitched the box aside and ducked underneath her burka, left a dusting of gaudy orange cracker crumbs upon the cloth.

"What's this?" I asked her, and held up the scrap of paper I'd gotten from Omar. As was her custom with infidels, she spoke to Omar who spoke to me. He said his father had called from Yemen and had told them he was stuck.

"Stuck?"

Monica-Safwah-Yusriyya leaned down once more and murmured at Omar who told me, "Yes, sir," who nodded and said, "Stuck."

I shook my head and gestured as if to ask, "Stuck how, exactly?" which proved occasion for more murmuring than I could graciously tolerate. The woman was a white-bread Episcopalian from the Hudson River Valley who had every right to make herself a torment to her parents with her halal mutton and her veils, her shawls, her shapeless clothing, with her salat prayers and her grubby hennaed feet. But I found her relentless piety an outright antagonism. She was Monica, for Chrissakes, from upper Dutchess County. I told Omar to tell his mother that she had best start talking to me.

I could see a little of her behind the gauze square in her burka, noticed that she persisted in watching the floorboards as she spoke. She told me Teddy's status had been altered in his absence, that the Immigration service had suspected Teddy's movements, weren't prepared to take on faith his mother's hysterectomy and were putting a hold on Teddy's travel until they could see just what they believed.

"Undesirable?"

She nodded.

"Teddy?"

I heard her snort and say, "I know."

Teddy, you see, adored America more than the two of us put together. He was a Snapple addict, a Yankee fan, a hot-dog connoisseur. He was prepared to believe most everything he heard on the nightly news, trusted in the heartfelt sincerity of movie starlets and politicians, would buy only American automobiles and smoke American cigarettes. He could mangle quotations from Benjamin Franklin, Will Rogers and Barney Rubble. At home in front of his TV, when our anthem played, he stood and sang. Teddy had even forgiven his meteorologist on the Weather Channel for the child that she'd conceived and dropped without him, and she was about as blond and corn-fed and midwestern as they get. I could hardly count the times that I had lain awake at night listening to Teddy play on his mizmar the shuffling *Andy Griffith Show* theme.

I suspected some pasty middle manager at the INS was simply seizing an opportunity to keep an Arab over there.

"You'll drive, won't you?"

And through her gauzy slot, I could see that Monica-Safwah-Yusriyya was looking directly at me now with a brand of uncommon intensity, pleadingly it seemed to me. With Teddy stuck and Monica leading a life of ritual devotion, there was nobody to make a living for her and Omar just then but me. The money I paid them to rent Teddy's sludge-brown Ford was all they had coming in, and if I let them down, I had to suspect, there'd be no ready recourse but a call to Dutchess County for the variety of loan that was sure to come with caveats and infidel conditions, was likely to be more bitterly bought than Monica could stand. So I had little trouble believing I was making a selfless gesture when I nodded and said to Monica-Safwah-Yusriyya, "Sure, I'll drive."

She praised Allah and then returned, I guess, to her Cheez-Its in the kitchen once she'd motioned to Omar by way of instruction for him to show me out.

I was certainly free to drive for Teddy. Sal had landed me a modern opera set on a planet in the sombrero galaxy in what was meant to look like a zoo. I was to play a specimen, a twenty-third-century civil engineer, and I sat throughout the rehearsals studying blueprints and schematics on display in an airless box with a glass front. The music was strident and painful to tolerate. The director quarreled with the tenor who sniped incessantly at the baritone while the soprano objected to her costume which looked to be made of foil, and she was pleased to show us all where it constricted and chafed her. Once the agents got involved and the coloratura came down with bronchitis, there was nothing to do but postpone the production and put us all out of work.

Sal compensated with the lead, I guess I'll call it, on a kibble commercial. I played a stock man in the pet-food aisle of a grocery store where I was freighting the shelves with a brand-new cat treat in a stay-fresh pouch. That treat, apparently, was an ordinary fish-flavored nugget, but the resealable closure was revolutionary. I was called upon to demonstrate it to a herd of cats. Not actual cats but wholly computer-generated felines who were added later which left me to talk instead to the grocery-mart floor.

I unsealed a pouch and sealed it back about four dozen times before the director, by way of congratulating me on my splendid performance, shook his head and exhaled. He told me, "All right, I guess."

Otherwise I had the occasional command mission to Staten Island. Bunny was suffering just then through an interlude of merciless introspection. He and his daughter, Carlina, had been warring over Brazilian Pino who was hardly of the Mediterranean stock Bunny believed she rated. Worse still, as far as Bunny knew, Pino had been lately gay, and who was to say if he could stave off that sort of urge forever? Carlina, of course, kept assuring her father that Pino was a capable gelding which left Bunny to picture a brand of logistics he'd rather not have entertained. So Bunny called me in for the odd repair and some freeform therapy.

We sat one morning, I recall, in the basement of a slummy building Bunny owned, an apartment high-rise with a serious service-panel deficiency. I was busy overamping assorted troublesome breakers in the box when Bunny began to speak of his feelings and his prejudices, touched upon various shades and kikes and roaches (he called them) he detested and wondered aloud if he was not maybe a little too ready to hate them. He seemed to want to believe that he'd be better off taking men as they came, even wiry gay Brazilians laying wood to his only daughter.

I was reminded instead of the greeting that I'd been charged to deliver. "Oh," I said to Bunny, "I almost forgot. Some guy named Giles says hey."

Bunny uncorked straightaway a corrosive slur and shot a glance at Danny who left off doing nothing so as to locate the hilt of his gun.

As for myself, I sort of liked Giles, admired anyway his efficiency. There was no wasted palaver with him, no wayward emotions, no second guesses. He was decisive, polite and given to elegant economy. There at the end of my two-week run for Teddy before he'd gotten "stuck," I'd carried Rachel to a tony Upper East Side doormanned building where Giles was waiting like he'd waited out in front of the Pierre. He was impeccably tailored, Samoan-protected, and once he'd made his arrangement with Rachel, he stepped over to give me instructions but shook my hand first and told me hello.

"Bunny sends his regards." I couldn't quite think of another way to phrase it.

Giles slipped me a half dozen twenties, neatly folded and crisp and new. He smiled in that winning way he had. He said to me, "I'll bet."

I once asked Rachel what Giles did exactly by way of making a living. Straightaway she told me, "Everything." We then rode for a stretch in silence while she considered, I have to think now, Giles's unsanctified range of pursuits. Rachel gave her head a baleful shake. She added, "Anything."

Rachel didn't seem to work for Giles exactly, but he certainly used her a lot. He supplied her to business associates instead of health care or stock options, recognized Rachel as the caliber of woman most men lacked the charm to win. It only seemed to be about sex sometimes and not sex inevitably, often enough just drinks and dinner and a kiss to cap the evening, concerts and soirées and Broadway productions, a bar mitzvah one night in Bronxville, a golf outing in Rockland County. I carried her clear to Philadelphia once for some stripe of thug buffet.

With Teddy "stuck" and me routinely behind the wheel of his Ford, I got to watch Rachel operate, had a rearview-mirror view of the finest natural actress I could ever hope to see. She had a gift for what gasbag theatrical types tend to call "commitment" which is to say that she was perfectly capable of doting on an ogre for hours on end without perforation or any need for relief. Giles occasionally threw Rachel in with low-life Eastern Europeans. They were vulgar and greasy and almost without exception about half drunk. Even still, Rachel could manage for an evening to seem smitten, and she'd never, once she'd shed one, give a sign or indication that she'd found the man to be a beast.

It got to where Rachel would call me directly, and I'd sweep into the city to carry her wherever she needed to go. Then she and Giles and his associates would routinely overpay me for the privilege of watching an unrivaled thespian work. I even managed to pick up a pointer or two, particularly where it came to listening, or where it came anyway to appearing to be enthralled. Rachel had a gift for seeming to find palaver intoxicating.

Oftentimes the men she kept company with, most particularly Giles's colleagues, were all but anesthetic with a line of talk. They'd tell Rachel about their business dealings, their cars, their sporting interests, frequently seemed compelled to speak to Rachel at length about their wives, and yet no matter the crushing tedium, Rachel evermore succeeded at looking something close to galvanized. She did it mostly with her eyes. They never strayed or clouded over but stayed focused upon the gentleman at hand. Rachel would pose the odd query as evidence she was authentically engaged and nod and smile to indicate she was wedded to the saga of some fellow's partridge hunt in the Bekaa Valley, the ups and downs of waste disposal, a layman's version of the science at the heart of recapped tires, the pedestrian pitfalls of life in the Volga basin with a loud ungainly woman who was equally enamored of Belgian chocolate truffles and chinoiserie.

In my capacity as a quasi-professional actor, I went to school on Rachel and made, I like to think, successful use of her techniques. In one instance my TV wife and I were out shopping for a cooktop when our afternoon was spoiled by the onset of spastic bladder syndrome. Or rather her afternoon was spoiled because hers was the spastic bladder, and she was called upon to inquire if there might not be some treatment that would cause a spastic bladder to relax. My role largely took the form of impotent commiseration, but while my TV wife seeped and wondered where she might find bladder relief, I studied her in the fashion I'd seen Rachel watch her men friends, with tenderness, that is to say, and all but bottomless compassion, and I soon met with reason to think that I had come across as loving.

My TV wife's boyfriend, the first assistant to the commercial's producer, came storming toward me while the camera was still rolling to tell me, "Hey, goddamn it," and point a menacing finger my way.

Rachel and I became friendly inasmuch as she would allow it. There was a coffee bar in the East Village on Avenue A just off the park where they made some sort of frothy mocha that

Rachel couldn't resist. She'd buy us each one while I parked the car, and we'd sit on a bench by the dog run drinking our coffees and watching the canines play, the owners snipe and quarrel. I'd try to tempt her to talk about herself, would set in with trifling questions in hopes of probing Rachel's secrets after a strategic while, but she was far too cagey to tell me anything worth knowing, and somehow I always ended up rattling on about myself.

Rachel was particularly partial to anything I could share with her of Neely. I got the impression she'd grown up in a soulless suburb somewhere and so was keen to hear whatever I could remember of home. It all started with a salt-and-pepper schnauzer in the run one day. He was doing what schnauzers tend to do which is meddle and intrude. He'd assumed, among the other dogs, the position of shop foreman and was touring around the dog run visiting all of his colleagues and charges so as to nip them and sniff them and poke them, when need be, with his whiskery snout.

I was reminded, quite naturally, of Itty Bit and mentioned her to Rachel, told how she'd died in her dotage compressed between a storm and panel door which Rachel allowed was the sort of news that called for an enlargement, so I soon enough found myself holding forth at length on Itty Bit.

One Easter my father dipped her in a pail of scarlet egg dye. He even went to the trouble to give her a yellow stripe around her midriff, and he kept her in our backyard to dry until very nearly dusk when he sent her home to scratch on the Kings' storm door and get let into the house. My father and I, I recall, were sharing the glider while we waited, and it only took about half a minute before Mrs. Phillip J. King screamed. As shrieks go, it was a sterling specimen, even by her standards, and once she'd charged onto her porch to scream again, my father called over to ask her, "What's the trouble, Helen?"

She sputtered at us initially. No words, just spit and agitation before she managed to speak of her scarlet dog who clashed with her décor.

"Kids probably," my father suggested, and Mrs. Phillip J. King (who was childless) responded with a hard unladylike piece of talk about adolescents before turning to charge back into her house while wailing her husband's name.

My father, hardly a religious man, appeared to find peace on the glider. He drew a rich breath of evening air, smiled beatifically and told me, "He is risen," to devotional effect.

Rachel couldn't get enough of that sort of thing. She'd reliably prime and prompt me, and we'd sit there drinking our frothy mochas watching the dogs fertilize the mulch while I acquainted Rachel with the heritage and the denizens of Neely, from the Epperson sisters with their taste for improvisational dance, to cousin Spencer in his mother's tropical-weight dresses, to the death of the bald Jeeter and Throckmorton litigiousness, to the virtually expired muskrat that wrecked Peahead Boyette's Ford Falcon, to the pigeon fiasco and the Christmas-pageant fire, to the ill-fated Labor Day picnic spoiled by a blend of bad crab salad, a nest of yellow jackets and a spot of spontaneous gunplay. Rachel requested on several occasions the tragic Pettigrew story which had everything from betrayal and heartache to suicide and a chimpanzee.

I'd readily oblige her as she was too beguiling to deny, but I would try once I had rattled on for twenty minutes or so to quiz her a little by way of fair return. I'd ask about her life as a child, inquire after her relations, her pets, her high-school boyfriends, broken bones and favorite foods. I was prepared to settle for almost anything she'd care to tell me which usually turned out to be nothing much at all. At length Rachel would punctuate our chat with what had become our coda.

"Oh, Marty," she'd say with a shake of her head and a hint of exasperation, and I'd pitch our mocha cups in the trash.

By the time I had need of a favor, we'd established a clear divide between business and pleasure. Behind the wheel of Teddy's sludge-brown Ford, I was Rachel's driver, but we were chums more or less on our bench in the park with our frothy coffees, easy and friendly with each other for something approaching an hour a week.

I'd worked up what I intended to say, had all but rehearsed it like a part. I'd walked around for three or four days practicing my phrasing, along the length of the promenade, down to the harbor with Omar and back, in my cloudy bathroom mirror, in my toaster oven's chrome, at night in bed with no lite-FM mizmar to distract me. When the time came, however, and I had brought myself to broach the topic, I bumbled around and said to Rachel whatever popped into my head.

"I've got kind of a problem."

I waited for her to invite me to tell her what the trouble might be until we'd passed a couple of minutes there on our bench in pristine silence when I volunteered particulars but not at all like I'd rehearsed them.

"I kind of need a girlfriend."

Rachel finally said, "Well . . ." but failed to come up with anything beyond it.

"A sculptress," I told her. "Saturday after next. My mother and father are coming up."

"Louis and Inez?" Rachel asked me. She probably knew more about me and mine than it was seemly for her to know.

I nodded. "They think I've got a girlfriend."

"A sculptress?"

I winced a bit and nodded.

"I made an ashtray once," Rachel told me, and I pictured her as a Brownie with badges and a sash, a little beret and (God help me) a D cup. She reached into her shoulder bag and came out with her date book. Rachel flipped two weeks ahead. "I've got Friday." I nodded again, and she penciled me onto the page.

"Louis and Inez," Rachel said once more, and smiled with sufficient savor to touch off in me a wave of nausea.

She handed me her empty mocha cup, and as I rose to toss it with mine, I told Rachel, "I'll pay you," said it as if I were offering to wash dishes but expecting to get dispatched to the parlor to sit and nap and burp.

Rachel snapped her date book shut and returned it to her handbag. She stood and smoothed her blouse front, with a toss of her head composed her hair. She did me the service of making an adjustment to my tie knot, tidied and tightened it snug, admired her work, informed me, "You certainly will."

4

MY MOTHER WAS ALL for taking the train until she learned that the Southern Crescent passed through Greensboro only once a day at 2:30 A.M. Then she suggested to my father they might prefer to drive instead. The only reliable car they owned was a 1984 Impala, a two-door coupe with a seepy water pump and a molting vinyl roof that my father drove to work and knew just how to tend and nurse. My mother's Bonneville would start only rarely on rainy days, and her electric windows had a way of opening unbidden which was irritating enough on a run to the Rexall but would have been punishing in break-neck traffic out on 95.

Once my mother had struck upon the notion of renting a late-model car or, barring that, driving over to Raleigh and catching the express bus, my father sat her down for a session at the breakfast-room table. Some years back he'd carried home a copy of *Aviation Week*, had picked it up at the brake-and-muffler shop where he was having his Chevrolet serviced. That garage was operated by Luther Sizemore and his sons—Buster and Jack and Desmond—who were a decent hardworking bunch, so decent, in fact, and industrious that if you went in for a tailpipe and the one who was hanging it for you noticed your oil-pan seal was bad or your rack and pinion had gone a little weepy, he'd tidy up that trouble at brake and muffler prices too. Those Sizemores couldn't help themselves, and drivers about were pleased to take corrupt advantage of them. Otherwise upstanding Neelyites, my own father among them, would make an appointment for new brake pads and maybe a dose of caliper grease while fully intending to steer whatever Sizemore they fell in with into a valve-lifter overhaul or a throttle-body rebuild.

There were usually, then, six or eight locals sitting around the waiting room trying to seem crestfallen and unpleasantly surprised over word they were getting a new head gasket or a repacked bearing when they'd come in for a tailpipe and a simple fluid check.

I have to think it was probably a blend of guilt with a natural itch for comfort that caused patrons to dress up the Sizemore waiting room the way they did. The place was maybe ten by twelve, with a cement floor and a pair of windows. One gave onto the garage while the other looked out over the parking lot. Originally the chairs were plastic and stackable in a pinch, the coffee table peeling veneer on chipboard, the watercooler ornamental and the magazines predictably several years old and freshwater-fishing-related.

The inaugural improvement was made by a Bigelow with a fractured motor mount. He'd taken his Skylark off-road inadvertently, and Jack Sizemore had welded up his motor mount for free. It turned out that Bigelow had some furniture he no longer required, a deacon's table and a love seat he was looking to get rid of. They weren't soiled and dilapidated in the usual way of local castoffs, just fussy and high-Edwardian entirely in his late wife's taste which he'd not warmed to while she was still about to inflict it on him and didn't imagine he would come to care for now that she was dead.

He hired a boy down the street with a van to carry the stuff to the garage, and he presented it to the Sizemores along with his personal check for the Skylark. Other customers noticed, naturally, and that Bigelow served as a trendsetter. In mere months the Sizemores' waiting room got entirely reappointed. The place got chairs and hassocks and curtains, a twenty-five-inch television, a satellite subscription with premium channels, fresh pastries daily, a coffee urn, a telephone with a couple of outside lines, a desktop computer with a broadband connection and a rather extraordinary assortment of monthly magazines from *Cosmo Girl!* and *No-Till Farmer* to *European Cigar Cult Journal* and *Dressage Today.*

It's little wonder, then, my father could come away from the Sizemores' garage with both a cut-rate valve job and an issue of *Aviation Week.* He'd carried off a copy that featured an article on basic aerodynamics. It had charts and graphs and was peppered with useful information on how jet engines worked and why planes left the ground and managed to stay in the air. My mother, who had always been a nervous flier, tended to worry increasingly about the mechanics of flight, poor workmanship on the sorts of assembly lines that made jet turbines, the competence of commercial pilots, the advanced age of the national fleet, and it had gotten to where my father was tasked with trying to stanch her fears just short of controlled narcotics and cocktails featuring dark rum.

Consequently he'd call her into the breakfast room to sit with him at the table for refreshers on practical commercial applications of thrust and lift. He'd show my mother the pictures in his pilfered magazine and reacquaint her with the basic physics of air travel. He was pretty sound at that sort of thing and patient with my mother, so after about an hour, she was usually prepared for talk of which bags she'd check. My father then was faced with the chore of persuading himself to leave the ground.

He had faith enough in the equipment and the airline personnel and had made his peace with the fact that airplanes sometimes fell from the sky. My father was nothing if not a helpless realist to his bones, and he knew that fittings failed and engines detached and spare fuel tanks exploded and that while pilots were not so volatile as postal employees, they could occasionally plunge into the ocean on an inky whim. So it wasn't the various risks of flight that plagued and troubled my father but more the caliber of paying passenger he shared the fuselage with.

In my father's view, people had gotten rather indefensible. He wasn't nostalgic and sentimental, hardly believed that there was anything terribly noble about the past or that our forefathers were necessarily better for having been quaint and courtly, but he couldn't approve of the general direction of modern humankind which, time was, he'd get reliable relief from on a DC-9. If my father longed for anything, it was the era of air travel when passengers used to actually dress to fly. They weren't necessarily finer specimens than passengers today, but a fellow could take consolation in the packaging. To my father it looked to have gotten to where people just rolled out of bed and put on whatever they'd found on the floor.

He was a bad one for sitting at his gate at the Greensboro airport and sizing up his fellow fliers at the check-in counter in their hockey jerseys and bicycle shorts, in their rustling pastel gym togs, in their cutoffs and sneakers and Nubuck sandals, in their tank tops and Wolfpack hats. He had a way of saying, "Sweet Jesus," with more vinegar and volume than my mother was usually prepared to tolerate in a public place. She would squeeze his hand with force enough to take his mind off of his upset and put it on his circulation instead.

She seemed to think my father was simply being uncharitable, but in fact he had a doomsday theory where it came to commercial flight. He had convinced himself that shiftlessness could reach a critical mass, that if enough sorry benighted passengers in their relentlessly casual clothing collected in a fuselage at once, they would function as the Lord's own chance to tidy the world a bit, and the pilots would be unable to keep the airplane in the sky. This from a man who believed that the Old and New Testaments were hyperpoetical bunk and who would as soon have gone to a veterinarian for spiritual guidance as a preacher, and yet he was mystically convinced that if he got onto a plane to find his ilk sufficiently outnumbered, he'd get reduced within the hour to a patch of sticky gristle.

My father once told me he'd know when it happened because it had happened before. Fortunately for him he wasn't on an airplane at the time but was out at the megacenter, the old one on the Danville Pike which was equal parts grocery mart and homewares store, so you could head to the register with both bacon bits and drywall screws. My father had gone for underwear. He made a run about twice a year once my mother had replenished her stock of rags from the top drawer of his dresser, and he'd done out at the megacenter what they depend on people to do. He'd started out bare-handed, had gone back for a basket, had returned that for a buggy and had filled the thing with items he'd been managing to do somehow without—yard implements, tooth whitener, wiper blades and batteries, drill bits, four pounds of taco chips, a bale of toilet paper, perfumed wipes moistened with both sea-mist air freshener and bleach and guaranteed to do everything about the house but pay the mortgage.

When he went to check out, he found the lanes clotted up

with people, and he was obliged to stand for a good twenty minutes leaning on his cart which gave my father a little too much of a chance to study his fellow customers and come by the chilling conviction that he'd be doomed at cruising altitude. He was persuaded he'd only survived the day because the megacenter was incapable of controlled flight into terrain.

My mother, then, was prepared to fly up to the city before my father had entirely steeled himself for the trip. He was the one who made the reservations and planned the itinerary, and he had a system for avoiding the flights he feared that incurious louts would take. He noticed that a preponderance of them tended to fly in the middle of the day which gave them the chance to wake up at half past ten and stop off en route for a Big Gulp, so he was keen to get the first plane out, but my mother nixed him on it. She'd been raised to believe it a sign of poor manners to arrive on a visit early in the day. Decent people showed up in the afternoon or even in the evening and didn't embark at the crack of dawn just to avoid some fellow in a Statler Brothers T-shirt and a Winston 500 cap.

She insisted on the flight that left Greensboro at 2:00 P.M. which gave my father nervous indigestion through the week before they came.

I was busy trying to figure out how to deal with my apartment. I had to make it look to my mother a fit place for a human to live which, in truth, would have called for more renovation than I could afford or effect, so I settled for aromatic varnish on the puckered parquet, cleaned the soot off of the windows and the fuzz off of the chair rail and bought an armful of tulips from the Korean market on Henry Street. I even changed the lightbulbs in the fixtures in the hall, swept out the stairwell and deodorized it and then had a little chat with Sal who my parents were eager to meet. I fairly begged him to watch what he said and, most particularly, how he said it. As conversational fill, Sal often resorted to blue profanity, most especially "motherfucker" in all of its guises and permutations.

I even tried on our bench in Tompkins Square Park to instruct Rachel a little. She was kind enough to let me carry on for half a minute about the class of delicate topics I was keen she not pursue. But she soon enough laid her upraised index finger to my lips and shook her head in such a way as to cause me to shut up.

I hired Mahir to carry me to La Guardia to pick my parents up. As my Yemeni car-service colleagues went, he was jolly and undercologned. Arab men, speaking generally, are often in the thrall of Aramis, British Sterling, Bulgari, Nautica Sport. Once you've combined cologne with stale cigarette smoke and essence-of-lilac car freshener, you might as well have swiveled around and clubbed your passenger with your shoe. Mahir usually just stank a little of Merit 100s and Safeguard. His Lincoln was cedar-scented, and he tended to hide his unsightly sweaters beneath a blazer that very nearly fit.

I rode up front on the way out from Brooklyn and provided Mahir instruction, told him to behave as if he didn't know me and had never seen me before which we practiced on the BQE and along the Grand Central Parkway, and by the time we'd reached our exit, Mahir had almost quit calling me "Loose."

My parents' plane was late because they'd had an incident in Greensboro. They were traveling in the company of a Presbyterian glee club, and one of the baritones had gone into mild diabetic shock. They'd been third for takeoff at the time, and all that baritone really needed was an apple juice or two to sugar him up and level him out. Apparently, though, there was a provision in the Patriot Act that prohibited flight attendants from providing passengers beverages on the runway, even in the case of a septuagenarian baritone with low glucose.

So the plane had to taxi back over to the gate where juice could be legally served, and everybody got ushered off so they might properly reboard which allowed my father the opportunity to retire to the concourse lounge where he buttressed his nerve with a couple of Johnnie Walkers and tap water.

The glee club, you see, was uniformed in scarlet vests and navy slacks, and they'd been guilty in the terminal and guilty in the concourse, guilty at the check-in counter, guilty down along the airway, and most especially guilty in the cabin of the plane itself of singing numbers from the Presbyterian-glee-club repertoire without overt civilian encouragement or even tacit invitation. Worse still, a woman had come along to sit squarely in front of my father who looked to be wearing a housecoat and had curlers in her hair. He'd gotten that megacenter feeling and had demanded from my mother the phone she mostly used on wet days when her Pontiac wouldn't start.

I was putting a sheen on my toilet rim when his call came through, and straightaway I could only hear voices raised in ragged harmony, what sounded to me a lurching version of "People (People Who Need People)."

I believe I'd said "Hello" maybe three times before my father managed a "Hey" and not so much by way of greeting but more in the vein of a frantic preamble. He then went on to tell me that their papers—their wills and deeds and documents—were in an accordion folder in the bottom drawer of the secretary.

"Where are you?" I asked him.

And my father informed me, "In the fiery bowels of hell."

Then he switched off his phone because he hated to use their free talk minutes which, left unsquandered, accumulated from month to month.

Once the diabetic baritone felt well enough to hold up his end of "Chim Chim Cher-ee," the passengers were invited back onto the airplane, and the thing even managed to overcome karma and rise into the air. My father had knocked back two Bloody Marys and had suffered in grim silence three verses of "Chattanooga Choo Choo" and a rousing rendition of "Fascination" before my mother would allow him out to use the toilet. On the way back to his seat, he stopped to quiz the woman in the robe and curlers. She was eating oyster crackers from a greasy paper sack and thumbing through the air-mall offerings when my father tapped a curler spike to gain the woman's notice and (before my mother could stop him) asked her, "Where in the world do you think you are?"

Fortunately he got drowned out by the Presbyterian glee club who were more or less harmonizing on "Lullaby of Broadway." The woman in the housecoat barked that no goddamn body touched her curlers, and she rolled up her air-mall catalog and flogged my father with it which had the happy effect of making the glee club clam entirely up.

I heard about all of this only later over dinner with Rachel, but I got a whiff of it out at La Guardia when I'd asked about the flight and my mother had paused to glare at my father before allowing it had been fine.

We were standing at the upraised trunk lid of Mahir's midnight blue Lincoln, were shifting the junk aside to make room for the bags when Mahir took occasion to tell my mother and father, "We are strangers, me and Loose. I saw him first time just today." And while my parents attempted to digest the news, nodded politely anyway, Mahir turned my way to wink and ask me, "Right?"

So on their way into the city, my folks were more nervous than they had true cause to be because I'd felt obliged to insinuate that Mahir was slightly unhinged. The traffic didn't help. My parents were used to Confederate-states driving which can be as erratic as Yankee northeastern-corridor car travel but is conducted on far less congested motorways at appreciably lower speeds. We found ourselves on the Grand Central Parkway with a cheek-by-jowl assortment of unconscientious wheelmen who veered (it appeared to the untrained eye) anywhere they wished most anytime they pleased.

By the time we'd reached the BQE and were sailing south toward the Williamsburg Bridge, my father's features were frozen in what I took for his megacenter expression. He might have phoned me again with word of his will if I'd not been sitting beside him.

After a spot of research that consisted largely of standing in a bookstore and consulting New York City travel guides, I had booked and paid for my parents' room at a new SoHo hotel. It was the sort of place with no marquee or any overt signage, just a street number in maybe sixteen-point chrome-brushed font above the door. A potential customer almost had to be blessed with lodging-house clairvoyance to entertain hopes of turning up the place. I'd walked past it three or four times when I had come to scout it out before I'd happened to see an exiting guest in the company of a bellman, or what passed anyway for a bellman at that new SoHo hotel.

He wore a shiny European suit instead of a uniform, had on a space age headset and was conducting over it a fairly lively chat as he made of himself no use at all to the guest he was escorting, a man hauling a garment bag, a shopping sack and a valise. That hotel must have wished to encourage its guests to be plucky and enterprising, because that gentleman set his bag down, dropped his sack and his valise and hailed his own taxi while the bellman spoke to Ashley (I heard him call her) about what sounded to me hardly anything at all.

He did actually deposit the shopping sack in the taxi trunk which turned out to be the only item that guest didn't wish to put there, so he fished it out and thanked the bellman for I can't imagine what and then tipped him what looked a ten-spot for I can't conceive of why. I looked on as that bellman folded the bill and pocketed it with a wink while he acquainted Ashley with one of his favorite uses for grenadine. I tried to follow him into the lobby, but he let the door swing shut behind him.

I'd hoped to see a room, but when I got inside, I couldn't find anyone willing to concede he was in the service business. The staff were all dressed like Parisian undertakers and were preoccupied with each other. They were talking either face-to-face or over their space age headsets, and the only human I actually chatted with turned out to be a guest, a woman who'd come all the way from Bolivia to shop at Century 21 and had yet to find an employee who would deign to give her directions.

I took her outside and pointed, fully intended to go back in but decided on the street that the hotel had the virtue of location and that I couldn't really muster the energy to impose upon the staff. I stood by the curb and booked a room over the phone instead.

The same bellman came out to greet us. He was having what sounded a similar conversation about some brand of clothing, some manner of cocktail, some species of haircut. He'd brought with him a luggage cart that looked as space age as his headset. It appeared to be made of Lucite with titanium adornments, the sort of item the Jetsons might transport their refuse on. He rolled it up to the fender well and left it there so that me and Mahir could load it as he described to Belinda (I heard him call her) an hors d'oeuvre he'd lately enjoyed, some manner of pygmy game bird skewered and grilled and dipped in chutney. Once the cart was loaded, he very nearly helped me push it in.

My parents' room was the size of a seventies-vintage luxury sedan with a window that looked across Greene Street to some manner of loft office where the employees appeared to be doing hardly anything at all. The bellman came in long enough to point out the sewing kit and the phone. I got displaced into the hall in order to make room for him.

We could all three be in that room together if one of us remained on the bed, and I was pretty quick to inform my parents that I'd paid already for their stay, that all of this big-city hotel splendor was entirely on their son.

My mother assured me immediately, "You're not paying for our room."

But my father was standing in front of the door reading the postings on it—the hotel policy sheet, the room rates, the escape route in case of fire. Without turning around, my father told my mother, "Sure he is."

We passed, my father and I, the next quarter hour crammed into the bathroom trying to figure out how to turn the shower on. The fittings were not so much postindustrial as bafflingly intergalactic, and it took us another ten minutes to flush the toilet and run water in the sink. I then suggested we go for a walk in the immediate neighborhood as if it had only just occurred to me that fresh air might be bracing. The truth was, however, I'd left no part of my parents' visit to chance and had spent a fair bit of the previous week reconnoitering.

I'd circulated through the streets surrounding their hotel

looking for points of interest we might simply happen onto, cafés and boutiques and ornate antique cast-iron building fronts. I steered my parents so that we'd happen onto a Prince Street pastry shop where I'd gone in the week before to check the atmosphere and crullers, ensure the mix tape wasn't loud enough to make a cranium vibrate. I sat them down and bought them complicated mochaccinos and then made mention of Rachel as if by wholly unplanned happenstance. Of course, I'd long since decided what I would say and how I would prepare them for the fact that someone like me had managed to snag someone like her. I could still pretty readily recall the reaction of my parents to Fay and the conversation I'd had with my father out on our front-porch steps.

As females go, Fay had been awfully easy to read, but I feared that my mother and father would take one look at Rachel and think, "Whore."

It turned out, of course, that I was being nervous for no reason. I was inflicting on Rachel my degree of mediocrity. As an actor, I could claim only semiprofessional skills and talents. I was like a utility infielder who spends his seasons in Pawtucket while Rachel had long since made the big-league team, if only to ride the bench. She wasn't a star exactly, but she certainly had the tools, and there was no lie that I managed to tell my mother and father about her that Rachel didn't confirm as gospel that night just by showing up.

She'd picked the restaurant, knew a place down below Canal where the music was low and classical and the waiters were solicitous, where the tables weren't shoved together and bar traffic was mercifully scant. We were there a quarter hour before Rachel hurried in, looking, I couldn't help but notice, like an authentic sculptress. She wasn't dusted with granite powder or hauling chisels in her bag, but she wore her hair pulled back a way I'd never seen her wear it, had on a blouse and trousers and only the merest functional coat of makeup, the sort of boots I had to imagine a real artisan might wear.

I saw her coming and rose from my seat, and she apologized on the way. She claimed to have gotten caught up in some ilk of gallery squabble and went directly to my mother and father and offered them each her hand. Then she stepped back around to where I stood all wooden and dyspeptic. She laid her fingers to my shoulder, told me, "Hey," and kissed me on the mouth.

My father helped her scoot her chair up once I'd required a quarter minute to muster spit enough to say to Rachel, "Hi."

She was splendid from the jump. I noticed she'd even gone to the trouble to get her hands a little dirty. She'd stripped the lacquer from her nails and wore a Band-Aid on one thumb. When our waiter came around, Rachel ordered a Negroni and told my parents that every Friday I would take her out for one. Then she reached over and squeezed my hand the way an actual girlfriend might. The nervousness I'd felt going in simply evaporated or was replaced anyway by the brand of warm contentment men must know when they've stalked and landed a female and are convinced that she's ensnared, are entirely persuaded she's devoted to them.

My father was a girls' guy, so Rachel proved absolute candy to him. And when I say "a girls' guy" I don't mean to suggest that my father was some stripe of goat. He was not remotely the leering lascivious type prone to sinning in his heart and in the privacy of his half bath at home, but he preferred even wholly innocent platonic exposure to women over any variety of human commerce with men. He'd explained to me once that men were transparent while women were opaque. He'd used the example of a frosted tumbler versus a jelly glass. You could glance at one and tell just what, if anything, was in it, but the other ordinarily required a spot of manipulation first.

So Rachel was precisely in my father's line of interest, most particularly since she was the megalopolis manner of opaque which meant cloudier even than the most intriguing Neely female, harder to get at and more of a challenge to know. My father essentially interviewed Rachel while my mother tried to forestall him, or spent half her time chastising him for prying where he shouldn't and the other half probing and prying a little herself. I could tell that my mother was well pleased by the want of an exposed midriff and no conspicuous indication of a tattoo, and Rachel was sharp and lively enough to give back as good as she got. She asked my mother and father after the Neelyites she'd heard of and extracted from them word of how the two of them had met which led to an involved discussion of men's couture, most particularly baggy trousers.

A discussion among them anyway. I mostly sat and watched, though Rachel from time to time would reach across and take my hand to pretty literally draw me into the conversation. My mother, naturally, told embarrassing stories about me as a child, caught up Rachel on my ungainly years and my paltry lot of girlfriends and then produced a harrowing quartet of snapshots from her purse that charted my progress into and almost out of the annals of dweebdom. Once my father had plagued Rachel with questions enough, she produced from her handbag a picture of a woman I have to think was actually Rachel's mother. She looked seventy, was preposterously brunette, wore a bathrobe and was standing by a stove. Rachel claimed to hail from up past Syracuse on toward Mexico Bay. She called her mother Annie and even misted up a little when she touched upon the woman's death from gallbladder complications.

We had appetizers, entrées, desserts and coffee, eau de vie, and there was never so much as a passingly awkward lull in the conversation. Whenever Rachel wasn't supplying responses, she plumbed for them instead, and I could tell that my mother and father both were utterly taken with her, relieved (I prefer to believe) I had graduated to an adult, a grown woman with sensible interests and what struck them as sound judgment. For my purposes Rachel served as a form of human compensation for my failed career in underwriting and my spotty acting prospects, for disappointments my mother and father weren't even remotely aware of yet. My shabby Dumbo apartment. My lawless Staten Island repairs. My car-service job. My agent and landlord, Sal "Little Pony" Delgado, who we were scheduled to see for lunch at Cooty's noon the following day.

We walked Rachel back to her building, or back anyway to a doorway on Thompson Street which looked like it might just give onto the studio of a sculptress. Rachel kissed my father's cheek and shook my mother's hand good night, and then my parents wandered up the block to give us a moment together which Rachel mercifully didn't spend in toting up the evening's charges.

"They're sweet," she told me, and she reached to shift a strand of hair from my face.

I was altogether smitten, and I plied her with one of my dreamy pathetic looks, a slack-jawed expression I'm partial to when I want to seem bewitching, though I can't recall an instance when it actually served me well. Rachel knew enough of men to sense what I was about, and she tried to bring me around by telling me, "Louis," as a corrective. Then she laid her hands to my shoulders and pushed me toward the street.

They talked about her the rest of the weekend, put to me all manner of questions about Rachel's art, about her people upstate. They insisted on hearing how we'd met which I was pleased to manufacture for them. I even took them up to Grand Central and showed them the very spot where I'd bumped into Rachel and knocked a sack from her hand. She mitigated everything the way I'd hoped she would. My apartment hardly seemed so grim with Rachel in the offing. My mother couldn't imagine, were we to marry, that Rachel would stand for such a place, most particularly once a sizable chunk of catalytic converter had dropped past my lone window and crashed loudly in the street.

Even Sal struck them as merely colorful while entertaining us at Cooty's. We had Cootyburgers, and Sal prevented my parents from eating the fries. The other four patrons, perched at the bar, were watching the hockey playoffs, were smoking and drinking Irish whiskey and manipulating phlegm, and when they'd get loud and rowdy, Sal would beg pardon and rise from the table, step over and tell them for fuck's sake to shut up.

We went to a musical on Saturday night, a revival of *South Pacific* featuring an actor who'd played a forensic pathologist on a TV drama which had never afforded him opportunity to leap to his feet and sing. I knew his costar from a cream-rinse commercial in which I also had appeared. She'd been called upon to walk down Seventh Avenue in the sunlight to display to very best effect her newfound body and sheen. I'd been charged to stand behind a man she noticed on the sidewalk and be the man she'd failed to notice.

She was blond onstage and looked voluptuous in her halter and shorts. Her voice was something on the order of a human trumpet, loud and metallic and sharp enough to keep everyone awake except for the fellow in the seat beside my father's. He'd brought his wife and children in from the suburbs, probably against his will, and he dozed off during the overture and snored through the first act, woke up only once his cell phone started ringing.

I drove them Sunday to La Guardia in Teddy's sludge-brown Crown Victoria. I told them (mostly the truth) that I'd borrowed the car from a neighbor and a friend. I parked in the short-term lot and visited with them in the terminal until they got antsy and decided that they'd best sit at their gate. I promised to come for a visit and assured them I'd pass on to Rachel their invitation for me to bring her along. Then I watched them through security and sent them off with a wave.

Azal gave me an incoming pickup over the radio, a woman named Driscoll who'd called from her L.A. flight on the Sky Phone after being brushed off, apparently, by the local Lebanese drivers and Egyptians. Azal informed me she was charming—actually, "chumming" is how he said it—which was standard Yemeni-car-service code for "You might want to watch your ass."

I fished my sport coat and tie out of the sack I'd stowed away in the trunk, wiped my milky square of Lucite clean and with a fresh grease pencil wrote the woman's name in tidy script approaching Times New Roman. Then I went in to stand with my colleagues near the baggage carousels while my parents, I figured, were waiting to board in Concourse C. That Driscoll was arriving in the early afternoon on what was supposed to have been the red-eye which meant she'd sat around LAX for four or five hours to ripen and stew. So she was pretty much a harridan by the time she got to me, came stalking down the escalator wrangling a couple of carry-on bags.

She looked far too ill and unhappy not to be my passenger, so I was fixed upon her well before she'd noticed me. I watched her scan with exasperation for her name among my colleagues. She finally found it on my square of Lucite and shoved both of her bags my way as she informed me, "You."

#@%&?/}#%!

1

ALMOST AN ENTIRE WEEK had passed, and I'd been in a fever about Rachel. I could hardly keep from recalling her in her sculptress clothes, would lie in my bed and relive the tenderness she'd visited on me. Of course I knew it had all been an act for hire, but I wanted still to believe that Rachel had gotten tempted by me to play the part in earnest. Every now and again when the light was right and my hair was lying just so, I could detect residual charm and allure in my medicine-cabinet glass. So I was equipped to believe that maybe I had slain Rachel a little once she'd seen me out from beneath the wheel of Teddy's sludge-brown Crown Vic and all dressed up with my parents in an elegant Tribeca restaurant. I worked to imagine her feeling about me the way I wanted her to feel.

As preoccupations go, it was a fairly consuming chore, and for a few days I wandered around the Heights fixated upon Rachel. I manufactured in my head all sorts of rosy futures for us. I was fond most especially of the version that had us moving down to Neely and living in the Pipkin place that had been torn down years before, knocked over to make room for a pharmacy with a cash station out front. In my head I never worked past the details of Rachel underfoot. Rachel in her skimpy leisure togs lounging around the Pipkins' parlor. Rachel refreshing my coffee. Rachel cutting hydrangeas in the back garden. Fuzzy naked Rachel bathing behind the frosted shower glass. I never got to the point where we made a living or had a conversation, argued over the checkbook balance, sat at the table through a meal.

So I roamed the neighborhood with lascivious fiction in my head and attempted, the way I tend to, to cobble up remarks I could try on Rachel the next time that I drove her. I wanted to seem both aware that we'd been playing at romance and yet open to the actual prospect of it which called for more skill at acting and talking than I could ever hope to possess.

I was up on the Promenade one afternoon contemplating my taste in clothing, wondering if I could make myself magnetic with a shift in style, when I walked past a bench and heard somebody on it tell me, "Hey."

It was Omar sitting by himself. He had his book bag with him, appeared to have come out to the Promenade instead of going home.

"Hey," I told him, and sat down beside him. "What are you doing out here?"

Omar shrugged. He plucked up the shoulder strap of his book bag and chewed on it.

"How's your mom?"

Omar shrugged again.

"Did your dad call?"

Omar nodded.

"Still stuck?"

Omar just managed a sort of grimace but otherwise didn't so much as twitch.

I started in with inexcusable bromides about patience and forbearance, told Omar all manner of rubbish about how trouble tends to play out. I let on that even monumental problems dissipate, that a fellow with a happy heart and a good thought in his head stands a better-than-average chance of putting his worries behind him. Omar chewed on his book-bag strap and glared at me in silence.

Then I held up my foot and asked him, "What do you think of these shoes?"

Omar responded by drawing his strap from his mouth and exhaling significantly. He stood up from the bench and wandered off, south along the Promenade while I rehearsed again a greeting I'd been cobbling up for Rachel and fussed with an unruly trouser pleat.

She called me on Thursday and had me pick her up in Chelsea at a cross street just off Seventh in front of a garden-apartment office. It was occupied, as it turned out, by some stripe of psychoanalyst Rachel went no more than once a month to see. The guy wasn't even an actual doctor, boasted on his etched-brass sign no proper psychoanalytical higher-learning degree. He was just some fellow, apparently, with a consoling manner and a gift (I'm only guessing here) for practical advice.

For Rachel's purposes I imagine he was merely a man she could pay, an antidote to the usual course of her evenings and small hours when she'd suffer her affections purchased and her female favors mortgaged. If she'd actually needed the counseling, she would have gone maybe once a week. I eased to the curb, and she gained the seat and reached for the door handle. I was just about to embark upon the sparkling peroration I'd practiced and honed all over the place the bulk of the previous week when Rachel sought my glance in the mirror and said to me, "Three bills."

I was trying to reason what brand of romantic overture that might be when Rachel finally offered an enlargement. "Four and a half hours at sixty per." She'd closed the door by then, had her daybook out and open and was consulting some notes she'd made. "I got to the restaurant a little after seven. Home at ten-forty, ten forty-five." She shut her book. She added, "I rounded up."

"Fine," I told her, and pulled from the curb nearly into a taxi. "Three bills." She laughed when I asked her if she'd take a check.

I spent most of the rest of the evening telling myself what a twit I was. I revisited my activities of the previous few days, all of the swanning around and the dreamy psychosexual suppositions, and I took pains to steep each enterprise in pathetic humiliation, had to wonder at how I'd succeeded at putting the commerce from my mind. I enjoyed occasion to throttle myself pretty soundly in front of Rachel's building once she'd gone in to freshen up and change, and I began to piece together a story for my parents which sent Rachel into the arms of a Frick Collection curator. It was the manner of tale that allowed me to be gracious in defeat, permitted me to acknowledge the virtues for Rachel of a boyfriend in her field who was sure to be an invaluable asset to her sculpting career. I was debating whether Rachel and I had managed to stay dear friends when she returned to the car in a gauzy off-the-shoulder number and directed me to drive her to an address in outer Queens.

We went to a street in Jamaica off Grand Central Parkway that was lined with commercial warehouses. Rachel had me park at the corner under a Powerhouse Malt Liquor sign and wait while she made her way a couple of doors down to a building with a sheet-steel landing and a trio of loading bays. She came out not a quarter hour later with an Estonian in tow. He was short and thick and would have been remarkable for his atrocious hair if he'd not been wearing a teal green suit. The material was slightly iridescent. The pocket flaps were piped in black. The pants were too long by a couple of inches, and the coat was far too skimpy. The fellow couldn't have buttoned that jacket with a gun to his forehead.

He smelled sourly of Eastern European cigarettes and faintly of what I had to figure for vodka, and he was rough (I noticed) with Rachel as he gripped her at the elbow and all but herded her into the car.

He said what proved the name of a restaurant on Park Avenue, though I couldn't begin to make out the words. His accent was thick and his clumsy bridgework nearly mesmerizing. It took Rachel to poke me and speak in plain English before I pulled into the road. He nuzzled her all along the way, and she giggled and staved him off, was evermore drawing his hand out from beneath her gauzy dress and making as if to find his chunky gold ring mesmerizing. He took occasional calls on his cell phone, screamed into it in Estonian. He had me stop at a liquor store just west of Rego Park, sent me in to fetch him a pint of Finlandia.

I didn't like him. Naturally, I didn't like any of the men Rachel "escorted" on account of the hopeless suitor interest I couldn't seem to help but nurse. But I most emphatically didn't like him, resented the way he handled Rachel, the liberties he took with her there in my backseat, the rude force he pawed her with. I kept checking the mirror in search of a sign, for the merest signal from Rachel that she would prefer me to stop and put Niki (his name was) out like trash at the curb. Then we could see by way of experiment if a drunk Estonian in a teal suit with a wretched thatch of brittle hair and a mouthful of brass bridgework could make his way to safety on a Friday night in Queens.

The one time, however, I caught Rachel's eye, she only smiled and winked.

They dined at some sort of Slavic place on a dowdy block in the Fifties, and I managed to squeeze in a couple of runs for Azal while they ate. I was up to Washington Heights and back, over to Kips Bay to a co-op where a woman with two terriers was leaving her husband in a huff. Rachel's Estonian was pretty well saturated by the time they came out of the restaurant. He didn't reel across the sidewalk, was not remotely a fall-down drunk, but he was gruffer with Rachel and, even by meager Estonian-hoodlum standards, noticeably more sullen and less polite.

Rachel directed me to the hotel she used sometimes near Gramercy Park, a little boutique of a place with a snug but altogether elegant lobby where Rachel had worked out an arrangement with the night clerk and concierge. He was one and the same. His name was Neal, and he was studying to be a nurse. He'd allow me coffee from the urn he kept hot on a mahogany sideboard. Neal once told me against my will exactly how a catheter worked.

Most usually Rachel remained upstairs for an hour and a half. She never stayed in that Gramercy Park hotel entirely through the night and carried there ordinarily Eastern Euro–trash like Niki who I figured would drop into bed and do more sleeping than anything else. So I wasn't surprised when Rachel was still upstairs after two entire hours, though I did get a little irritated once another half hour had passed. It was fast approaching the three-hour mark when the two of them finally came out, him first in his hideous suit to light a cigarette on the sidewalk and Rachel a few steps behind him moving (I noticed) rather gingerly.

She didn't look injured exactly, at least not right away. She just impressed me as tentative and perhaps a shade reluctant, not quite the woman who three hours before had gone inside with that fellow. As she crossed from the building toward the car, she jauntied up a little, shot me a smile and winked as if to say that everything was fine. She eased onto the backseat. I slipped in under the wheel, and together we waited for Niki to finish his cigarette on the sidewalk as he made a series of phone calls and screamed, it sounded, at underlings.

I watched Rachel in the mirror. She had to work to settle, and then she winced in such a way as to cause me to ask her, "Are you okay?"

Rachel nodded and patted her stomach. She told me, "Borscht."

Niki shut off his phone. He spit and flicked his butt into the street, fairly flung himself onto the seat beside Rachel, bumped her over a bit with his forearm. Then he announced an address that Rachel leaned up to translate which caused her shoulder strap to shift a bit and exposed to me some flesh that looked to be bruised, or at the very least blotchy and discolored. I recognized the impression of a man's fingers, the outline of his thumb.

I've never been given to violence outright. I know more of a gift for simmering constipated unexercised rage, the brand of anger that almost never results in simple assault charges but just perforated ulcers and hemorrhagic episodes. I'd only once previously thrown a punch and had hit a Rothrock with it. Not even the Rothrock I was aiming for but his little sister instead which had resulted, as wayward punches go, in enough humiliation to keep me for a while from even balling my hands into fists. Like most people, when I get angry I get uncoordinated, or more uncoordinated than I ordinarily am, so it was probably a valuable lesson for me to hit that Rothrock's sister. If I'd successfully hit that Rothrock himself, I might have gone on a punching spree and broken digits against doorframes or fractured them on jawbones and misspent an adolescence getting soundly beaten up.

Instead I was given to rue and thrombosis and nagging gastric acid, the usual side effects of cowardice and physical impotence, but on this occasion I yielded straightaway to unchecked fury and shrugged Rachel's hand from my shoulder as I threw open my door. She knew exactly what I'd seen and seemed to fear what I'd be up to but not enough to keep me from getting about it before she intervened.

She said, "Louis," as I gained the curb and jerked open the back door. She didn't say it, however, sternly or with starch enough to stop me but more like women say "maybe" when they mean "no" or "yes" when they mean "perhaps." It was the sort of conditional "Louis" that would absolve her if I killed him, and I'm delighted to say I very nearly did.

Niki was full of vodka and pretty well spent from his exertions, both the actual lovemaking and the Greco-Roman foreplay, so he came up like Slavic deadweight when I jerked him out by his jacket and flung him onto the sidewalk.

"You son of a bitch," was about the only thing I could think to tell him in addition to the odd pedestrian obscenity which I favored him with as I kicked him, as I punched him, as I stomped him and made him pay both for what he'd done and what I knew I'd never do. He'd had Rachel, after all, if only violently and for a fee while I drove her and doted on her and, even on the night I'd hired her, had let her get away with just a kiss.

I pummeled that drunk Estonian until he was senseless on the pavement, until he'd even stopped groaning every time I caught him flush which was along about when both Neal and Rachel intervened. Neal had a kind of conniption on the sidewalk. Rachel laid her hand upon my arm and told me simply, "Stop."

Neal reminded Rachel of promises he'd extracted from her when they'd first made their arrangement and he'd agreed to supply Rachel a room. Neal fretted openly over his job and his pricey nursing-school tuition, couldn't help but believe some guest had probably phoned the police. Then he came my way and charged me to explain what I'd been thinking, how exactly I'd seen clear to spoil Neal's night and scotch his prospects which I was working up some hangdog mumbling and a shrug about when Neal noticed a cut on Niki's cheek. I'd laid the flesh wide open and could still feel the sting in my fingers where I'd punched against the bone.

Neal pointed and told me, "Stitches. Seven. Maybe eight." Then he squatted down and had a proper nursing-student look at what proved to be a clean break in the skin. The healer in Neal took over. He grabbed Niki by the feet, directed me to hoist him at the shoulders, and together we carried Niki into the hotel laundry room where we laid him along the length of a pressed-wood table by a mangle. Neal, excited now that he'd seen the gashes and inspected the scuffs and cuts, excused himself and ran upstairs to fetch a kit he carried, a tackle box (it turned out) overflowing with medical implementa that Neal wasn't, in fact, licensed yet to use.

In his absence Rachel examined Niki. She shook her head and told me, "Christ," in a tone I couldn't help but take for marginally scolding.

"What did he do to you?" I asked her.

Rachel slightly shook her head. She continued to study Niki as she told me, "Not enough."

Neal had only local anesthetic in a can, the aerosol variety that got sprayed on baseball players, and the first blast he laid on Niki almost served to wake him up. We decided instead to let just the Finlandia make do, so Niki got cleaned and stitched and sutured with only vodka to numb him, and he was beginning to rouse himself by the time Neal finished up. He got coated with Vaseline at the last and so looked like a failed contender as we ushered him from the hotel basement out to Teddy's sludge-brown Ford. Niki was mumbling by then, was asking after a woman he called Gina who had stolen from him, by the sound of it, and who he fully intended to kill.

I tried to tempt Rachel into the front. I mounted, in fact, a bid to direct her, but she shot me a look to confirm she went only where she wished to go, and she wished to go on the backseat in order to tend to Niki who was singing what sounded like some sort of Baltic chantey. Before she ducked into the car, she told me I should take them back to Jamaica.

Then she added, "I don't know what he'll do," and I knew she didn't mean Niki.

It was probably half past one by the time we got there, and Niki had long since left off singing. His face had begun to puff and swell, and he'd just sat in the back and groaned for the last few miles past Metropolitan Avenue and Kew Gardens. Rachel climbed out and pounded on the door at the top of the sheet-steel landing, and I think I even whimpered a little when Giles's Samoan came out.

Rachel went in for a couple of minutes while Giles's man stayed on the stoop. He just hulked there above us and kept his eyes on the car until Rachel came back out with Giles and led him to the Ford where he opened the door and peered in at Niki, asked him, "How are we doing?"

Giles instructed me with a look to help him get Niki inside, or to help anyway his Samoan who all but took Niki up like a child and fairly carried him into the warehouse proper without contribution from me. I just brought up the rear back of Rachel and Giles and found myself quite shortly on the tidiest warehouse floor I'd ever seen. Pallets were organized in rows with crates and boxes stacked neatly upon them. The concrete floor was so clean and shiny that it reflected the overhead light. We followed Niki and Giles's Samoan into an office against the far wall that was lamplit and cozy and boasted an impeccably clubby décor. A man inside (Rudy, Giles called him) was poring over a ledger. A matronly assistant with vague pinkish hair was changing the filter in the coffee urn.

"Rudy," Giles said, and with tilt of his head caused Rudy to clear the sofa, a big burgundy chesterfield item that was freighted with paperwork—canceled checks and invoices, tissuey bills of lading. Rudy made short work of the clutter, and Giles's Samoan laid out Niki on the couch.

Rudy took in Niki's sutured cuts and gashes. He said, "Big Frank?" to Giles who shook his head and pointed at me.

I couldn't help but wonder if that warehouse office was the last place I would see, with its framed foxhounds, its cast-bronze lamps, its globe, its mahogany bookcase, its massive etching of a bull moose set upon by wolves.

"It's Louis, right?" Giles asked. I nodded. He stepped to the door and beckoned with his fingers. "Walk with me."

I followed him down off the landing to the street where we waited for a moment in silence until Giles's Samoan had joined us, and I couldn't help but picture myself racked and broken by that fellow who, even by generous Samoan standards, was burly and oversize. He only followed us, however, proved deft at hanging back discreetly while Giles and I left the ruptured sidewalk and walked along the street.

Giles had me tell him my side of the incident, and he failed altogether to quiz or interrupt me as I talked but just allowed me to spill everything I intended to tell him of Niki's offenses and a few errant choice items about my interest in Rachel I'd not meant to say. Giles had a gift for that sort of thing, was capable of saying nothing for long enough to cause a fellow to try to fill the hollows up. So I told him essentially everything, dribbled it out along the block, and by the time we'd reached a rubbishy pile of cement at the road end between a derelict warehouse and what looked a Con Ed transformer graveyard, I'd pretty well established myself to be a courtly fool.

Fortunately for me, Giles approved in a general way of courtliness. He liked rules and mores, appreciated standards of behavior. I think he was even a little fonder of Rachel than he could afford to let on. So he was going to do me a favor, he told me, and patch things up with Niki who Giles identified as a "merchant" of some standing and some use. Giles was big on favors and chits and markers and binding obligations, and once he'd announced he'd spare me, he offered up his hand for me to shake.

As we walked back toward his warehouse, Giles allowed me to be relieved. He permitted me a half a block of routine respiration and no active threat of an avenging Samoan hanging over my head, and after I'd enjoyed for a couple of minutes the fact I'd go on living, Giles provided me occasion to do him a favor in return.

"Bunny," he said, and stopped in the road. "I need to run across him."

I'd called him once myself when I was running behind

schedule. "I've got his number somewhere," I told Giles, and shrugged. "I think he's in the book."

Giles smiled and shook his head. He said, "I need to run across him."

"He's got these day-old—"

Giles wagged a finger at me. "Somewhere else," he said.

I told Giles about the Sicilian restaurant on Spring Street. I warned him off the lobster fra diavolo. "Too hot," I assured him, "for a human to eat."

2

IT WAS AN UNREMARKABLE Tuesday. I recall that we were at orange alert, and two abandoned police boats were moored for show beneath the Brooklyn Bridge. Omar had stopped by on his way to school to share with me news of his father who'd phoned, like he tended to, in the middle of the night. Teddy, it seems, was capable still at the time of taking consolation in the sorts of arid assurances issued by embassy flunkies. He was re-submitting documents, enduring interviews and was desperately missing his wife and his son and (most likely) the Weather Channel.

Teddy had charged Omar to ask me to check the oil level in his Ford and start, if I got the chance to, his badly battered Lincoln which we'd decided not to tell him had been towed the month before and was somewhere out at a city garage in the ass end of the Bronx accumulating compound storage charges and penalties. It would have cost far more to spring the thing than it was worth. In the night Omar had completely disassembled a hair dryer, and he showed me the resistor that had melted. I laced up my sneakers and walked with Omar to his school on Middagh Street, left him thinking I was on my way for a run on the Promenade, but I stopped instead for coffee and what tasted like last week's Danish, hunted down a spot of sunlight and had my breakfast on a bench.

I dialed my parents up around half past nine which was not at all my custom. I tended to call them in the evening just be-

237

fore they'd sat for supper, about the latest point in the day when my father would answer the phone. He'd been for years disposed against nighttime telephone conversations, disapproved of the sorts of people who'd dial up, say, after eight unless, of course, they'd called with dire news. He preferred to read the Greensboro paper uninterrupted and watch the occasional public-TV show about wildfires or grubs.

I almost never called them in the morning, had been avoiding them, in fact, and hadn't phoned them in the early evening either because my mother was keen to get me down some weekend soon with Rachel, and the last few times I'd spoken to her, she'd pestered me for dates. She had no way of knowing it was a painful topic for me, that every endearment I had to generate, each scrap of trivial Rachel talk, was a galling chore. When I tried to suggest that Rachel was too caught up in sculpting affairs for a trip out of the city in the near term, my mother just fished out her calendar and flipped it some months forward in an attempt to nail down a weekend or even cement a holiday.

The last time we'd talked, I'd been obliged to mention the Frick curator, had invoked him as a distraction and a punctuational ploy, had allowed I couldn't be absolutely certain he was a rival, but I owned up to nagging suspicions, and I hinted at my fears and suggested that there might not be sound reason for a visit.

I'd been pretty effectively putting off an update ever since, until at least I had some morsel of authentic news to convey, and Sal had armed me with one the afternoon before. It turned out my purgatory for having fought with the podiatrist had come to an end in the form of an actual television part. I was to play the operator of a methamphetamine lab on a show about the passions and the vagaries of our legal system. Or rather a show about the love lives of the prosecuting attorneys and the abiding shiftlessness of the people they put on trial.

A producer of the show had caught my cat-kibble commercial and had tracked me down because of what he'd called my "rural look." He wanted a cracker innocent to play a methamphetamine kingpin. He had used (apparently) an overabundance of criminals of color in the past and so had ordered up a white-bread part. Worse still, I was to employ undocumented migrants and pay them something well south of the going gangland rate which opened me up to felony charges and NAFTA infractions both at once.

I was to be laconic, Sal had informed me, and have but a couple of actual lines beyond the privileged murmurings I poured into my lawyer's ear. But I'd be on screen looking wholesome for a pretty considerable while, long enough anyway for my father to figure out how to turn on the recorder and seek out a videotape with space. It was a topic other than Rachel that we could bandy about, and I was sitting there in the sunlight licking Danish glaze off my fingers when I pulled out my telephone and dialed them up.

I didn't get an answer. The machine picked up, the one they never debriefed. It sat on the nightstand in the spare bedroom behind two years' worth of *McCall's,* and while I do believe that my parents sometimes harbored thoughts to check it, they never quite seemed to get around to playing their messages back. Most particularly once they could be assured their friends and all their relations knew it was fruitless to leave a message and consequently never did. I decided they had fine weather like I was enjoying and were out on their morning walk.

By that time my father was working only intermittently, or

rather was driving to the office usually one or two days a week and otherwise running what numbers he needed to on the breakfast table at home which Meridian had struck upon as an economizing tactic. They were doubling up on real estate and rejiggering workforce standing so they might deprive employees of health coverage and the like.

Mornings when weather allowed, my parents often drove out to the park, not the one along the creek bed with the toads and the mosquitoes but the exercise park that had been built on fill from the shopping plaza—dirt and stumps and morsels probably of uncooperative tradesmen which had gotten dumped into a gully until it made for level ground. The fill had not, however, been packed and tamped sufficiently to keep it from being susceptible to sinkholes and eruptions, and soaking rains would usually float up finish nails and scraps of Romex, making of the path a bit more of a challenge than it was intended to be.

Exercise contraptions were scattered throughout the place. They were made from a combination of treated timber and galvanized piping, and each came with a sign attached bearing instructions for its use. The one that looked like a pair of cold frames was for high-stepping thigh enhancement. There was a jungle-gym sort of an item for chin-ups and lumbar stretches, a set of parallel pipes for balancing, a brace and a board for crunches and a couple of suspended rings for God-knows-what. It hardly mattered, however, what those bits of equipment were for since local people only ever perched upon them and smoked.

Three circuits were a mile, and my parents used to go for six around most mornings, before breakfast usually when the heat wasn't bad and there was nobody out there much. My mother was permitted on the exercise path to speak, if she wished, about Jesus, mount one in her series of futile bids to win my father to the Lord as they made their counterclockwise progress from the gravel parking lot out past the weedy drift of jonquils and the bed of canna lilies that the city had planted but couldn't be bothered to water and then over around the sewer pipe and under the willows before they turned back through the marshy bottom toward the parking lot.

So when I failed to reach them, I could picture where they were. Sitting on the Promenade in the sun with a view of lower Manhattan, I imagined my parents circulating along a cinder path in a half-assed exercise park that had been a gully once.

I didn't think any more about them until I got the call. I had noticed that traffic was light on the bridge and sparse on the expressway which convinced me to take the Crown Victoria out for a midmorning shift. Azal favored me with a fare to Newark, and I even managed to snare one back. An Austrian tourist with but scanty English and no feel for the currency was about to get played by a gypsy cabbie (Senegalese, he sounded to me) who was near to striking a deal to drive him to midtown for what it might cost in the honest world to get a ride to Detroit. I stepped in and undercut the guy by about 3,000 percent, and he put (I have to think now) some sort of malediction on me.

That Austrian, as it turned out, was on the elder-hostel circuit, had slept in a special homemade percale sack in church basements all over the world. He had a pocket dictionary for helping to cobble up commentary, and he told me in fractured and, on occasion, wholly senseless English ("She say cake axle happy, no?") about all the cities he had seen and the splendid hikes he'd taken. He seemed to have eaten some sort of seasonal fricasseed insect in Iquique, had walked into Slovenia across the Julian Alps. He claimed to have nearly been perished (he called it, after a bit of a scour) by a thicket of stinging nettles on the Serengeti Plain. He'd gotten ill on chorizo in Lisbon, had suffered a rat bite in Australia, some sort of toe fungus (it sounded to me) on American Samoa, and he confessed at length with a wink and a hardy Tyrolean laugh that he'd enjoyed the sexual favors of a fellow traveler, a Romanian woman he'd met on Mull, and he informed me of her "throw weight" which he'd either miscalculated or she was the size of a light-duty truck.

I learned that the coffee at elder hostels was universally unpotable. That thievery was rampant and the dorm rooms smelled of feet. Then my Austrian fare inquired after an Automat for lunch and refused to believe me when I said he was fifteen years too late.

Azal kept me going through the early afternoon with outpatient-surgery pickups and Upper East Side doctor visits. I helped a woman move an alarmingly heavy pressed-wood TV cart, loaded it into the Crown Victoria trunk and fetched it out at her destination, a building on West End Avenue where she was making of it a gift. I hauled a whiskery white-haired gentleman to a Columbus Avenue thrift shop with what appeared to be every sport coat he'd ever bothered to buy—crested blazers and seersuckers, tweedy tartans in nappy wool that all smelled like they'd passed a couple of years in an elder-hostel dorm room while their owner reeked of fried rice and yeasty twelve-pack beer.

Traffic was manageable, even crosstown, and the city was splashed with sunlight, precisely the conditions to inspire me to optimism, infect me anyway with a sense I could succeed where I had floundered and win with a little concerted effort everything I'd not yet won. It was a familiar brand of utterly unmerited well-being that I was given to stumbling onto from time to time. When the weather was good and my skin was clear and my blood sugar (I guess) was balanced, I could pretty readily persuade myself I'd finish my lizard novel, would harden and sculpt my muscles through the daily use of free weights, would become with conscientious study fluent in Italian, would give up calzones for sea bass, Singha for Poland Spring and might even meet a woman I'd not have to pay to date.

The sensation always passed, of course, but I savored it while I could and planned for myself a rather triumphal and resplendent future while exiting through the Midtown Tunnel and leaving the city behind for Queens. Azal had offered a La Guardia pickup that no one else had wanted. A gentleman in from Toronto needed a car into the Village, and I sailed out Grand Central Parkway and scooped him up. He was carrying a knapsack and wearing a Maple Leafs jersey. He had matted white-boy dreadlocks and a scraggly scant goatee. As his grunge was Canadian, it was largely faux-foul and cosmetic. He had lovely manners. His clothes smelled freshly laundered and were pressed.

He'd come, he told me, for the weed, and as we motored toward the city, he laid out for me the virtues of steady marijuana use. There were three, apparently, which he presented as ten or twelve since he couldn't keep a firm hold on the thread of his presentation. There was something about tars and carcinogens. Something about consciousness expansion. Something about a Canadian snack food that I'd never run across. He told me his given name was Gale which was why he went by Rowdy. He owned up to a personal preference for what he called "Thai shit" which led to a rambling disquisition on Southeast Asian climates that yielded somehow to talk of the Blue Jays' salary cap.

I was carrying Rowdy, per his instructions, to Washington

Square Park where even I knew there was nothing approaching "Thai shit" to be had. Only the task-force flunkies with quotas to meet had authentic marijuana. The Rasta dealers all sold hundred-dollar bags of oregano, moved the stuff to students mostly who'd occasionally find the pluck to come back and entertain whole pockets of bench loungers with indignant demands to get their money back.

Now ordinarily I would have carried Rowdy directly to the park and wished him happy hunting, but because I was in the throes of one of my optimistic spells, I decided to warn him off the place and so broke the news to Rowdy that unless he was angling for Central Booking or hoping to cook marinara, Washington Square was not remotely the place he wanted to go.

Once Rowdy had soaked in the wretched news, had said to me anyway, "Huh?" and had slouched against the seat back while I repeated and enlarged, he looked so close to tears that I drove him downtown to a Nassau Street storefront where it was widely known the traders and the brokers bought their dope.

As I watched Rowdy head into that storefront, I felt, I'll confess, like a bit of a cosmopolitan ambassador, a fellow who knew on the island of Manhattan exactly what was what. And the glow persisted up to Houston and east to Avenue A, stayed with me while I parked the Ford and fetched a mochaccino, only began to ebb once I'd perched upon our bench before the dog run which I was obliged to share with an elderly woman in a housedress and knee hose who smelled like livestock and scratched herself as a sort of avocation.

While I watched a pair of terriers fighting over a chunk of bark mulch, I couldn't help but think of Rachel with a sour stab of regret. Things had not been remotely the same between us since I'd throttled Niki which Rachel had managed to see for the heartsick enterprise it was. I had gone and promoted myself from driver to man friend with a special claim. I don't suspect I was very successful at disguising the longing, never really intended to be since I had hoped she'd sniff it out.

I'd last carried her to the Waldorf to meet a gentleman from Boston who owned and operated a bearing factory outside Ellsworth, Maine. He had tickets for some kind of brass ensemble at Avery Fisher Hall, a dead wife, a toupee and a defibrillator. He had a suite on the upper floor, a titanium hip and a personal driver, all of which Rachel informed me of as we traveled up Park. Into the viaduct, up and around the terminal at Grand Central and onto the upper avenue with its balky lights and swarming cabs. Rachel took a schoolmarm's tone as she listed her date's features, provided them to me as proof he wasn't worth the bother to beat up.

She tried to make it all out as a joke when we stopped before the hotel. She laughed and gave me a twenty to keep and told me to be safe. On the way to a York Avenue pickup, I balled up Rachel's money and pitched it into the street.

I'd come to our bench as confirmation that I was all right, that I was capable anyway of continuing without her, could readily pass for satisfied and make a show of being fine without rue and bile and rank regret bubbling up to swamp me. Rachel was off by then with a yogurt magnate, a fellow with a house in Bermuda whose wife had been, for a couple of years, in and out of consciousness. She lived (after her fashion) in a private-care facility in Westchester County where she was well seen after while her husband went on with his life which was largely given over to business but partly to Bermuda and the sort of recreation a girl like Rachel could provide.

So Rachel was out of reach, at least for the moment, of Eastern Euro–trash which I was prepared to take for consolation. I recall that I had noticed a leggy creature in the dog run. She had about three gross of ear studs, a shirt that quit at her top rib, a pair of low-cut jeans designed to put her pelvis on display. Her hair was maybe seven colors, none of them found in nature, and when I first saw her, she was screaming for her dog, a shivering hairless vermin of a canine named Mabel. That girl was an outright spectacle even in the heart of the East Village, one of those females who probably heard all of the time from her mother and her aunts what a beauty she would be but for her taste in clothes and her rainbow coif. She was pretty thoroughly tattooed as well. One arm was almost covered, but she'd left her midriff unadorned except for navel jewelry, an elaborate platinum item that looked a little like a night chain. It caught the sunlight as she twisted and bent and all but hypnotized me.

Naturally I gawked a bit and just as naturally got caught at it. She ignored her dog for a moment so she might turn and ask me, "What?"

I would have been stung and embarrassed if I'd not been taking her for proof that there was leering adenoidal life for me beyond the reach of Rachel, that I was alive enough to the virtues of women to get detected inspecting one. So I was enduring something more in the way of relief and satisfaction than my usual bout of cringing consternation when my telephone rang.

"Louis?" the voice on the line said to me.

"Yes."

"It's Phil King."

Phil King? I'd never once heard him abbreviated before and so couldn't manage at first to place him. It was as if the Savior had dialed me up and called himself J. Christ.

"Phillip J. King?"

"Yeah," he told me, and then I heard Mrs. Phillip J. King say something to him. It sounded her usual sort of directive though not quite in her usual tone. She was a little louder and higher-pitched, a little more excited. I took anyway for excitement at first what turned out anguish and despair.

I had a moment there when I was giddy because it was all so unforeseen. I'd been caught staring at the navel of a woman when Mr. Phillip J. King, of all people, had rung me up on my cell which struck me as odd and funny and somewhat miraculous.

"What's up?" I asked it lightly, had yet to work through in my mind the sorts of things that would have to be up for Mr. Phillip J. King to call me.

He exhaled. He said only, "Louis," again and then failed for a moment to speak, long enough for me to make out Mrs. Phillip J. King in the background. Her breath was shallow and labored and humid. She was sobbing like a child.

3

I SORT OF KNEW the boy who'd hit them. I'd once held him in my arms. He was the infant son at the time of the sister of a friend of mine from school, a guy named Matt who I'd gone home with for one reason or another, and his sister was there with her newborn that she was offering around. She seemed, I recall, predisposed to believe I was anxious to hold him, that I was of an age to savor the earthly miracle of an infant when, in truth, that baby smelled a little of the barnyard to me and I would as soon have tossed him across the room as taken him into my arms.

She insisted, however. Polly, her name was. She told me what to cradle and showed me how and advised me not to squeeze. Then she gave him to me, and he wailed in my face. I remember he was toothless and homely and stank up close of mother's milk and processed succotash.

He was all of sixteen and driving a truck his parents had bought for him. The thing was new and shiny, with oversize tires and automotive-product decals. One for the company that made the lifters, the company that made the injector cleaner, the company that made the struts, the company that manufactured the sound system and a large sticker on the rear cab window for the rubber-bed-liner concern. It was powerful and overtorqued, as midsize pickups go, while the boy behind the wheel was just your standard middling-octane teen.

I heard later from a county police officer who had me call

him Deputy Dale that Brendan (the name, it turned out, of Matt's nephew and Polly's son) had been fiddling with his radio and had taken his eyes from the road. Deputy Dale went on to tell me that settings could be complicated on a state-of-the-art sound system in a flashy midsize truck.

Deputy Dale was standing in my parents' front room at the time, and as he spoke, he inspected my mother's gimcracks on the mantelpiece. A couple of pewter songbirds. A Depression-glass vase with two dusty silk lilies in it. A tarnished pan from an old ornamental scale that held rubber grapes and match-books. A picture of me and my Grandpa Buck and my dad fishing at Nags Head. A length of scarlet Christmas ribbon that had never been thrown out.

Deputy Dale took up the photograph and confessed to a weakness for fishing which he detailed for me at some length. Deputy Dale was a Zebco man. He was partial to night crawlers for bait. He liked to soak his bass fillets overnight in a bowl of salted milky water, dredge them in cornmeal and crushed saltines, fry them in peanut oil. Deputy Dale professed to re-calling having been sixteen himself, having driven his daddy's Monterey and his uncle's Ram half-ton. He owned up to having been a little shiftless as a driver where it came to signaling turns and making proper four-point stops. But otherwise Deputy Dale was pleased to allow that he'd been careful and even still had managed to have a couple of ding-ups (he called them) himself.

The point for him was that Brendan didn't seem to be at fault. The point for him was that sometimes car wrecks merely up and happened. Deputy Dale then fingered the Christmas ribbon briefly and put it back.

As I watched him pluck from the tarnished pan a rubber

grape and compress it between his finger and his thumb, I went to the bother of recalling having been sixteen myself. The unchecked hormones. The ruptured skin. The spotty coordination. The wholly unjustified interludes of pristine self-assurance. The baseless opinions. The abominable haircuts. The haplessness behind the wheel.

"I guess what I'm here to tell you is, we can't say yet about charges." Deputy Dale then showed me the grape that he had buffed between his fingers. "Muscat," he said and returned it to the pan.

I opened the door and stood alongside it. I told Deputy Dale, "All right."

They'd had rain, not a downpour but heavy enough to send them to the mall instead of to the park built on shopping-plaza rubbish. The Neely mall was something well shy of a thundering success. It usually had a third or more of its retail space on offer. I can't imagine the rent was all that high, but business was deplorable, mostly because the locals were loyal to shops they'd patronized for years. They preferred the Rexall to the CVS and Harmon's to the Hudson-Belk, couldn't be tempted in any regular way into the chain store for shoes when them and their parents and probably even their parents' parents before them had bought all of their footwear from Lucy Messick in her junky shop downtown.

So part of the trouble was simply small-town retail intransigence, but the local mall was also an eyesore and a structural depressant. None of the light was natural. The plants were artificial. The fountains had proven seepy and so had been drained and kept dry. The music they piped in was all but criminally insipid. Both of the escalators were unreliable, and the rubbishy homewares boutique had saturated the place with the stink from its scented candles. Parking was even a problem because of poor drainage and substandard paving, so there was only a meager far-flung portion of smooth acceptable lot since the rest was either ruptured or swamped if not the both together.

My father flatly refused to go to the Neely mall when the stores were open, but when the weather was poor—too wet or chilly for the exercise park—he'd drive out with my mother, and they'd circulate clockwise between the darkened storefronts and the empty tiled mall fountains. While the place was a bit of a bust for commerce, it was a popular strolling spot and so afforded my father a rich opportunity for commentary. He could look in store windows and belittle the merchandise, take shots at their fellow walkers in their sneakers and their pastel marching togs.

And that, of all places, was where they were headed when they got done in by some kid who'd had his license for all of seven months and was trying to drive while operating the sort of radio that Deputy Dale had assured me was fairly bristling with features from megabass to cold rinse and air fluff. My father had been taking his customary shortcut off the boulevard, down past the middle school, the propane works, the dollar store, and he and my mother just happened to be rounding a curve in their '84 Impala when Brendan met them while drifting across the center line in his midsize truck. He bucked directly up over my father's hood, busted out the windshield, crumpled both of the front stanchions and all but pancaked the Impala roof. Then he rolled off sideways and slid about thirty feet on his door panel before fighting his way through the airbags and climbing out unhurt.

A guard from the middle school, a propane-truck driver, a fellow weed-whacking grass in the ditch were all drawn by the racket of the collision out into the street. My dad's Impala had bumped against the curb and stopped. Brendan looked around and said by all accounts just, "Damn."

I've seen the pictures. Deputy Dale allowed me a look at the file once he'd plucked out a couple of ghastly photos he didn't think would suit. There were snapshots of middle-school children, gawkers and rescue-squad workers and firemen. Even the fire chief in his little blue hat like a saucepan with a bill. In one of the photos, two men in red jumpsuits employed a pneumatic contraption to lift the roof off that Impala and open the car like a herring tin. My father was crushed and punctured and lacerated, hardly more than half alive. Deputy Dale allowed me to see a snapshot of him on a gurney. I could make out behind him, beyond the torn headliner and the ruptured vinyl upholstery, a meager piece of my mother's sky blue patterned top. They'd been some hours removing her from the car, had worked with care and at their leisure. Through a crack where they could see him between the roof and racked door panel, my father had told the guard from the middle school, had told the propane-truck driver, had told the man cutting grass in the ditch that my mother was already dead.

It was one of those tragedies that might have been designed and ordained for Neely. It occurred at the top of the business day when people were out and about, and it was a gruesome spectacle near the middle school where citizens with a taste for carnage could find no end of parking in the bus lot. The way I heard it, word got around pretty fast as the Bearcat police scanner had largely supplanted the power juicer as the local appliance of choice. So people heard Deputy Dale and his colleagues over their radios and got wind early on of casualties and vehicular devastation.

I can readily imagine local sorts convinced my father had it coming. He was always too blunt and pointed, far too wry for that sort of place. But my mother was of them and for them, sympathetic to their urges, and I still sometimes against my will conjure up onlookers. They loiter curbside watching the rescue squad crew shear away the Impala roof. They are grim and respectfully silent. They are sorry my mother is dead.

Mr. and Mrs. Phillip J. King just happened onto the scene. They had escaped for the morning from the steely grip of Shropshire Glen Estates. The place had been conceived as a kind of subdivision snare with houses inside the stone gates and, just out on the roadway, precisely the sorts of shops the residents would probably need. The trouble was with the pricing. That development was almost eight miles out of town, but the residents might as well have been living on the Azores given what they paid as a sort of retail surcharge for convenience.

Once every couple of weeks, then, Mr. and Mrs. Phillip J. King would mount an expedition. They'd fill a thermos with coffee and a cottage-cheese tub with nut brittle and set out in their green Biscayne for a shopping tour through town. They'd call at the megacenter and swing by the Red Apple, stop in at the Rexall and buy a tank of gas at the Sunoco. Then they'd routinely stop in at the mall so Mrs. Phillip J. King could see if the coat she refused to pay full price for had been closed out or marked down.

It was their usual custom to bicker recreationally as they drove, and they were pretty hotly at it when Mr. Phillip J. King took the middle-school shortcut around one in the afternoon. The way I heard it from him, there were scarlet flares still burning in the roadway. There were a couple of guys from the wrecker service, Brady and his assistant, sweeping glass and bits of plastic out of the road and into the drain. Brendan's truck was already out at the dealership for an assessment. What was left of my father's Impala was canted up on the wrecker hook.

Mrs. Phillip J. King said, just in her usual general forlorn way, "Oh, my," which was how she simultaneously acknowledged a misfortune and gave thanks the wretched business had not been visited upon them. But in this case it had, and she sensed as much only once they'd eased past the wrecker. She sucked wind and instructed Mr. Phillip J. King to stop.

She'd recognized my father's bumper sticker. He'd bought it at a South Carolina Stuckey's years before. It was weathered and faded and blistered, a bit puckered on each end but still legible from maybe twenty feet. My father referred to it as his cri de coeur. It read in full "#@%&?/}#%!"

So they got it mostly from Brady and a little from Brady's assistant, a cousin Brady'd had no practical recourse but to hire. His name was Kim or Kelly, and there was little he preferred in life to a good vehicular crack-up and some attendant carnage. He was excited and eager with insensitive details, told Mr. and Mrs. Phillip J. King more than they'd hoped to hear before Brady could jerk him by his collar and cause him to shut up.

"Dead?" It was all that, between them, Mr. and Mrs. Phillip J. King could say.

"Her," Brady told him. He added, "Him," and shook his head and shrugged.

That was just about all the Kings had found out by the time they'd called me. They'd driven directly from the middle school out to my parents' house, had let themselves in the side door that was hardly ever latched and had plundered around through the kitchen and back hall looking for my number. They wanted to call me before the likes of Deputy Dale did and break the news with what grace they could muster. But after they'd found my number on a notepad in my mother's hand, Mrs. Phillip J. King went to hysterical pieces, and she was only just recovering when Mr. Phillip J. King (by force of habit) wondered rhetorically if he should be making a long-distance call on my parents' telephone.

I believe that Mrs. Phillip J. King elected to hit him with a book. So he was grim and a little battered on his end of the phone when I answered his ring and heard him tell me, "Louis?"

I can't say how I felt exactly. I barely remember driving home, and by home I mean across the Manhattan Bridge and then underneath the motorway to my apartment building. I told Sal. I stood in his office door and watched him shake his head, watched him rise and come across and try to be consoling. Sal indulged in a litany of everything I shouldn't fret about. My rent. My gas. Electric. Upcoming acting jobs. The heap of lamps and toasters and power tools in the corner of his office that I'd not managed to work repairs on yet. Sal promised to take care of everything and even patted me once on the forearm although Sal was not remotely the forearm-patting type.

I arranged for a flight, dialed up Azal to make apologies for my shift, found Omar in the hallway and had him fetch his mother who reached out from beneath the folds of her gown and touched me with her hand. I went down meaning to catch a cab, but Mahir was waiting for me. In his argyle sweater, his tweedy blazer, his tan polyester pants, Mahir was leaning against his fender well looking genuinely stricken.

Mahir climbed out at La Guardia to shake my hand on the departure ramp. He then unfolded some sort of kerchief and spread it on the sidewalk, dropped to his knees and saw me off with a Muslim prayer for the dead which a pair of Port Authority officers took as an affront. They approached Mahir, and one of them poked him with his rubber baton.

I had no practical notion of what to do, which arrangements needed making, and I jotted a list on my cocktail napkin which my seatmate kept stealing glances at until I'd finally showed him the thing. He studied my napkin, read what he could where the ink hadn't seeped and bled. He asked me, "Who died?" and by all rights I could have said, "Everybody," which was by then a fact on the ground I'd not met up with yet.

I rented a puny and wholly inexcusable two-door Buick, a kind of rolling penalty for having failed to reserve a proper car. The thing had no features to speak of. The dash was all blanks and divots where knobs and gauges might have been. The gas pedal was about the size of a bar of three-week-old hand soap. When I'd find it with my foot and press, the motor would need a moment to think.

I got lost in Stokesdale. They'd rerouted the road around an eyesore of a shopping center and a strip of hyperilluminated nationally franchised crap, so you no longer turned where you once had to get on the blacktop to Neely, and I was very nearly to Walnut Cove before I'd realized my mistake. At the time I felt like I was racing to my father, was equipped somehow with a brand of mystical genetic family connection that would allow me to perch at his bedside and effectively will him to live. But he proved to be more thoroughly crushed, more punctured and lacerated than even (I guess) a prince of a child could likely have undone.

They had him in the Amos Collins Wing with its motel ambience, and when I stopped at the nurses' station and identified myself, the two ladies behind the counter went identically grim together, and one of them took up a phone receiver and announced that I'd arrived. I knew I was too late when she saw fit to refer to me as "the son."

Buddy came down along the corridor in his teal green lab coat with its tailored fit and embroidery on the sleeves. His rank cheese smell preceded him. He extended his beagle-fondling hand and told me, "Louis," that he followed with a slight nod and a wince.

He had a nurse take me to see him, a large black woman named Mavis who was as human as anything afoot in the Amos Collins Wing. She was sad for me and meant it. She spoke tenderly of my father, and when she walked me into the room where he lay covered on a gurney, she talked directly to him as if he were alive. I only peeked under the sheet, could see he was a carcass already and had passed into something that didn't remotely look to me like sleep.

Mavis told me he'd come out of surgery and into her care in the ward, the same ward (I imagined) where Aunt Sister had expired. I pictured it in my mind's eye—the half dozen beds, the failing patients, the pulsing from the monitors, the gurgle from the breathing tubes. He'd awakened for a moment, Mavis said as she steered me back into the hall. He'd raised up as best he was able and had looked around the room, and Mavis told me she was going to supply him what comfort she could when he faded and expired. "When he passed," was what Mavis preferred.

Mavis was wedded to a New Testament theory about death and transforming salvation, and I allowed her to visit it on me down along the corridor and back to the nurses' station where I was given forms to sign. I nodded every now and again in a show of sympathy which was altogether fraudulent since I had my own opinion as to what had likely transpired. In my view my father had suffered a final megacenter moment. He'd awakened with a dead wife and stopgap surgical repairs, had reared up to find himself in a room full of critical cases. Expiring was the only way that he could say, "Well, shit."

Mrs. Phillip J. King had more or less moved into my parents' house. She was making as I arrived ambitious funeral arrangements, or rather was entertaining bids from our local morticians over the telephone in the alcove my father had built for it in the hall. She'd dragged out my mother's gilt vanity chair to perch upon while she talked, and she was berating one funeral professional or another over his sky-high casket prices when I came in through the front door and fairly seized her notice instead.

She shoved the receiver at her husband and came charging directly at me. Mrs. Phillip J. King had changed into her slippers, had stripped off her makeup and applied some sort of unction to her face which she was keeping her hair away from with an unbecoming headband.

She said, "Oh, sugar!" with torment and volume both and then threw herself upon me and sobbed for about a solid minute. This was the woman who'd once, when I had baited Itty Bit into the shrubbery, assured me she intended to snatch me bald.

I could only manage to lay a hand to her bony back and pat it. I felt not numb exactly but muffled and at an odd remove from the world. The sight of my parents' house impressed me as just slightly wide of normal with their clothes in the closets, my mother's coffee cup by the settee, my father's varying strengths of reading glasses strewn about. I suspected I'd find in their Coldspot evidence of last night's supper along with the usual crumb-dusted stick of butter and pitcher of cloudy tea.

Mrs. Phillip J. King assured me she would handle the arrangements and thereby leave me otherwise unoccupied to grieve which was all good and well since I'd no idea how to put a funeral together, but I also soon discovered that I had no knack for grief.

I hardly knew what to do with myself. Friends of my parents' and neighbors carted food and sympathy, but Mrs. Phillip J. King handled them as well. She laid a buffet on the breakfast-room table and sent Mr. Phillip J. King to fetch disposable plates and flimsy plastic utensils. Mrs. Phillip J. King was of a mind it didn't pay to pamper mourners because most of them would prove content to mope around all day and eat.

As best I could tell, my job was to sit in the front room and be consoled. I entertained from callers commonplace stories about my parents, lengthy and hopelessly convoluted bits of pedestrian business devoted to a final sighting of my father at the gas mart or a valedictory greeting bestowed on my mother at the dairy case. There was talk as well of the food which looked to me uniformly awful. Even in Neely few people troubled themselves to cook much anymore. They got by on freezer fare, boxed Stroganoff and rotisserie chicken, and were hardly so deft as locals once were when called upon to cook.

We ended up with eight or ten identical green-bean casseroles—straight unimprovised back-of-the-cream-of-mushroom-soup-can fare. Multiple versions of a noodle dish flavored with a seasoning packet. Various quarts of store-bought coleslaw turned out into bowls. A couple of undisguised buckets of the Colonel's crispy chicken. A few grosses of his biscuits. A tub of his whipped and gravied spuds. A lady from my mother's church circle carried over a tureen of what turned out to be quite unintentionally fermented ambrosia, and the Younts from up the street brought a rice salad that featured a couple of cups of converted long-grain they'd very nearly cooked.

Consequently I didn't much find that I was tempted to dine myself, so I sat around drinking weak tea with entirely too much sugar in it while entertaining commentary from a steady stream of mourners who were acquainted, most of them, with my work in the spastic-bladder commercial and were pleased to congratulate me on my wholly persuasive turn.

The viewing was, if anything, a more wretched experience. Bad food got replaced at the funeral home by my parents in their caskets. Mrs. Phillip J. King had elected to go with the Womacks on the bypass, Macy and Pitt, who'd been joined in the funeral business by their daughters' husbands and had lately relocated from their original digs downtown to their new facility (they insisted on calling it) out by the nursing home. The buildings shared a parking lot and, for all anybody knew, were linked by a geezer-size pneumatic tube beneath the ground.

Pitt considered himself a cosmetologist of appreciable artistry, and he always took a bit too much conspicuous pride in his work. He personally displayed my mother and father in their brushed-aluminum coffins. He ushered in me and the Kings and a second cousin from Charlotte who had arrived for the viewing two hours early due to uncommonly light traffic and nagging personal pathology. For the reveal (Pitt liked to call it), he'd taken off his smock and put on what looked to me a smoking jacket. It was blue with sateen piping and about a size too large. Pitt tugged at the sleeves as he led us past the baby's breath and lilies. With no little ceremony, he raised the coffin lids, did everything really short of saying, "Ta-da!"

I have to imagine that Pitt was accustomed to shrieks and helpless blubbering, to women collapsing at the sight of his work into the arms of their relations, sobbing to see their loved ones just as they had been in life if not slightly rosier and better coiffed. My parents looked like they'd joined a touring company of *Oklahoma!* and had gotten each a little scoured by wind sweeping down the plain. They were ruddy and looked of waxworks, seemed more replaced than dead, and I doubt Pitt would have been much gratified by the sour wince I managed, so it was fortunate that Mrs. Phillip J. King could be counted on to shriek.

She wailed and keened and blubbered, pitched into the arms of her husband and generally paid to Pitt the compliment of being deranged by grief while I just stood and wondered what those creatures were before me while my second cousin, a man named Wally who I hardly knew, explained to me once again that he'd decided to leave his house at three-thirty because of the threat of bottlenecks from roadwork on 85. As Wally talked, I touched my mother's cheek and came away with a scarlet finger.

Conversation at the viewing turned, naturally, to auto wrecks at length which gave way in due course to talk of general tire wear and gas mileage.

I can't really recall but bits and pieces of the funeral itself. The Reverend Mr. Shelton gave the eulogy which was dry and larded with Scripture. We sang "Jesus, I My Cross Have Taken" and "There Is a Land of Pure Delight." Some girl from the Methodist children's choir performed solo "The Lord's Prayer" as if it were a ballad from *Evita,* and the women's auxiliary hand-bell ensemble played "Oh, Promise Me" with such artless brio that I half expected my father to find some way to get up and leave. Sal had sent a throw of carnations that rested on my mother's coffin as if she'd just won the Preakness, while the most extraordinary wreath of ivory roses I ever hope to see rested on an easel at my father's feet. The card read "Giles and Rachel" though I figured mostly Giles. Meridian Life and Casualty had sent a vase of tulips I wouldn't have given on the occasion of a tonsillectomy.

The Reverend Mr. Shelton rode with me and the Kings in the family limousine, and he plagued me on the way to the cemetery with beatific piffle. Knowing that my mother had been fond of him, I failed to put him out in the street.

She was waiting, had come out early and gotten properly situated. Mrs. Vestal was sitting in a chair by the open graves just alongside her practical nurse who held a pair of crisp new linen handkerchiefs in her hand, entirely free of their cellophane wrappers and in fit shape for flinging.

The graveside ceremony was brief and fairly arid. A passage of Scripture followed by a prayer. Then a fistful of dirt on the part of the reverend and the ordeal of Mrs. Vestal struggling with the aid of her practical nurse up from her folding chair. Her latest minor stroke had served to compromise her speech, so she spit out a "Farewell, brave souls!" after a chewed and highly lubricated fashion and made a rather miraculous toss of a handkerchief into my mother's grave. Center shot, and she seemed to have aimed it with a calculation for windage since it started wide and drifted to hit the absolute heart of the hole.

My father's handkerchief was another matter. It fell short and struck the railing, bounced off the bright brass pipe of the casket-lowering device and fell to the Astroturf at my feet. I plucked it up and shook it, let it uncrease and hang loose, even crumpled it some like I had to guess my father would have preferred before I held it over the open grave and let it drop to join him. I wandered out from beneath the canopy and into the afternoon sun.

What followed was more deplorable food and all-but-debilitating chatter. People lounged about our house with go cups and Chinet. They stayed too long and talked too much, ridiculed the food as they consumed it. A deli platter from the megacenter came in for particular abuse. It was all cheese cubes and pressed meat ornamented with black olives. It made the green-bean casseroles seem by comparison savory cuisine.

Late in the day, my friend Matt's sister brought her son Brendan over. She'd made her husband—some lump of suet named Carl—come along with her as well, but he was clearly the sort of fellow who simply served in life as ballast since he straightaway spied the cubed cheese and the sweaty rolled bologna and asked me as he shook my hand, "Is that for anybody?"

Matt's sister informed me that Brendan had something he wished to say, and Brendan (who'd clearly been made to put on a sport coat for the occasion) rolled his eyes and snorted, endured a shove from his mother and with a huff saw fit to tell me he was, you know, kind of sorry about the accident that had killed my parents. He added that if he could bring them back, he figured he probably would.

I noticed that Brendan was carrying folded in his jacket pocket a dealership brochure for the latest model of Chevy midsize truck. I recognized that he was not, in fact, so much as remotely sorry or affected at all beyond the irritation he seemed to feel at having been made by his mother to put on his sport coat and air rehearsed regrets. He was impatient and bored, the sort of kid who went just where he wished and never failed to get just what he wanted.

I told Matt's sister I'd appreciate a word with Brendan alone, and I laid a hand to the young man's shoulder and steered him toward the kitchen, out the back door off the breakfast room and into the yard, deep in the lot to the bottom where my father had grown tomatoes until he'd wearied of feeding the rabbits and squirrels. This was really more than Brendan had signed on to tolerate, and before I'd spoken to him, he'd told me twice he had to go. He assured me he had stuff to do and people waiting for him. He looked irritated that the apology he had recently unfreighted hadn't served to settle his debt to me.

I plucked the Chevy brochure from his jacket pocket and asked him what package exactly he was in the market for which brought Brendan to life a little, and he described to me the suspension he was after, touched upon the rally wheels and the virtues of a viscous differential. He showed me the color combination he'd picked out. Then he asked me what I drove which did me service as an opening, and I told him I didn't actually own a car. I told him I lived in the city, and I described the place a little, and I allowed as how I'd made in my time up there no end of friends. Some were honest, I said, and decent and lawful. Others, I informed him, weren't.

Then lowly and without any trace of ire or irritation, I told Brendan that on a day of my choosing I would have him killed. I winked and gave him back his midsize-Chevy-truck brochure, delivered a chuck on his arm and suggested, "Live it up."

SPECIAL PROVIDENCE

1

EVERYBODY RECOMMENDED THAT I should take my time deciding just what I wanted to do exactly and how I should proceed. People proved keen to acquaint me with misjudgments they had made and decisions they'd acted on in their grief that they had come to rue—property they'd sold and papers they'd burned and effects they'd hauled to the landfill when they wished instead that, for a few weeks, they'd just sat and thought.

I had one fellow tell me, a Phelps who sold lawn equipment, that he knew for a fact it was hard on a man to lose his mama and daddy just up and of a sudden and both together at once.

"Lose yours?" I asked him.

He paused to think for a moment before confessing, "No."

I had no plans to do anything, quickly or otherwise. In fact, I couldn't so much as begin to decide just what I might best be up to. I went down to the bank where my parents had done all of their business for years and had got grief counseled by a perky young loan officer named Patty who gave the impression of having lately attended a seminar on the very topic of dealing with mopey men in my circumstances. She made compassionate noises and eye contact. She offered me a beverage and supplied me with bank booklets that she felt might be germane which I left behind her ficus on the top of her credenza and went instead to see the lawyer who'd prepared my parents' wills.

His given name was Alan, but he'd been saddled for years

269

with Winky which even he couldn't begin to account for any longer or explain. He was a generous pile of a guy with a puny hideously paneled office that had nowhere near the storage he required. There was paperwork heaped everywhere, contracts and files and titles held together, some of them, with the clamps that cabinet joiners use. The heaps were, for the most part, pitched and perilously balanced so that a client come to discuss with Winky a lawyerly sort of matter could be forgiven for wondering if he would get out of there alive.

Winky had my parents' pertinent documents in a folder, and for a moment there he made as if there were a principle by which his monumental office clutter was ranked and organized. Winky stood anyway and surveyed the place as if it were conceivable that he employed a system for causing the papers he needed to come to hand. But then he just grunted and sat back down with force enough to alarm me. I was watching the folders to my right as Winky told me, "Well."

He called in the secretary he shared with an accountant next door and charged her with locating the folder that he needed which she managed, quite miraculously, in just four business days. So Winky got on the job of settling everything he could settle while I mostly sat around and thought about handling everything else. The Kings kept insisting I join them for dinner at Shropshire Glen Estates, and I did for three or four evenings running until I had finally succeeded at persuading Mrs. Phillip J. King that I was sane and stable, wasn't sulking about the house debilitated with grief. In fact, I'd moved into a motel, the new one out at the bypass exchange with the pseudo-Moroccan restaurant and what they insisted on calling a spa—a room with a couple of treadmills and ten square feet of exercise matting along with the sort of fiberglass sauna you could order through the mail.

I'd spent a couple of restless and uneasy nights at home listening to the floor joists pop and the water heater gurgle and all but besieged by memories of my life there as a boy. The courtesies I'd failed to extend. The kindnesses I had belittled. The fits I'd pitched for no good reason. The lies I'd told and resentments I'd nursed. I could only seem to recall myself as a peevish spiteful ingrate who'd waited a bit too long to know the chance to make amends. So I was kept awake by the itch of opportunity squandered along with the ceaseless racket of an old and ever-settling house.

I took to dining in the pseudo-Moroccan motel restaurant where I was comforted by the sight of a briarwood mizmar they'd hung on the wall along with what looked to me Shriners' fezzes and a map of Africa. I'll let the cuisine off as fusion, though I'm not entirely convinced that a dish of spareribs and dirty rice served on a hammered salver should be called on even a bypass motel menu a tagine. The food, however, was usually tasty enough and the patrons mercifully scarce, and I'd dine and pass my evenings stretched out on my king-size bed watching ordinarily the Weather Channel.

In the course of my week at the bypass motel, I came to understand and honor Teddy's abiding fascination with his weather girl. Once during the global weather update as she defined a williwaw, she seemed to be speaking expressly to me alone.

Daylight hours I spent at my parents' house. When people dropped by, and people dropped by pretty routinely, they'd usually trouble themselves to ask me just what I was about. I'd take occasion to glance around whatever room we might be in, and I'd tell them, "Oh," would tell them, "tidying up."

In truth, I was mostly sorting and rifling indiscriminately

through drawers and cupboards and boxes, the odd accordion file. I once passed, I would imagine, a good three-quarters of an hour standing before my parents' closet looking at their hanging clothes. I allowed their food to spoil in their refrigerator, played my mother's radio on the kitchen countertop and left it tuned to the easy-listening Burlington station she'd been fond of where the saccharine music yielded occasionally to uplifting New Testament flotsam and scraps of sunny doggerel.

Local people, at an absolute loss, I guess, for anything else to do, kept bringing me ovenware dishes freighted with unsavory food. Casseroles and cobblers and Tetrazzini and a puzzling wealth of Swiss steak, puzzling anyway until I'd found a recipe from the *Chronicle* that my mother had clipped out and saved along with everybody else. I was as gracious as I could manage, given an orphan's allowances, but I'd invariably rake the food into the garbage straightaway, squirt a little Ivory into each dish and leave it to soak in the sink.

Deputy Dale called on me one afternoon in the immediate wake of a Jeeter, a woman my mother had done some kindness for when her sister by marriage had died. That Jeeter had dropped off a custard pie which I was just about to dump when Deputy Dale stuck his head in the house and shouted out, "Hey here!"

He was essentially casing the front room when I came out of the hallway with that Jeeter's pie plate resting on my hand. Neely historically has, like most small towns, a wayward-deputy problem. There's an awfully fine line on the county force between lawman and thug on account of the vigorous head knocking and routine white-trash wrangling that decent people need police to be about. So deputies tend to be unduly tough and ready sorts, decisive and passably fearless, not the type to take eight credits toward a criminology degree into a fight with drunken cousins armed with knives and hatchet handles.

The price to be paid was in deputies ranging a little wide of the law. They were brawlers and drinkers as often as not and notoriously sticky-fingered, and I could tell by the way that Deputy Dale sized up my mother's knicknacks that he probably had more than the common share of larceny in his heart.

"You Benfield?" he asked me, and while I was nodding, he took up a candlestick, a big honking cut-glass monstrosity that had belonged to my grandmother. Deputy Dale seemed pleased with the heft of the thing and told me approvingly, "Damn."

He had a file folder that looked crammed with photographs, and he laid it on the coffee table which freed him up to circulate with both hands available for whatever items caught his eye. He took up our pewter tree squirrel perched upon his pewter limb, admired my mother's porcelain milkmaid and her fractured salt-glazed jug which he upended and examined for some sort of maker's mark.

He picked up a framed snapshot and set about telling me how he fried his fish as I made a move toward Deputy Dale's file folder. I could see a corner of a photo sticking out, what looked to be a picture of my father's crushed Impala. Without glancing to see if I took any heed, Deputy Dale told me sternly, "Uh-uh."

I dropped onto the sofa holding that Jeeter's custard pie, and from there I watched Deputy Dale pass briefly out of the front room proper so as to satisfy himself there was nothing of burning interest in the den before he headed back to occupy the cushion alongside me. He even handled his folder briefly in an officious sort of way, neatened up the exposed contents by knocking the spine upon his palm as he studied that Jeeter's custard pie in silence.

"What's that?" he asked me at length, and I handed him the plate.

I would have fetched the man a knife and fork, but he didn't let on to need them, was hardly the sort to be thwarted by a pie just because it wasn't sliced. He picked at the crust around the rim and scooped out a bit of custard, produced a nose rag from his hip pocket that he wiped his fingers with.

"Good stuff," he told me, and went on to list the virtues of that pie which included crisp and tender crust and well-set silken filling, but he shook his head and added, "A little heavy on the nutmeg."

He'd come by to tell me that they'd decided not to bring charges against Brendan, informed me they'd largely gotten out of the business of laying vehicular blame. "It's one thing if a fellow's drunk," the deputy told me and nibbled a crust crumb. "But ain't no law for stupid, at least not in these parts."

"Good thing, huh?" I asked him.

He grinned and told me, "Shit."

That's when he elected to show me a select few of his photos which included the one of my father's gurney and my mother's blouse. "Drifted over, looks like," Deputy Dale informed me and indicated the position of Brendan's truck a couple of feet across the centerline.

I just sat and looked and nodded when Deputy Dale seemed in need of a nod, even bobbed my head once he'd informed me Brendan was a decent kid and it didn't seem right to ruin the life of a boy just for his driving. "Might have been me, you know?" the deputy told me. He added, "It might have been you."

That's when I plucked out a picture he'd not meant for me to see. Too much buckled Detroit steel liberally splashed with carnage. I tapped the thing with my finger and told Deputy Dale, "Was me."

"Well," he told me. "Yeah," he said. "Sort of. I guess," he managed as he shut his folder and plunged his foremost finger into the pie. He drew it out and licked it clean of custard. Then Deputy Dale stood up with a groan and did a passable community-theater job of airing an afterthought.

"Oh," he said like maybe the question had just popped into his head. "What exactly did you tell that boy?"

"Brendan?"

I could picture Brendan's mother at the county police station raising holy hell about me with her son and husband in tow.

"He was shopping for a truck. I told him I'd go with a Ford."

"Not what his mama said," Deputy Dale informed me.

I squinted as if I were casting back. "I don't recall his mama was there."

Entirely satisfied, Deputy Dale bobbed his head and snorted. "Some mouth on her," Deputy Dale confided. I could picture her jawing at him.

He took a last long scour around the room, and seeing where his gaze lit, I stepped over to the mantel and fetched away the cut-glass candlestick. It felt like it weighed about fifteen pounds, was ugly enough for twenty.

"Here." I shoved it at Deputy Dale. "For your help," I told him.

He was touched. He loosed an admiring "huh" while he examined that candlestick which was exactly (given the chance) the sort of thing he would have pilfered. He stopped and turned at the doorsill, and, in an effort to be decent, Deputy Dale told me, "You're all right. I don't care what they say."

Only once Fay had found me out at the motel on the bypass

did an agreeable plan of action finally coalesce in my head. I was eating a chicken-thigh preparation that would, in Morocco, have been goat and so probably would need the raisins, the apricots and cinnamon spicing that boneless skinless chicken thighs could hardly hold their own against. Fay came in the restaurant and marched directly to my table, didn't pretend that she had only strayed across me by happenstance.

She pulled out a chair and sat down beside me and asked of my supper, "What's that?"

Matrimony appeared to agree with her. She was tan and lean and newly tattooed, had gotten some manner of flower inked into one of her collarbone hollows which I complimented her on straightaway.

"Thank you!" she told me, and appreciably more emphatically than it rated. Then she added that Doug had needed two weeks to even notice the thing.

"How is Doug?"

Fay shrugged and tasted an apricot which she spit into my napkin. "Doesn't do a thing but watch the goddamn TV." Then Fay paused for a minute and had a thought. "Hey," she said, "sorry about your folks." She reached for my hand and held it in both of hers. "Poor baby," she told me, and thereby confirmed just why she'd found me out and what, if I were game, I might be in for.

"Is there anywhere," Fay asked me while eyeing my room key on the table, "me and you could maybe go and talk?"

She passed a moment or two in silence imbibing the décor of my room. Fay was taking just then an Elon College night class in interior design and so felt academically fit to sneer at the curtains and say, "Christ!"

Then she shoved me onto the bed the way I'd seen it done in

movies, and she chose to sit astride me while we had our little chat. Fay was wearing, of course, a tube top and low-cut skintight jeans which, unlike the run of slutty trashy sexually active women, Fay was anatomically qualified to wear. She was all sinew and impeccable tan, and she sat perched there on my package confessing that she hungered for me and couldn't bear the touch of Doug.

Fay had been thinking, she informed me. Fay had been thinking of me, and she passed a few minutes reminiscing about pleasures we'd enjoyed which she couldn't seem to manage without the odd pelvic gyration. Fay wondered if I recalled the session we'd held in my Honda wayback, the one that had involved floor-mat burn and boysenberry jam. Then she reminded me of an evening we'd passed at the Stokesdale drive-in in the back of her brother's pickup atop a quilt her great-aunt had made.

"Good times," Fay told me, and worked her hips like she was grinding meal.

I managed, I think, to nod and tell her, "Yeah."

Naturally I knew where this was going, could picture just how we'd end up which was in a naked sweaty heap atop the deep-pile carpet, but I was plagued by the sense of what a bad son it would make me out to be. I already accounted myself about a middling to sorry offspring. I'd never done for my parents when I'd had the chance the way I'd seen some parents done for. I'd never thrown them lavish anniversary parties or sent them away on cruises, flown in far-flung relatives at my own expense, arranged for sentimental Mother's Day extravaganzas. I'd never offered to join them on vacation after my eighteenth year. I had, however, given up Fay and had traveled to New York in order to get fired off the job my father had landed for me.

Even sprawled on my motel-room bed with Fay astride me making friction, I couldn't help but see how yielding to my appetites and urges would be a crowning insult from a severely shiftless son.

I told Fay, "Look," and, with all the strength I could muster, bucked her off me.

I explained to her as delicately as I could manage that my parents hadn't liked her. That my mother had disapproved of her midriff-baring wardrobe while my father had known an instructive experience with a female much like Fay.

Fay was not remotely offended. She said, "There's nobody like me, sugar," and then she cleaned with her tongue the entire outer fluting of my ear. She left off long enough to tell me, "Anyway, they're dead."

I know that people are given to pointing to moments when everything altered for them, key instances when a word or a look or a wayward galvanic notion served to ensure that nothing would be exactly the same for them again. I'd always believed that sort of thing was the product of willful reconstruction. If a fellow, say, had overhauled his life, had given up drinking or gambling or whoring, he could look back when he was straight and pure and cobble up just why. I hardly suspected I'd be able to recognize in actual time an instant I knew to be utterly transforming.

But there it was.

Of course, I'd known they were dead in the pit of my stomach every morning when I awoke, in my comprehensive emotional numbness, in my attention to their affairs. But I'd not until that moment felt what losing them had meant. It came to me in the form of a duty and an obligation, a conviction that I was finally fully prepared to be their son. It started with Fay. I steered her just like my parents would have wanted out of my room. She saw fit to uncork an altogether salty assessment of me and then tugged at her tube top and snorted and went back home to Doug.

I got in my wretched rental car and drove to my parents' house, parked and didn't go in but stepped instead next door to speak to the neighbors, the couple from Danville who'd bought and overhauled Mr. and Mrs. Phillip J. King's place. The husband (Shawn his name was) had approached me tentatively a few days before. He'd called to me over the boxwood hedge while I was standing on the front walk sizing up the sorry neglected state of my mother's Boston ferns. He'd asked if we might have a little talk.

Shawn had inquired with a fair bit of grace if I was meaning to sell the house, had informed me that he and his wife would be rather keen to buy it. He made no secret of the fact that they would only knock it down so as to open up space for a new wing on their present place. Shawn couldn't imagine that sort of thing was what I had in mind, but he and his wife had decided they should ask me nonetheless. Then he said kind things about my parents he seemed to actually mean and spoke of a time when he had driven my mother to the bakery. It was raining, and she couldn't get her Pontiac windows up.

I knocked on their door, and they had me in and introduced me to their children. We sat in the sunroom off their kitchen to negotiate a price.

I've never had much use for stuff, am not the sort to grow attached to hall trees and chests of drawers, dining-room tables, hassocks and upholstered chairs. I collected matchbooks once as a child. I kept them in a shoe box but carried them out one day on a whim to incinerate them with the trash. I mislaid the pocketwatch my grandfather left me upon his death and cherished his Dobbs fedora up on my closet shelf only until it mildewed and began to stink. I've no possessions left from my childhood. I broke or chucked them all.

So I was either exactly the wrong guy to dispose of my parents' belongings or more likely, I'm inclined to think now, precisely the right one. I started out by having Mr. and Mrs. Phillip J. King come by and select an item as a keepsake and remembrance. Anything at all they wanted, I was fully prepared to let them have. They were restricted, however, by their scanty space at Shropshire Glen Estates, had already packed too much furniture into far too little square footage, so the wardrobe Mrs. Phillip J. King had always had her eye on was altogether too monstrous to fit. Mr. Phillip J. King asked after a metric-socket set of my father's which I hunted up and presented him with while Mrs. Phillip J. King decided she'd take the candlestick off the mantel, the big ugly honking thing I'd already given to Deputy Dale.

When I told her I'd knocked it onto the hearth and shattered it accidentally, she flopped on the settee and blubbered for a while. She made do with my great-grandmother's entire silver service instead.

Otherwise I only called in my Cousin Ethel once removed. She was a sour spiteful woman with a grudge against my mother. Cousin Ethel had always insisted my mother had stolen a cake plate from her. It was a hideous thing my mother, in fact, had bought at a Burlington flea market. It had daisies on it and, around the base, a garish porcelain basket weave. I wrapped the thing and put it in a box for Cousin Ethel, told her my mother had quite specifically wanted her to have it and neglected to mention I'd taken my father's clawhammer and broken the thing to bits.

I very nearly packed up a few items to keep, had located a stack of *Chronicles* with the intent of wrapping some glassware when one of the Reverend Shelton's columns captured my attention. He was sharing glad news in this instance of a man named Dewitt DeKalb. Dewitt DeKalb lived in Waycross, Georgia, and was, after a fashion, charmed. He'd led a life of near calamity and glancing misadventure. Planes he'd held tickets for but had missed had crashed. Ships he'd almost taken had sunk. He'd retired from his job at a ball-bearing plant the very day before a colleague had brought weapons in from home and thoroughly shot up the place. Dewitt DeKalb had survived a tumorectomy that was ordinarily killing, and a tornado had once made a harmless circuit around his house.

Dewitt DeKalb enjoyed, in the Reverend Mr. Shelton's view, special providence, and as a tribute to the guiding hand of Jesus in his life, Dewitt DeKalb had volunteered to deliver food to Waycross shut-ins. He made himself and his Astro van available once a week which hardly struck me as fit compensation for the Lord's care with his carcass.

I drew a lesson from the reverend's column, though certainly not the one he intended. I was proud of my parents who, with no special providence to keep them, had braved the weather and struck out for a jaunt around the mall. They'd been just unlucky. It seemed the best thing I could do for them was go ahead and live. So I called in a guy, a Womble who owned a U-Store-It operation which looked like a string of glorified car sheds out on Greensboro Road, and I paid him to pack up my parents' things and haul them to a unit which I knew even then for the first leg of their progress to the dump.

I found in the drawer of the secretary my father's broken ashtray, his scallop shell with GRAVEYARD OF THE ATLANTIC painted across the bowl. My mother had busted it up in the sink, and it was in a half dozen pieces. I had to think my father had hoped to glue it back and make it whole. I wrapped those bits and shards in the story of Dewitt DeKalb from Georgia. That ashtray was the only thing I kept.

As my flight out of Greensboro lifted off, the young woman alongside me chose to ratchet up the volume of her nattering a click. She'd started in at the gate about the internship she'd been awarded, some coveted stint at a rather prestigious marketing concern. Then she'd moved on as we'd taxied to talk of her apartment, and she'd rattled off information about the girls she'd share it with. With the wheels up and the scattered lights of the county out the window—the bright junctions and the townships, the suburbs and the shopping sprawl—she set in with a bubbly recollection of a drill-team trip she'd been on to perform in the 1997 Macy's Thanksgiving Day Parade.

I reached over and took her hand which startled her a little. I leaned close and smiled and told her, once she'd let me, "Please shut up."

2

SAL EXPLAINED HE HAD a cousin in flowers when I thanked him for the casket lay. We were dodging detritus up on the roof of our building at the time. Sal had told me already by then about his mother's Catholic funeral which had been peppered and adorned, as funerals go, with what Sal called "the damnedest things," Sal who admitted to having been laggardly in his church attendance, Sal who confessed that the incense and gold plate and Latin gave him the creeps.

"The Virgin Mary," Sal said with a sour sneer, and puffed on his cigar. "I'm here to tell you a little of her can go a hell of a long way."

Then he tousled my hair again, had been in a curious hair-tousling mood ever since I'd gone downstairs to show up at his office door. In my absence Sal had repaired a curling iron for one of his wife's relations, had fixed it so well, in fact, that he'd set a bit of his office clutter on fire and had singed what would have ordinarily served him as his tousling hand. It was salved and wrapped, so Sal went at me lefty, and he proved altogether clumsy at it. Truth be told, he didn't tousle so much as paw and smack and tug.

Naturally then I was keen to have Sal understand I was perfectly all right, or fine enough anyway to get by on conversation alone. As we watched a hunk of retread drop from the motorway above, I acquainted Sal with my determination to make my parents proud, told him the story of Dewitt DeKalb and his special providence and spun out for Sal my alternate view of how men best might live which Sal soaked in with the occasional grunt, the odd telling puff on his robusto, but when I'd finished, he told me, "Aw," and reached for me with his left hand.

Omar had heard me come in the night before and had crossed the hall to join me. And in the way of children—not knowing exactly what he ought to say—he sat in his usual chair and told me nothing at all beyond, "Hey."

I gave Omar two sacks of airline peanuts, a squat bottle of airline water. He told me he and Yon-Min had found a dead crow over on Fulton Street but hadn't touched it because it was infected. He said one of his GameBoy batteries had leaked acid on his hand. He told me his mother had cooked a curry that had made the both of them sick and that a woman had jumped from the Brooklyn Bridge aiming, he guessed, for the harbor, but she'd landed on the pilot house of a Circle Line boat instead.

"Ouch," I said.

Omar nodded. Omar told me, "Ouch."

He finally got around to Teddy who was stuck still off in Yemen but was filling out fresh papers and knew a man who knew a man who'd promised, for a fee, to make an introduction to an embassy functionary, some State Department hanger-on Teddy had not begged help from yet.

Sal had work for me. He was one of those back-in-the-saddle guys, and my spastic-bladder performance had won me fans industry-wide. I discovered, however, that I had been typecast as an attentive husband, the sort of fellow who—when his wife was about to fill her Underalls—failed to leave her to it and run away. If I could seem somehow to adore a woman with a spastic bladder, then (the thinking went) I could probably gaze with loving eyes on creatures afflicted with yeast infections, eczema and morning yeti breath.

So I had work, but it was tedious work. My wives did all of the acting. They were rash-ridden halt discolored vaporish insomniacs who I was charged to treat with all-but-saintly understanding. I got bored enough to take a Metropolitan Opera job that I knew going in would call for unflattering leather pantaloons and a stint downstage pretending to drink ale from a pewter tankard.

I drove for relief. The "Loose!" they gave me once I'd signed back on was about as touching and stirring as anything I'd ever heard. For my first few days, Azal insulated me with tourists. I went from La Guardia and Kennedy in to hotels, from hotels out to restaurants. I drove a couple from Phoenix to see their new grandson over in Park Slope. They showed me pictures they'd been sent. They told me all about their daughter who'd confessed to them that she'd been happier back in Scottsdale. They spoke of her husband at some length while we sat in traffic. He rated caveats and sundry misgivings, helpless resignation at best. I carried them to the airport once they'd finished with their visit, and they were teary all the way out, held hands and hardly spoke.

I had about an hour's wait for a pickup in from Chicago, which gave me time to write the gentleman's name (it was Baxter) on my Lucite. I opted for Palatino and used up a half a grease pencil getting it right. I was standing at the foot of the escalator with my colleagues when I spotted her by the baggage carousel. She looked positively stunning, was with a gentleman I'd never seen, a fair fellow with sandy hair and some manner of crest upon his blazer. He had on the sort of slacks and loafers that brought to mind Andover and Choate. He didn't look like the stripe of guy who'd knowingly hire a girl like Rachel, more the type that Rachel might have seen the chance to cultivate.

I tried to catch her eye, stepped just inside the baggage railing and gave a little wave to attract her notice with my Lucite sign. She was waiting for luggage from a flight out of Miami, looked windswept and bronzed by the Florida sun. I only intended to say hello and thank her for the funeral flowers. She had spent, after all, a perfectly pleasant evening with my parents and might, I thought, want to say a thing to me now that she knew they were dead.

When she finally saw me, however, Rachel merely shook her head, little more than twitched it discreetly so her sandy-haired friend with the blazer, slacks and loafers wouldn't know.

She didn't even look back once their bags had come around and they'd struck out for the exit. I watched them climb into a taxi driven by a turbaned Sikh. I was holding at the time my square of Lucite low and sideways against my leg which caused Mr. Baxter in from Chicago to have to bend to read it which he was not, apparently, in a mood to tolerate with grace.

He unshouldered his garment bag, shoved it at me and said, "Here."

I didn't need to drive. I really didn't need to do much acting since I had money my parents had squirreled away, a fairly handsome amount, along with the price the neighbors had agreed to pay me for the house. I could have moped and lounged and taken my sweet leisure with my grief. I could have moved to better digs, relocated to Manhattan, but I stayed where I was and felt all right just doing what I did. I even went once more to Staten Island at Bunny's invitation long after his crisp one-hundred-dollar bills were meaningless.

Sal called me down to his office one morning, and I found

Danny waiting for me with news of a problem Bunny had dire need of me to fix. I supposed I could have refused to go, but I'd not seen Bunny in a while, so I climbed into Bunny's Fleetwood and allowed Danny to drive me down the Gowanus and across the Verrazano onto Staten Island. Danny carried me to Wolfe's Pond Park where I had first met Bunny, and he was waiting by the water in the same place as before.

Bunny had heard I'd had tragedy in my life, and he greeted me with a grave handshake which he followed up with some manner of Sicilian benediction, the words a priest in Siracusa (he told me) had buried his sainted mother with.

I thanked him, and he got directly down to business. The freezer I'd repaired for him what seemed a lifetime back had, just the previous evening, left off running once again. For whatever reason, Bunny trusted only me to fix it, and he produced from his jacket pocket his wife's violet sleep mask which stank still of night cream and Final Net. We went on the ride we'd taken before through the byways of Old Richmond and fetched up at the curb in front of the same house. Danny led me inside. The radio was tuned to the sports-talk channel. The place smelled of scalded shortening. Danny ushered me down the stairs and into the musty cellar where I was deposited behind the freezer and instructed to unmask.

The back panel had already been removed, and some one of Bunny's henchmen had called on the freezer vendor and had come away with all of the pertinent parts that unit could possibly need. They were in a carton beside an open tool kit—brand-new and unused and complete with a platinum-plated socket set. There were men again, as there had been before, standing just out of reach of the lighting. I could see their trousers from the knees down and their impeccable shoes.

It was the compressor this time. Spent and shot and well beyond repairing, so I unbolted and unwired it, fished the new one from the box and had that freezer up and running again in probably twenty minutes. There was muttered relief in that Staten Island basement precisely like before, and as most of his colleagues climbed the stairs, Bunny remained with a lone associate. Once the two of them had closed on me to speak, I could see that the man was Giles.

Bunny gestured toward me and said to Giles, "You know Marty, don't you?"

Giles nodded at Bunny and offered his hand to me. He said, "I do."

Giles visited on me condolences, and I thanked him for the flowers. He told Bunny that he was going my way and would be pleased to carry me home.

We rode together in the back of his Town Car while his massive Samoan drove and proved himself a bit of a heedless fright along the roadway, not as bad as Danny in a rage but pretty close. Giles didn't look anxious so I attempted not to look anxious as well, and I told him I guessed things had worked out between him and Bunny. Giles smiled. He had a way with a smile. It was winning, was reassuring, and he told me he couldn't help but feel he owed me one.

"Here," he said, and produced from his inside jacket pocket a business card. It was heavy embossed ivory and had a number on it. No name. No address. Just ten phone digits punctuated in the European fashion. He placed it in my hand. "If you ever need anything," he said, "just call."

I looked at that card and thought for a minute. I asked him, "Anything?"

Giles nodded, gave me the opportunity to cobble up a request. "Do you happen to know anybody," I asked him, "at the INS?"

I thought I was only dreaming. Not two weeks later, I was asleep in bed suffering through another installment of the nightmare I'd been enduring for probably eight or nine days straight. I was on the open ocean well out of sight of land in a dilapidated rowboat with a pair of broken oarlocks, and I was trying to paddle the thing with an oversize barbecue fork—one of those long-handled newfangled items with a thermometer built in—while tolerating advice from my mother and father sitting on the stern seat, recommendations that seemed to have nothing to do with being adrift at sea.

My father supplied me with the benefit of his actuarial knowledge and spoke at length one evening about the carburetor on his Lawn-Boy which required, he informed me, delicate adjustment with a slotted screwdriver. He told me how to prime a water pump and tie a Windsor knot. My mother on one occasion described in stultifying detail her method for making Brunswick stew from scratch. She suggested I'd do well to commit to memory the book of Ezekiel and advised me to stay away from sandals with their spotty arch support.

The talk was dull and numbing, and I might have awakened from sheer boredom, but the nightmare part came in when I spoke to my parents back while trying to paddle with my barbecue fork. The water temperature was always (I noticed) sixty-eight degrees. We were making little progress in the chop and against the current, and I can't say that I knew where we were headed anyway. The constant palaver surely didn't help, irritated me, in fact, so when I'd finally find a spot to interject a comment, I would tell my mother or my father just, "For shit's sake!" back.

It was precisely the manner of thing I would have never said to them in life, and in our shabby rowboat out on the open ocean, they had a way of glancing at each other that conveyed their wholesale mutual disappointment.

Consequently I would wake up agitated and distressed, nagged by regret and self-recrimination, and only once I had decided that I'd best apologize would I recall that the two of them were dead.

I was contemplating medication, had asked Sal about narcotics, and he was making inquiries of relatives in the trade when we were joined one night in our rowboat by a Canada goose. My mother had acquainted me with her sundry personal views on pilaf, and my father was speaking of the practical difference between loam and vermiculite when that goose began to sound off, and we turned to look upon her. I couldn't recall having seen her fly into the boat. She was perched on the bottom between the thwarts and in the brackish slosh from our persistent leak, and she sounded in pitch like a regular goose but appreciably more melodic. She was squawking, as best as I could make out, a version of "Too Late Now."

I started awake and managed to locate myself in my apartment. I recognized the wash from the streetlights, the clatter of traffic overhead, the sweet smell of fermenting garbage from my long-unemptied bin. And after a moment or two of lying there and remembering who I'd lost, I realized that somehow or another I could still make out the goose.

Teddy was on the fire escape in his Members Only jacket. When I stuck my head out the window, he smiled and told me, "Hello, friend." He'd been abused and all but jilted by the nation that he loved, and me and Teddy and Omar passed a few days just walking around the area to give Teddy occasion to vent. We'd make a circuit down by Cadman Plaza and up the Promenade and then back toward home with a stop in the park at the Fulton ferry landing with its view of the towering Brooklyn Bridge and the lower-Manhattan skyline.

Teddy had usually spent a fair share of his agitation by then, and he'd stand looking out over the water, would often shake his head and sigh, would occasionally turn to me and say with a wounded smile, "Win-win."

3

SHE IS FLYING INTO Kennedy from Milan on Alitalia. Azal spelled her name for me two times over the radio. Dechiara. We have decided between us, in the wake of uninformed debate, that the *ch* is very likely hard. Mahir tried to raise a dissent from up in Riverdale somewhere, but his gain was weak, and he got swamped by static.

I take Atlantic Avenue instead of the Belt Parkway, and I pay with roadwork and sluggish traffic and lumbering carting trucks. I pass ever so deliberately through shifting neighborhoods with tony boutiques and restaurants yielding quite precipitously to bodegas, to nail salons, machine shops, automotive-repair concerns. I creep east, sit through two changes of most every traffic light, but the plane was held for maintenance and is flying against headwinds, so there's precious little chance I won't be waiting when it lands.

I drive exclusively at night now. Teddy is capable of days. He went for almost three full months consumed with irritation. Irate and insulted, bewildered, really, and stung. He came over one evening to find me working on my lizard novel and conscripted me into helping him write a letter of protest. It was a rather exhaustive catalog of the qualities and assets that made Teddy the sort of gentleman this nation should embrace. We mailed it off to our junior senator who wrote to thank us for our input. She responded on heavy embossed congressional stationery, was respectful and incisive, and I

293

don't think Teddy noticed that her signature was impressed with a stamp.

As I sit behind a fuel-oil truck at Empire Boulevard, I'm obliged to shift and scratch and search the glove box for my ointment. There's a price, I've found, to be paid for wearing leather pantaloons, even well downstage in the cool of the shadows where I just hold a tankard while a tenor sings about his one true love who's disguised as a man.

In the short-term lot at Kennedy, I sharpen my grease pencil and get her name down on my Lucite after two aborted tries. It's centered. Not just top to bottom but also side to side, and I've managed a satisfying blend of Courier and Verdana, just the sort of script that (I decide) I'd take some solace in were I arriving from Milan two hours late on a Wednesday evening.

As I approach the terminal, I see a gaggle of my colleagues. They are milling about at the base of the escalator between the carousels with their box ends and scraps of paper, their fares' names inked in ballpoint, with their wrinkled trousers and their linty acrylic sweaters, with their undersize sport coats and dilapidated shoes. I feel for them something verging on professional mortification. Once inside among them, I can smell the dinners that they ate—heavy on coriander and mustard oil.

She will be fashionably dressed and underfed. She'll wear those glasses Italians favor with the Bakelite frames and the copper-tinted lenses. She will have stopped at the ladies' room down by the gate to work on her airplane hair, apply a spritz of eau de Lombardia and a fresh layer of lip gloss. She'll be on her cell phone—impossibly tiny and sheathed in resplendent chrome—while simultaneously attempting against all federal prohibitions to light a Rothman. She'll fairly toss her carry-on bag my way. She'll ridicule my driving. She'll complain about the charges, about the route I've chosen. Once I've stopped in front of her hotel, she'll attempt to pay me in lire.

They come in tides, the passengers do, in freshets and in dribbles, and I finally see a woman I choose to take for Signora Dechiara. She looks sour and weary, unnaturally bony. Her hair is the color of lacquerware. Her glasses may well have served as goggles in another life. She toys with a platinum lighter as she rides the escalator. She squints down to where we drivers are collected and penned in.

I'm so sure, in fact, I've nosed up and have singled out my fare, that I fail at first to see the creature come to stand before me. She allows me to shift and find her. She is willowy and lovely.

She points at my square of Lucite. She smiles as she says, "Me."

ABOUT THE AUTHOR

T. R. PEARSON's widely acclaimed novels include *A Short History of a Small Place, Cry Me a River, Off for the Sweet Hereafter, Blue Ridge,* and *Polar.* He lives in Virginia and Brooklyn, New York.